Look Not Upon Our Sins

a novel by

Georgette Symonds

Paradise Found Publishers

Paradise Found Publishers
P.O. Box 1064
Largo, Florida 33779-1064

Library of Congress Control Number: 2006932147

ISBN-13: 978-0-9788410-7-2
ISBN-10: 0-9788410-7-7

Printed in the United States of America
Edited by Dorothy Dowling of DRD Associates
Author's Photo by Karen Dawn Munson

Publisher's Note

This book is a work of fiction. Names, characters, places
and incidents are either the product of the author's
imagination or are used fictitiously, and any resemblance
to actual persons living or dead, business establishments,
events, or locales is entirely coincidental.

This book is printed on acid-free paper

If you have built castles in the air, your work need not be lost; that is where they should be. Now put the foundations under them.

Henry David Thoreau

Dedication

To Eileen,

You not only encouraged me to dream and dare to build my castle in the air...

You held steady the ladder with your unending support as I climbed up each and every rung.

Acknowledgement

To all my family, friends and colleagues who always asked how my book was coming along, to Marian Lawe and Theresa Darcy for being readily available to answer my questions about Ireland, to friends Ann Favicchia, Una Warde and JoAnn DeSalvo for being my first readers, to my daughter, Mary Beth Perri, not only as a first reader but for your words of encouragement, to Karen Munson not only as a first reader but for all your tech support, to my grandson, John Bevilacqua for your awesome advice, to Dorothy Dowling for your wonderful editing job, to Bob Finn for giving me that last push, to Bridget Warde a fellow passenger on the *Franconia*, to Saint Theresa for giving me a rose and especially to Eileen Konowal without you I would have never written another word after 9/11, to each and everyone of you a sincere and heartfelt THANK YOU.

~ Chapter One ~

Bridget Donahue's heart stopped. And, in that moment, a torrent of guilt and regret swelled up consuming her. Before her, under a mound of fallen leaves, a piece of faded red cloth protruded. Bridget's heart again began wildly beating, pounding the blood against the walls of her veins, as it raced through her. Her body pulsated. Salty tears washed over her hazel eyes. Before her could be the answers to her questions. Before her could be the end of her searching. Through the lump in her throat, her voice cracked as she dared to ask the question.

"What is that?" she spoke barely above a whisper. Peter was only steps away.

"In only seven years it will be 1900," mindlessly Peter was babbling on. "Think of th…" he stopped dead in his speaking. His hand tightened on the coppiced knob handle of his shillelagh when he also saw the deteriorating fabric. Bridget and Peter had walked together through this wooded area on the north side of Glencar Lake many times over these last four years searching for some telltale sign of Meg.

Why hadn't we seen this before? she thought.

"Stay there Bridget, I'll examine it," Peter ordered. Apprehensively, he walked towards the pile of lifeless leaves. Its grave-like size and shape could easily have entombed a young women's body. At one end, a branch stuck out as if it was a marker.

Peter placed his blackthorn walking stick on the ground as he knelt beside the mound. It would be too sacrilegious to poke around at the ground cover with it, for indeed, this might be Meg's grave.

Nature feeling the gravity of the moment kept everything around them still and silent. Awkwardly, he started wiping away the top layer of freshly fallen leaves.

"What do you see?" Bridget asked. She brought her hands up to her mouth trying to hold back her emotions when he did not answer. Her long flowing auburn hair lay limp upon her shoulders. Deep lines furrowed across her face making her look years older then seventeen. Through her tears, she watched Peter. He was the youngest and the runt of the Kelly boys. He was neither to inherit his family's farm nor its stature. Nevertheless, to Bridget no one ever stood as tall as he did. He was Peter…her dependable Peter… her confidant…her *anam chara*.

Two weeks ago, they planned to come again to Glencar Waterfall saying then it was because it had been Meg's favorite place. Everything up until this moment had been perfect. The usually changeable weather had stayed especially pleasant. The breeze was cool. The crisp Irish air refreshing.

The ride in Peter's jaunting cart was comfortable. Fairy Dancer, his prized Connemara pony, was strong with an easy temperament. They followed the winding road that went along Glencar Lake. The mist hung low on the pastoral shores that lined it, as black face sheep stood knee deep grazing in the lush green grass. A pair of swans gracefully glided across the mirror lake. In formation, a flock of geese landed in its waters. The steep slopes generously covered with wildflowers and heather perfumed the air with their sweet fragrance. Traveling through this tranquil setting in the Sligo Mountains, through this enchanted land of fairies; it was easy for Bridget and Peter to forget the origins of their Sunday trips.

The sun tried to send its rays through the thick canopy of foliage above them as they hiked up the woodland path. Songbirds flying over them carried juicy berries in their beaks back to their nests.

In the distance, they could hear the sound of pounding water as it cascaded from the waterfall. They followed the gently rippling stream towards it. Once there, it was easy to see why Meg loved this magnificent place so. They sat watching the racing waters fall to the waiting pool below, being refreshed by its spray. It was only while they were making their way back down the mountain that they saw it... that faded piece of red fabric.

Earlier that morning Bridget and Peter had prayed in church that this would be the day they would find an answer. They prayed this would be the day they would find Meg. And now they prayed and begged God that He wouldn't answer their prayers. Not today...not here.

Bridget watched searching her memory about that piece of cloth. Hope began filling her as she remembered that Meg was not fond of that color. It quickly left. Through all her years of searching for her older sister, Bridget knew that she really did not know Meg at all.

Peter continued to work his way down to the beginning of the scarlet material. The rich smell of the composting leaves filled the air. The stiffness in his body loosened when he found it.

"I have it," Peter said. Smiling, he turned and held up what he had exhumed for her examination.

"It's just a nest," Bridget said as the tears she had desperately tried to hold back began falling freely.

"Not just a nest. A mighty fine one at that," Peter said holding in his hand an example of an avian architectural masterpiece. Its maker had planned for a soft lining as she had woven other birds' feathers and strips of crimson colored rags into it. Unfortunately, it was evident that this fortress had come to a violent end as it lay there with the branch it had fallen with. What once had been the potential for three new lives were now just broken, dried up eggs. They had no further chance for life.

But, for the moment at least, Bridget had the chance to hope again of finding Meg …alive.

~ Chapter Two ~

"*Oh, it was a beautiful morning,*" Michael Donahue began the tall tale as his young daughter, Bridget, climbed up on his knee. "The mist was sitting on the Garavogue River as I took me walk. There before me half-awake eyes was our beloved St. Bridget, herself." Her father never changed so much as a single word in any retelling of it. "St. Bridget was standing by our well that she blessed so many years ago. In her arms, she held something wrapped in a white blanket. She beckoned me to come and see what she was holding. As I open the blanket, what do you think was in it?" Michael asked. As a child, Bridget loved watching the twinkling in his eyes as he told the tall tale to her.

"Me," she cheerfully answered, knowing the myth of her birth on February 1, 1875 by rote.

"Yes, indeed. It was you," Michael continued. "Just a wee little thing you were. Bridget, you were the most beautiful baby that God in His Heaven has ever sent down to earth. 'She is a gift from God to you and your good wife Mary,' was what St. Bridget herself said to me as she gave you to us on her feast day."

In truth, the day of Bridget's birth was a damp and dismal gray day with a coldness that penetrated down to bones. Their first child, James Patrick, known as Jimmy, was fourteen years old and Margaret Elizabeth, whom everyone called Meg, was five.

Twenty-five years after the Great Hunger in Ireland, its effects were still palpable. The famines that started in 1846 had taken the lives of a million and a half. However, it was not in the large numbers of those that died that killed the spirit in the living. It was all the single deaths. It was the loss of their caring mothers, loving fathers, dearest sisters and cherished brothers. It was the seeing valued neighbors and close friends die. It was in the watching of their beloved children's tender lives being taken away by starvation and disease. The unremitting hunger and illnesses ate at the Irish spirit. The constant helplessness and frustration made them numb. There was no mercy. The famine was cruel. There was no real help forthcoming. They were alone and isolated. The famine forced a million of Irish families to emigrate to other countries including Canada and America.

Nevertheless, Michael Donahue would have none of that in his telling of the miraculous events of his youngest daughter's birth. For generations the Donahues had lived on and tended this farm. Norse warriors and Anglo-Norman invaders could not take their land from them. The home, rich in intertwined Celtic and Catholic traditions was where Michael was born in 1836.

Even then, times were hard when he was a boy. However, he and his family felt rich. "We've more than enough turf and potatoes to provide for our family," Michael's father told anyone who came to their door. "There is always room for one more at our table."

It was commonplace for friends and neighbors to gather together at the Donahue's for a *Céili* where the lively music from fiddles, flutes and concertinas intermingled with laughter, singing and the sounds from the quick steps of Irish dancing all filled the air. An evening spent at the Donahue's would not be complete without one of their famous tales.

That was all before the Great Famine. Now, Michael Donahue was the last of his father's house. Drink easily numbed his pain and even if only temporarily, erased his memories.

"For sure, we'd be hearing the sound of a *cipin* beating on a *bodhrán* drum if we listened to your chest," one of his chums said to him in the pub. Indeed, in the same pub where Michael spent hours listening to others recount their problems without talking of the pain he carried in his own heart.

Mary Murphy Donahue, Bridget's mother, was quite a different sort. Money and food was sparse. Life had been hard for their mother Mary. She had seen the death of four children and with each of their deaths, a part of her died. The outside damp dismal gray day of Bridget's birth was warm compared to the coldness in her mother's heart. Mary Donahue did not want this child. She wanted no more children as she feared to love them, dreading that they too would be taken from her. Using all the strength she could command, Mary put up a wall between Bridget and herself. The wall of her own making, over time, made her a prisoner from reaching out to anyone. Mary found no solace in drink. She chose, as her mother before her, to hide behind her religion.

For the Murphy's family creed was *entomb your feelings*. An act blessed by the church, as with each of their offerings they earned the graces for a better place in Heaven. They laid to rest and buried all their wounds and unsatisfied desires in the rich soil of their souls. Layer by layer each generation added their avoided feelings. Thinking this apparently simple act would keep them safe from these unwanted emotions. Never realizing the soul is the center of life and that everything planted there lives on forever. Unaware these seeds would germinate and sprout into the flowers that would be their everlasting legacy to their heirs. For generations, obscure feelings of resentment, bitterness, depression, self-doubt and foreboding took deeper root as each new generation added to the compost. This was Mary's inheritance and one she was willing to pass down to her heirs.

In spite of the difficult conditions surrounding her, Bridget's childhood was a happy one.

"Jimmy, take me," Bridget would ask.

"I will," Jimmy answered. He loved walking down to the tracks to watch while the train sped by. Many a night, he brought his little sister with him.

"It's coming. It's coming," Bridget yelled as the steel rails beneath their feet rumbled long before they could see the train coming. Eagerly, they watched for the approaching cloud of smoke and listened for the toot. As the train hurried past, Jimmy and Bridget caught glimpses of its passengers. The train quickly vanished. The soot it left behind always burned her eyes.

"Where is the train going?" Bridget asked the same question each time.

"It's traveling all the way to Dublin," Jimmy answered each time with the same excitement as the last. "Won't be too much longer and I'll be on her. Then onto another grand train all the way to Queenstown. And then, Bridget, I'll sail on a fine ship all the way across the Atlantic to America!"

"That will be grand, Jimmy, won't it?" Bridget worriedly replied. "Will you take me with you?" wiping her eyes, she asked. "Will you take Ma and Da? Is Meg going?" There was never an end to Bridget's questions. Sweeping her up into his arms, Jimmy swung her up into the air and placed her on his shoulders. There she sat, while he carried her all the way home telling her his wonderful dreams.

"That will be grand," Bridget repeatedly said.

Crossing over the town road, the hint of warm yellow lights coming from their farmhouse windows became visible. No matter how cold the weather, just the sight of it warmed them.

"Bridget, when you are older, I'll send a ticket for you and for Meg to join me in America," Jimmy made the same promise each time he took her off his shoulders.

There was only five years difference in the girls' ages. Yet, Meg was a mother to Bridget. Lovingly and gently, she watched over her. Bridget feared the days when Meg was not around to protect her.

"Mind what you do and don't get under Ma's foot," Meg ordered. Unfortunately, it was next to impossible for Bridget to avoid doing so.

"Get out of me way!" Mary Donahue's voice was sharp. "Stop that singing!" her voice bitter, as she chastised Bridget's loud playing, as though Bridget had stolen the laughter from her dead brothers and sisters.

Only on the days when a letter from Mary's brother came, would there be any pleasant change in her temperament.

"I picked up the package that Uncle James sent," Jimmy would announce to his mother and sisters.

"God be praised," their mother happily said. "We'll open it after supper." Hurriedly they cleared the table. Michael would take his seat. Mary sat beside him with her sewing basket.

"Jimmy, you may begin," Father said as soon as Meg placed his whiskey bottle and glass in front of him. With a grin on his face from ear to ear, Jimmy carried the package into the room.

"Bridget, will you help me take off the wrapping?" he asked. Jimmy opened the box. The contents repeatedly were the same, two envelopes and a gift for the children. The first envelope with *MARY* written on it Jimmy handed to his mother.

"Thanks be to me brother, James. It's a good month we'll be having," joyously Mary said counting the money that was in it. James Murphy had done well for himself since he traveled to America in 1842.

Anxiously, Elizabeth and Meg waited for Jimmy to start reading the letter in the second envelope marked *FAMILY*.

"Well, what do we have here?" Jimmy joked with his sisters.

"Get on with the letter. We all know it's a puzzle, Jimmy," Mother snapped, wanting to hear the adventurous stories of her brother's life.

No one made a sound as Jimmy read the letter.

Mary, Meg and Bridget did not want to miss a word. Always, Jimmy read the offer for them to come to America. To which Michael had the same reply:

"If God wanted us to be in America, He would have put us there." Michael's tone made it know that he was the head of the house and there would be no further discussion.

Looking directly at his father, he said, "When it is time for me godson and namesake Jimmy to come to America, I'd be mighty pleased to find him a find job." Jimmy knew this sentence by heart.

"You always were more of a Murphy than a Donahue," his father would mumble. Jimmy continued reading. When Jimmy was almost finished, Michael took two spoons and started playing a tune. Each time he started a different tune by rhythmically hitting them between his hands and his leg. It never took Meg more than a few seconds to pick up the beat and recognize which one he was playing. Up she would jump and start dancing. Bridget would sing. Mary continued her mending, not looking up or joining in. By the time Jimmy finished reading, "As always, I remain your loving brother," the celebration had begun. Jimmy would join Meg in dancing. Michael poured himself another glass of whisky and raised the glass.

"To our great benefactor, Uncle James," he would say sarcastically.

"To Uncle James, To Uncle James," Bridget would chant.

"Stop it! Stop it!" Mary would demand. Michael leaned over to his wife, trying to reach in behind her stone wall.

"Frimsy Framsy, who's your fancy?" he would ask her. Mary turned her face away. Again, Michael tried to coax her.

"Come now, fair maid Mary. Frimsy Framsy, who's your fancy?" he asked now with a sweeter tone in his voice.

"Michael Donahue that's who," Mary said forgetting herself. Michael with a wide grin on his face leaned over towards her.

"Don't you get any craziness in your mind," Mary ordered. Michael leaned closer and kissed her full on the mouth. The children roared with laughter. Something in the sound of happiness always snapped her back to her senses and reminded her where she was.

"Michael, now stop this! I have work to do," Mary's sharp and cutting voice made it know that this merriment was now ended. She picked up her mending and left the table. Michael may have been the head of this house. But, it was Mary who was the heart. And, it was her heartbeat that set the rhythm for its daily life. After hearing the sound of her shrilling voice, Michael poured himself another glass of whiskey and stood up.

"To James," he said seriously. He took a sip from the glass. Looking up to heaven, he solemnly lifted his glass in salute.

"To Patrick and Liam," he whispered and then he gulped down the rest of the whisky. He slammed the empty glass down.

"I'll be home later," he announced putting on his cap. He closed the door behind him.

The children watched in silence. Once their father was gone, Jimmy brought out the puzzle their

Uncle James had sent last month. The children had been working on putting it together for weeks. Not an easy undertaking, as all the wooden pieces had been cut on the color lines so there were no easy transition pieces. Deceptively, some of the pieces had the same cut so they would temporarily fit where they did not belong. Moreover, if that hadn't make the puzzle difficult and tricky enough, it was a two-sided puzzle with a different picture on the front and back of each piece. The red box it came in had no picture or description on it to give a hint of what the puzzle would look like upon completion. The three Donahue children would have to wait until it was finished for that.

the 4 of May, 1880

Dear sister Mary and beloved family,
    I am in first-rate health and me spirits have never been better. I have read your last letter over and over. It was with the outmost of pleasure that I have obtained a promise of employment for our Jimmy. There is a great need for good laborers on the construction of the Brooklyn Bridge.
    Mary, you would not believe your eyes. It spans across a great river. This is a good land and it will make a fine and respectable place for Jimmy to make a decent living. The work is hard but there is great opportunity here for those who know where to find it.
    There are Murphys, Kellys and O'Briens in the hundreds, so Jimmy will not be missing the company and talk of his kinsmen. And me own son, your cousin Sean, wants me to assure you, Jimmy, that life

here in America has added to the beauty of our young Irish women who can be found here healthy and in good spirits. I have made arrangements for Jimmy to sail on the *Abyssinia* from Queenstown.

I am also enclosing enough money for him to buy his bedding, cooking and eating utensils at the wharf. I have put in a little extra for any other items he may need. It is with a happy heart that I look forward to looking upon his face.

As always, I remain your loving brother,

James

As Michael Donahue had requested, Jimmy waited until after his nineteenth birthday to make his fortune in America.

"I promise, when you are old enough, I'll send you a ticket to come to America," he told Bridget the night before he left. It did not help. Tears kept falling down her face, as they walked together to the train tracks. Watching the grand train and its passengers travel pass, knowing tomorrow he would go, Bridget had no questions for him.

"Come have a drink with me," Michael said as he woke his son up. Jimmy obliged. Sitting in the kitchen in the hour before sun up, Michael handed Jimmy something wrapped in a clean hanky.

"It was me brother's, I want you to have it. It keeps good time," his father said. "In time, I expect you will be coming back home again to see us."

"Thank you, Da," Jimmy said, holding his father's prized pocket watch in his hand.

"Here is a little extra pin money. Make sure

you hide it so that you don't get your pockets picked?" Michael quickly added before there was any chance for either of them to become more sentimental.

Mary Donahue spent the morning fingering her rosary beads. She never uttered the words goodbye to him. Meg and Bridget would not stop kissing him. Nevertheless, in too short a time Jimmy was gone. Meg tried to take Jimmy's place of reading Uncle James letters. But it wasn't the same for them without him there. Now they eagerly awaited the arrival of his letters from America. If only for a few minutes his jovial sense of humor livened up their lives.

As it does, one day turned into another and time passed. By the time Bridget turned thirteen, Meg was a full-grown woman of eighteen. Meg's oval face with its high cheekbones and full lips was beautiful. Her long raven colored hair fell softly on her shoulders. The paleness of her skin accentuated her deep-set bright blue eyes.

Bridget was in awe of her sister's good looks. Meg's smile would light up a room. Her walk made the boys stop talking and look. Bridget wanted to be her. Bridget was shorter, rounder face and had rather a plain look about her.

Bridget could only see the differences between them. Meg never thought about it. A stranger would always be able to tell they were sisters.

It started innocently enough. One morning Meg was nauseous. The smells of the barnyard upset her stomach. Eventually, every morning she began vomiting. Bridget became concerned.

"I should tell Ma, she can give you something,

she said.

"No, No… don't tell her. She'll only get upset. I'm fine. Something I ate is disagreeing with me." Meg begged her not to tell their parents.

"Are you sure you're alright?" Bridget asked.

"Look at me," Meg said flattening her nightgown on her stomach. "If I was really sick, I'd be losing weight. You can see I'm gaining some." Bridget deferred to Meg's judgment.

"Why not? Meg isn't losing any weight so she can't be to sick. Actually, Meg's face looks a little plumper," Bridget thought.

"Don't tell anyone," Meg ordered.

"I won't" Bridget answered.

"Not even to Jimmy in a letter," Meg said.

"I won't," Bridget again answered. This decision became an act she was soon to regret.

~ Chapter Three ~

As Bridget remembered it, Meg was starting to feel better for only a few days before she disappeared. There was no indication that last evening was going to be the last they spent together. They not only shared an upstairs room, they shared a bed. Together they said their prayers and then they said good night. Sometime during the night, Bridget rolled over and Meg was not in the bed. She gave no thought to it and went back to sleep. When she woke up at her normal time, Meg was nowhere to be found. Their father was not at home. Their mother was cleaning up in the kitchen. Mary's attitude was indifferent when she answered Bridget.

"I have not seen her. She may have had an errand to run." Mary was not concerned.

Something was wrong. Bridget felt it. All day at school, she could not keep her mind from worrying about her sister. She ran most of the way home to see if Meg was there. She wasn't. Michael and Mary were in the kitchen when Bridget burst in.

"Is she home?" Is Meg here?" Bridget questioned them. She did not wait for a reply and was calling and running up the stairs to her sister. Michael sipped on his drink. Mary busied herself.

"Where is me sister?" Bridget interrogated them

when she came back into the kitchen. Neither of her parents answered.

"Where is Meg...What is wrong?" Bridget commanded.

"We don't know where she is. I have looked all over for her and I couldn't find her," Michael simply stated.

"Couldn't find her? How can that be?" Bridget questioned.

"We think she ran off," Mary chimed in.

"Ran off...with whom... Meg wouldn't do that. She would have told me. Something has happened to her," Bridget was rambling.

"I asked all through town. No one else is missing. No one has seen her," Michael spoke as if this was enough of an answer. Bridget stood looking at him in disbelief.

"It was the Tinkers. Been awhile since they took anyone from around these parts. Must be about time for them to start that up again. Mind where you go. Mind who you're with," Mary said giving motherly advice for the first time.

"Could have been tinkers. Heard there was a band through this way a few weeks ago," Michael added. Bridget had heard the stories of tinkers all her life. She had never seen one. For that matter, she heard stories of fairies and leprechauns who she had also never seen. However, these she knew to be true, as she had heard for herself the sounds of the fairies when she went by the Fairy Mountains.

Her parents were so calm and resolute in their belief that tinkers abducted Meg. It was incredible to Bridget that they were sitting there calmly having this conversation.

"No need to get all worked up this soon. Meg might just have run off. She could be home in a few days. Heard stories of girls doing that same thing from time to time," Michael finished talking and went out. Mary went back into her solitude.

Life as Bridget knew it was gone. There had to be an answer. Bridget went back up into their room to see if she could find it. There were no marks on the windows or door. There were no sign of tinkers prying anything open. Nothing was out of place. Nothing of Meg's that Bridget could see was missing.

Bridget came down to help her mother with dinner. Without speaking, they worked together. Michael had not come home from his visit to the pub. Mary and Bridget ate in quiet. The silence was deafening.

They're keeping something from me, she knew it. After she finished her chores, Bridget walked to the tavern. She had walked to O'Donnell's many times to fetch her father. However, on this night as she walked along the dirt road her stomach quivered. She had to find Meg. Something was horribly wrong and she could feel it.

What did they know? Is it true that tinkers stole her? Did she run off by herself? Did she go for an early walk and drop dead in a field? Is she sick somewhere? Did she fall in the river? All Bridget could do was to think of questions. Meg always knew the answers. Meg was the stronger of the two. She took care of any troubles. If Meg couldn't fix it, her father always could. But Meg wasn't here and her father didn't seem to care. Bridget made her way to the tavern and for the first time in her life, she felt truly alone.

Her hand trembled as she turned the knob of the pub door. Once opened the stale smells of stout, whisky and body odor rushed out to free themselves from confinement. Bridget's eyes squinted as she looked for her father among the men in the darkened room. It was an easy task. Michael sat in his favorite chair at the table in the far corner. There was no music playing. There was no merry singing. Michael Donahue sat quietly while his chums were busy doing all the talking. A quivering feeling ran across her lower back as she mustered up the courage to talk to her father.

"Da, Ma sent me," Bridget lied. "You must come home now. It's important."

"This had better be a most serious matter to be bringing me home at this hour?" her father answered.

"It is," she stated plainly enough. Michael Donahue finished his drink before he got up from his chair.

As they walked along the dirt road towards their home, Bridget's body shook as she tried to find the right words.

"Da, where is me sister? Meg would not have left without telling me." Once she started the questions kept coming from her. "Where is she? What do you know? Why aren't you worried about her?" Michael did not break his stride as they walked together towards home. There had not been enough time for him to acquire his usual end of the night of drinking stagger.

Michael Donahue did not look at the desperate face of his daughter. There was no twinkle in his eyes as he began to answer all her questions. By his unnaturalness, she knew this would not be one of his tall tales.

"When I was a boy I had two older brothers Patrick and Liam. I know you know their names, Bridget, but I have never told you their story." Michael Donahue's steps slowed as he searched and struggled to find and say the right words to her. The air was crisp for the clearing of his mind.

"In the Summer of '47 it was with terrible sad hearts that me parents gave their blessings to me brothers for an undertaking of such awful importance. Me father had gone to Lissadell House and asked the landlord, Sir Robert Gore-Booth, for enough passage money to pay for me brothers to sail to Canada. There was no future for Patrick and Liam here. No one could promise them that if they stayed they would be well and live full lives. Sir Robert was a decent man and gave me father what he asked.

There was nothing joyous in the departing. For us it was a funeral. We said our goodbyes without knowing if we would ever see each other again. Me mother cried. Jesus, I cried. We hoped they would send us money back from Canada. Me parents knew there was no other choice. Me mother said I was too young to go." Michael Donahue's voice cracked as he spoke. Bridget motioned her father to a rock by the side of the road where they both could sit. Michael Donahue just continued walking as he talked.

"The Great Hunger started back in September of 1845 when the potatoes went black. The bloody blight rotted the potatoes and withered their leaves making them uneatable. Some of the starving did eat them though and sickness and death followed. A horrific hardship covered all of Ireland.

Patrick was eighteen and Liam was twenty. Oh, how young and filled with great dreams of adventure they were. Stories of opportunities for wealth in Canada were ringing in their ears.

The boys had never before been outside our own parish. They had gone to the ticket agent on Market Street to pay for their passage." Michael's voice was stronger as he now spoke. Bridget was listening intently to every word.

"The *New Prospect* was the name of the ship they would be traveling on. The ship's name alone was inspiring. They felt her name was a foretelling of what was to come. The ticket agent gave them a flyer with a picture of the ship on it. You could see her traditional clipper bow and a squared off stern. Amid ship there were two enclosed paddle wheels and a straight smokestack.

She was fully rigged with square sails. For her power was a two-cylinder steam engine. But the steam pressure on that bloody ship could hardly lift the lid off a teapot so it was the sails and wind that were to help her. Me brothers boarded the vessel the *New Prospect* with great optimism. They could have set sail on the *Saint George*. That ship would have conjured up in their minds vision of dragons being slayed. There were other ships with gentler names such as the *Bark Mary*, the *Rose* or the *Agnes*. Sailing on one of them would not have changed the outcome. The name did not matter. They were all coffin ships." Michael stopped walking.

They both stood before the High Cross on the side of the road. The tall stone cross' intricately iconographic designs was Celtic. Below the ring on the south panel skillfully carved in high relief were scenes of David in the lion's den and the sacrifice of Isaac. This would be a respectable place to continue with what happened to his brothers and so many others. He motioned for Bridget to sit with him on its plinth.

"Thousands boarded these ships that summer and thousands died. All these packing ships were the same. At one time they were used to transport cargo from one port to another. Now they were ill prepared to take Ireland's sons and daughters to a new beginning.

The passengers were cramped into dirty quarters with little privacy. They slept braced against beams or on the bare wood deck. Some were lucky enough to have brought some bedding from home and others slept on bare canvas bunks. The ships did not carry enough water, food or medicines.

Me brothers went on that bloody ship not knowing that the last time their eyes looked at our beloved homeland it would be the last land they would ever see.

I must admit, the years of the famine were not kind to anyone so they were probably not in the greatest of health at the beginning of the journey. However, they did not die from lack of fortitude.

A young sailor from the ship, neither his name nor his rank was passed on to our family, relayed their story. He told it to Father Dowling the priest at Grosse Isle who buried them. The sailor who was around the same age as Patrick and Liam took a liking to them and they became friends. Right from the beginning, they all got along. Patrick and Liam watched and listened as the sailor sang his chantey while he did his routine jobs. They learned the words and joined in. Liam would play his concertina and Patrick would sing along.

On the passenger's side of the fore deck was a fireplace for them to cook their meals. The sailor would come there and trade stories. There was much gaiety on that side of the ship. Father Dowling said the sailor was touched by the frame of mind of these poor displaced persons. The conditions were horrid. Yet, they were light hearted and found something to dance and sing about. The young sailor spent hours with them and watched as Patrick and Liam would liven up the evening hours with their music and foolishness.

It was said of them, as well as of me father, there was never a man who enjoyed a good time more. To them every man was a friend or kin. The sailor would stay there during the evening prayers.

At first, the crossing was going well but it soon became apparent to everyone that there were not enough supplies on board for all. Provisions were made to ration the food and water. The ship met up with bad weather and the voyage that they thought would take less that a month was now up to twenty-seven days and they had a thousand miles yet to travel. The ocean surrounding them looked to be no smaller than the universe above. The waters swelled up and tossed the ship around with such force that passengers thought they were facing the wrath of God for having gotten on that bloody ship.

"My God, my God, why have you forsaken me," must have been part of their daily prayers as everyone battled to cling on to life. The fresh water that had been stored in old dirty barrels was now contaminated and bad. The passengers were in poor health to begin with and a daily death was common. With the lack of food, water and medicine, many more were dying each day. The fever spread throughout the ship to the sailors. The passengers began to fear there would not be enough of a crew left to sail the ship. Patrick and Liam helped the sick and gave comfort to the newly orphaned children. They attended as each body was thrown into the deep ocean. They still made time for the music "to heal the soul," they would say. The sailor said there was no one who tried harder to keep everyone's spirits up than the two of them.

They had almost made it to Canada's shore. Only eight days before they would have docked at Grosse Isle, Liam started with the fever. Patrick took loving care of his brother. He would sit and for hours tell Liam of all they would do in Canada. He had great dreams for them. From the day that Liam became sick, the sailor had told Father Dowling that the music in Patrick left. He would sing softly the songs from home to Liam but he would not join in with any of the others. He would not leave his brother's side for any longer than he needed. The sailor came and brought what food and water he could. He promised to do his best in taking their place in helping the others.

Patrick also entrusted to the sailor the name of our good mother. He made the sailor promise that if anything where to happen to them that he would get word to her. The sailor did not make light of the situation and say anything as foolish as stating that nothing would happen. Instead, he took down all the information needed.

Patrick came down with the fever three days after Liam. Together they lay in the bottom of that rancid smelling ship without a bed. They were sick, hungry and thirsty yet these two tried to keep their dream alive. I must admit that to this very day when I hear the gospel about the Beatitudes I think of them and that nameless sailor. Sometime during the darkness, Liam died on the day that the ship was to dock at Grosse Isle. The sailor was with Patrick in the morning hours when he took his last breath.

The sailor told Father Dowling that Patrick did not know his brother had died earlier. He could say this because Patrick in his delirium was still talking to Liam as if he was still there. To meself, I have always thought that Patrick would not leave his brother's side and that Liam came and told him it was alright for him to go home.

The sailor, using his knowledge of knots and with the greatest of respect, tied the two bodies of me brothers together. He said he did this to insure they would be buried together. He then made his way above deck.

A small boat rowed toward the ship. In it were an oarsman, a priest and an official looking man. The official called up to the first mate and informed him that he was the medical officer from Grosse Isle. He inquired if there was fever on board. He accepted the first mate's response and did not see any need to verify it. He told the first mate that he would send word back to him when they would be allowed to have the passengers disembark for quarantine. His duties done, he was prepared to leave.

Father Dowling was the priest. He asked for

permission to board the vessel so he could bless the dying and pray with the sick. The young sailor approached the priest as soon as he boarded. He asked him to come to the lower deck and bless his friends. In an understanding tone, Father Dowling said he would go there after awhile. He first wanted to bless the dying as their souls might be in need of making peace with the Lord. The sailor made it apparent that he would not take no for an answer. "Who's to say when the soul leaves the body?" the sailor argued. He added that knowing these two as well as he did, he was sure their souls would be hanging around waiting for a blessing. And, for good measure, he added he wanted to be able to let their good mother know that they were blessed.

Father Dowling, tired and weary from his duties on the Isle, did not have the energy to be discussing theology and thought it best to start down on the lower deck by blessing these two men. Even after the hundreds of times he had done this, the smell was still something difficult to tolerate. He covered his nose with his handkerchief as he anointed Patrick and Liam. He saw no reason why they could not be blessed tied together. However, he did ask the sailor to help by positioning and holding their heads for the anointing with holy oil.

If they had died one day earlier their bodies would have been buried at sea. The sailor took great pains to make sure that he gave the good Father Dowling their names and parish they came from. All that was sent back to our family was described as a common pocket watch.

The sailor also added that he took the shoes from their dead bodies to give to two other men with families on the ship who were in need of them. He said that in his heart he knew that Patrick and Liam would approve greatly. The sailor stayed watching as their bodies were carried off the ship.

The men doing the work were complaining about the smell and the weight. One of them suggested that it would be easier if he cut them apart. The sailor pulled his knife out of its leather sheath and held it facing the men, yelling he would kill the man who separated them. It would have been the start of a fight except that as the sailor drew his knife he dropped Liam's concertina and it fell making the strangest of noises. The sailor picked it up and said he would carry them off himself if need be. The workers were really good and decent men and stopped their complaining. They did as was asked.

Later, the sailor told Father Dowling the story saying he knew he could not be forgiven for that sin. He also stated that he would not be asking for any forgiveness since there was no way he would have allowed the two brothers to be separated. Father Dowling assured him anyway that no sin was committed.

Patrick and Liam were laid to their eternal rest unwashed and in the filthy cloths that they died in. In the rope with its sailors knot was the only outward sign that these two had been loved. The sailor prayed for them as they were placed in the mass grave with seventeen nameless others. He threw in the concertina before the dirt was placed over them. Father Dowling thought it was a pagan thing to do. Yet, he thought it best not to make a fuss over it in front of the sailor. He sprinkled some holy water on the musical instrument, blessing it and thereby making it a sacramental, knowing Liam would have also used it during religious songs.

Me two brothers and all the others were Ireland's heroes. They deserved so much better. The pagan Vikings who came to Ireland centuries earlier wore a hammer pendant, the sign of their great god Thor. A hammer he used with such might as to make thunder and lightning. These pagans sent their fallen comrades to their final resting place with a proper send off. Food, provisions and other earthly possessions were placed along with them in a fine ship that was set ablaze.

We sent our heroes with pendants of a cross, the sign of our God, a loving Jesus. The cross with such self sacrifice that they were to offer up all their hardships without complaint to gain rewards for a better life in Heaven.

If the two of them could have held on to life a day longer, there is no way to say that things would have been better for them. *The New Prospect* stayed anchored off shore for three days. Her passengers waiting there for room to be made for them on Grosse Isle. Many of them died in the waiting. Many more died on Grosse Isle.

The little island was only one-mile long and a half-mile wide. That little island held the hope of our nation. The doctors and priests worked long and arduous hours tending to the sick and dying with little provisions. Our emigrants stayed in tents and sheds long enough to determine that they were healthy enough to travel on further. Many of our children became orphans there. Daily burials were the rule. The emigrant ships keep coming pouring in these wretched souls. The fact that so many lived and did make it to enjoy a future is a testament to the good people of Quebec.

May God bless them for all their hard work and help. May God bless all those souls that died from the hunger. May God bless the souls of me brothers, Patrick and Liam."

Bridget watched her father finger his vest pocket which once held Patrick's watch. His eyes were wet and his face red as he finished.

"Bridget, this is a hard land. Life is cruel here. It takes away from us those we love. A man came into the pub today and told me the tinkers had taken his daughter. Bridget, they have taken Meg, and there isn't anything we or anyone can do about it." Michael was resolute. Tears ran freely down his face. This was the only time she had ever seen him in such a state. The heartbreaking sight of it made her cry with him.

This was not Michael Donahue. This was not her father, the man who could fix anything. This was a man she did not know. Life had been hard on him and this final act broke him.

Holding his head in his hands, Michael Donahue sank into the stone support of the Celtic cross. He sat sobbing at the cross' base, the foundation of his proud people.

"Da, let's go home and I'll get you a drink," Bridget tried her best to comfort him. They walked home together in silence. There was nothing else to be said between them.

He was beaten and did not have enough fight left in him to go and get his daughter back from these roaming devils. If indeed they were the ones who had her. There was no one for her to count on. It was going to be up to her alone to find her sister. It was going to be up to her alone to bring Meg back from God knows where.

~ Chapter Four ~

The dark bedroom was empty without Meg. There was nothing or anyone who could shield Bridget from the lonesome feeling that was beginning to encompass her. Memories from happier times flooded her thoughts as she tried to write a letter to her brother, Jimmy. She sealed the tear-stained envelope. Meg might have written him. She may be in contact with him now. Nonetheless, Bridget believed contacting him would be fruitless.

Jimmy had done well for himself in America. His first letters home came filled with exciting stories of his building the Brooklyn Bridge. He wrote each line knowing they would be read, savored and enjoyed over and over again. The letters always contained money. He continued the practice of sending back puzzles to the family. It was more of a challenge for them without him. However, over time, with much practice, Meg and Bridget became skillful in finding and arranging these non-interlocking, oddly shaped wooden pieces into colorful pictures.

In one of his letters, Jimmy wrote he met the girl of his dreams and he was planning to ask her to marry him. They waited eagerly for his next letter. It was months before it came and without a reason the tone of his letters changed. He was opening

Donahue's, a restaurant in Brooklyn. From his subsequent letters, it was obvious to them that he was very successful as he sent larger sums of money. Yet he did not write anymore of personal things. His tone was more factual...more business like. He continued to send offers for them to come to America if they chose. Over the years, in his letters Jimmy no longer resembled the young man she remembered.

Perhaps, Meg had taken him up on his offer. Perhaps, Jimmy held the answer but Bridget did not think so. It would be weeks before she would have his reply.

Exhausted, she made herself ready for bed. There was no safety for her in this room, if indeed; tinkers had kidnapped Meg from their bed. From a drawer she took a roll of black thread and bells. The first bell she tied to the bedroom doorknob. The second bell she tied onto a long piece of thread. This she attached to the window's sash lock. The remainder of the bells she tied onto two other long pieces of thread. These last two pieces she crisscrossed from wall to wall in her room, attaching them about six inches off the floor. No one could now enter this fortress without her hearing.

The next day was Saturday. After completing her chores, Bridget began her search for Meg. There was only one place from where she would set out on such an arduous task. She crossed the town road and went through a little forest path that led to the River Garavogue. Just before reaching the river, she took the well-worn path to the left. There in a clearing in the foliage was St. Bridget's Well. The water from this blessed well was highly prized. As it was on that very spot, on that very day, that the beloved

St. Bridget herself preached that these waters sprang forth.

Bridget tied a piece of cloth to the rosebush next to the well and offered a prayer. She splashed some of the well's water on her face. Here, her father had said was the place of her birth. All of Ireland attributed the well's water with great healing powers for the eyes.

"Let me eyes see me sister's face again," Bridget begged her beloved saint as she splashed the blessed water into them. She was ready. From here, she set out to crisscross the countryside, searching for any sign of her sister.

"Have you seen me sister, Meg?" was the greeting she gave to each and every person she met.

"Sorry to say, I haven't," was the usual reply.

Bridget walked all the way to the footbridge outside Sligo town. There by the shore of the River Garavogue a group of young men stood fishing. In the mist of them was Peter Kelly, a boy she knew from school.

Peter noticed her long before she did him. He walked right over to her.

"I heard the terrible news of your sister. Those bloody tinkers should all be run out of Ireland. And those of them that won't go should be burned alive," angrily Peter said.

"Who told you? Has anyone seen them?" Bridget was reassured to finally have someone who was as angry about what had happened to her sister as she was.

"Everyone's talking, but I don't know a soul who had seen them. I heard tell that a band of them devils were seen up by Knocknarea Mountain." Peter willingly offered the information.

"Then it's to Knocknarea, I'll be going," Bridget announced.

"That's a good stretch of the legs. There's no way you could make it there by foot at this hour," Peter advised her. Before she had a chance to reply he added, "I'd be pleased to take you."

Peter pointed over to his waiting horse and wagon. Fairy Dancer was a handsome horse. At fifteen hands high, she looked to be too much of a horse for him to handle. On the contrary, her gentle ways balanced her size, strength and speed. He took great pride in her appearance and in the care of his wagon. He did not appear to have the same pride in his own disheveled looks.

In actuality, the first-class horse and wagon were out of place with him. Besides his scrawny build, he had an oddly angular jaw and ears that stuck out too far from his head. In spite of this, Peter had kind, sparkling blue eyes and a wide smile that pulled all the oddities together and softened his look. He gave such a grin to her.

Without thought, without hesitation, her face cracked and stung as she smiled in response. Peter took her hand to help her up into his jaunting wagon.

"Do you know your way around Knocknarea?" Peter asked.

"I do," she answered. "But if you're asking do I know the way to the secret passage, I don't."

"I don't know a bloody soul from these parts that does," Peter said. "But it wouldn't surprise me at all if those damn devils found it and that's where they were hiding."

"Do you think we'll run into them?" Bridget

asked.

"No, not really. Heard they left along time ago. But it can't hurt to check it out," Peter assured her.

"I agree," Bridget said and let out a loud sigh. They settled back into silence as the wagon jostled about. The sounds from the wagon's wheels set the background rhythm for the signing birds. The warm hillsides gave up their lingering sweet primrose fragrances. Bridget and Peter reached the grassy track of road that led the way to what was known to be the burial mound of Queen Maeve.

"Where have you looked for her?" Peter asked nervously, having found the courage to break the silence.

"I've walked all through the neighboring farm lands then made me way by the town road to where I met you. That's all," Bridget replied.

"There are so many places you should go. When we get back, we should stop at the ticket office. With a girl as pretty as Meg, she'd be remembered having purchased a ticket," Peter said with authority. Bridget's body relaxed. The strength in Peter's voice covered her with a blanket of relief.

"We should check out the Abbey, Fairy Mountain and Castle Park," Peter was rambling on with the names of places of where Meg might be. Bridget nodded in complete agreement, which made him continue to think harder.

"I'll go with you tomorrow to see the priest after mass. He always knows what is happening in these parts." Peter showed no signs of nervousness as he said this. Even though it had been years since he had set foot inside the church, he was fearless.

In the distance was Knocknarea Mountain. The

entire upper half of it was shrouded in a swirling mist, so fine it looked like snow. After they finally arrived at the base, Bridget watched as Peter first tended to the care of his horse. He was the person she needed in her life. He picked up two rocks from the ground and gave them to her. As they walked up through the tall green grass towards the peak, the mist evaporated into clear skies. There were no signs of tinkers. There were no signs of Meg. At the summit was a large cairn. Together they walked around this great mound of stones. They could find no evidence of a hidden passageway to the tomb of Queen Maeve. They could find no evidence of Meg. They stood at the pinnacle from which on this clear day they could see all of Sligo and Donegal.

Bridget placed the two rocks on this spot for luck. Peter wrapped his hands around the dark brown blackthorn shaft of his grandfather's shillelagh. Acting like a Celtic chieftain, he held it high above his head. He vowed to God and to his grandfather that from this day forward he would not falter in helping Bridget find Meg. The powerful wind began to stir up around them. In their ears, they could hear the mumbled voices of the iron-willed Queen Maeve and her fallen soldiers blessing them.

This was the beginning of their partnership. This was the beginning of their quest. Over the next four years, they entered abbeys, churches, cathedrals, friaries and monasteries. In each of these sacred places, they asked for answers and prayed for help. They searched the ruins of fallen castles. Entering under the machicolations that once protected these impregnable fortresses they remained unharmed.

They searched their courtyards. They walked the curtain walls from towers to turrets. And from the small donjon windows they viewed the countryside. Bridget and Peter traveled from the megalith sites of Magheraghanrush and the Giant's Griddle to Moytirra. They crossed over old crossings of huge flat stones. They went through open fields spotted with wild flowers and climbed over dry-stone walls. As they unearthed mounds of fallen leaves to look for signs of Meg they talked of idle matters. Unaware that what they were really revealing was themselves to each other.

With Meg and Jimmy gone the Donahue household was quieter. Michael still went out each night to meet with his friends. Mary was now forced into talking to Bridget more. Bridget dutifully tried to bridge the gap between them.

Days went slowly by at first. Then they quickly turned into months and eventually into years. Memories of old pains grew dim. Jimmy never came home to visit as he had promised the day he left. He continued to send short notes, money and the ever-loved jigsaw puzzles. Bridget kept up with the tradition of working on them but Peter was the only one who ever joined her. Many were the nights he stayed for hours looking for just one more piece before he went home.

No matter how small the note, Jimmy always ended with an offer for them to come to America. A place Bridget stopped dreaming of going.

"If God wanted us in America he would have put us there," she would now say, repeating her father's words. After all, who would take care of her parents? She was the last of her father's house.

In truth, she loved her homestead and the living from the soil. A backdrop of fields and distant hills framed her farmhouse. To her Ireland was breathtaking and beguiling. Whitewashed cottages with thatched roofs and ivy-draped buildings all created the beautiful settings of tranquil scenes. She had traveled every inch of it as she searched for Meg.

What she loved most was Peter, their relationship and the time they spent together. It seemed to all that there would never be any change in it. That was until in 1905 when Michael Donahue died.

~ Chapter Five ~

As it was their custom, Bridget and Peter walked up to the well. Peter was quiet which suited Bridget's mood. She was deep in thought about the responsibility of taking care of her mother and the farm. Walking towards the well she could see there was something strange about it. The rosebush was covered with different colored ribbons all tied onto its branches. It was usual to see some ribbons on this bush, as others from the village came here also to pray, but never this many.

"'Tis a grateful thank you or a mighty request that someone is asking," Bridget said looking for an empty place to tie her ribbon onto.

"Bridget Donahue, it all depends on you," Peter solemnly stated. She turned around to look at him. Peter knelt before her. The moment would have been a serious one except that Peter knelt on a broken piece of rock that had him jumping right back up cursing and carrying on.

"Bridget," he finally said when he had himself composed. "I own no property. I have no money to speak of. There is only one thing of value in me life and that is you. I love you, Bridget, and I offer you this love forever. Will you be me wife?" Bridget threw her arms around him.

"Yes! Oh yes," she lovingly answered. Before they left, Bridget picked up that piece of rock.

"The ribbons then are a thank you," Peter said as they were leaving.

Once married, time passed quickly and their life fell into its own routine. With the responsibility of the farm on his shoulders their walks to find Meg soon stopped. By the time Fairy Dancer died, Peter and Bridget had three daughters to care for and love. Elizabeth was born in 1907, Margaret in 1909 and Kathleen in 1911.

They worked together. They spent time together. Theirs was a happy family. The girls loved getting letters from their Uncle Jimmy in America and the biggest treat was the puzzles he continued to send. The Kelly girls were never frustrated as they worked the intricate different patterned pieces to fit into these wonderful pictures. These times would have been perfect moments except for their grandmother Mary.

Mary Donahue did not like Peter, feeling he was too much of a dreamer. When Michael was alive, Mary had kept this dislike to herself. However, from the moment that Peter came back to the house and asked for Bridget's hand, Mary did not hold back her sharp tongue. Mary eventually consented to the marriage and Peter moved into the farmhouse with them after the wedding. From that moment on whenever she had the chance, Mary would cut Peter down with her words.

"He only married you for the farm and for the steady money your good brother Jimmy sends." That was her favorite statement. For a while, Bridget was able to convince Peter, as she had done to herself, not to listen to it. Eventually, Mary Donahue wore him down. Not in the way that over time continuous running water will smooth down rocks. More like the way a jackhammer indiscriminately smashes anything in its path.

Mary Donahue made evening time uncomfortable with her constant complaining. Peter began leaving the house when his meal was finished. The silhouette of him walking with his shillelagh and his dog at his side going towards the tavern was a familiar sight for all townspeople. Peter loved his wife and daughters dearly but by the time Mary Donahue died in 1912, the damage to the home and family was done and irreversible.

Peter and Dog, and that was the animal's name because Peter could think of no other, were walking home from the tavern by way of the town road. The night was clear and lit by a full moon. Peter had no more to drink then was his usual custom and needed to relieve himself. *No man makes it all the way home with all the stout he has drank.* He joked to himself stepping off the town road into the woods to find a private place. Dog waited on the road for his master's return. Peter finished his business and picked up his shillelagh to begin making his way back when a ruffling noise startled him. Peter turned to see what made the sound. There was nothing. Peter continued his way back towards the road. Unfortunately, in his drunken state, he did not realize he had turned himself around and was not heading for home at all. He was going deeper into the woods, straight towards the cliff and the thirty-foot drop to the river below. Dog sensing something was wrong started going after him. Peter singing and swaying his way to the river never heard the dog's bark. Peter passed one more tree and took one more step too many. He slipped and fell. By the grace of God or his guardian angel, he grabbed hold of a tree root that jutted out from cliff's wall. Peter screamed for help. Dog was there in an instant. Nonetheless, it was an instant too late. If it were not for Dog no one would have heard him.

"Go and get Mammy. Get me help!" Peter panicking cried out. Dog ran home.

"Go! Go away, you crazy dog!" Bridget yelled at the poor animal not understanding why he was making such a ruckus. Dog ran back to his master. Peter had settled in. He had found rocks upon which to brace his feet making it easier for him to hug the earth. Whether it was from the drink or his good-natured optimism, he was comfortable with the situation and awaiting help.

"Where's Mammy?" Peter surprisingly asked, not believing in Dog's inability to do his job.

"Now go and get her! Be quick about it." Sobering up, Peter authoritarian tone returned.

Dog ran back and this time he would not leave without Mammy. He bit at her apron and skirt. At once, Bridget knew something was wrong.

Kathleen saw her mother running out of the house after Dog.

"Elizabeth! Margaret!" she screamed. Her older sisters came rushing down from upstairs.

As the three raced to catch up with their mother, Elizabeth saw two men walking in the distance. She began running towards them.

"Kathleen, go with Ma!" Elizabeth ordered.

"Margaret, go get the neighbors!" The two

younger sisters without question did as she ordered. Bridget's heart was beating fast as she ran following Dog through the woods. The moonlight cast eerie shadows as she searched for some sign of Peter. Dog's barking hid the sounds of the crunching leaves under her feet. Then Dog sat in silence looking over the edge.

"Did you get her?" she heard Peter call up to Dog.

"I'm here," she yelled in response. Bridget stood looking down at him. She would have stayed frozen in fear except she knew she had no time to waste.

As Bridget stooped and looked over the sheer drop, she could not believe what she saw.

"Peter, I'm here," her voice quivered as she tried not to show her fear. Peter looked up. His body relaxed. His good wife would get him out of this situation.

"Women are you daft? Why didn't you come right away when I sent Dog to fetch you?" Peter said his last words. The rocks, under the strain of Peter's weight, loosened and without notice gave way. The earth and stone took Peter with it. His body plunged to the waiting River Garavogue below. From Bridget came a horrific cry as she watched his body bump and bounce off the precipice as it descended into darkness.

Bridget fell to her knees. In the darkness, Peter was lost. From the darkness came the rushing escalating sounds that led in a final crash. Then…nothing…only silence.

Kathleen stood over her mother horrified. Elizabeth and the men reached them. Through her wailing, Kathleen told what had happened. Bridget stayed kneeling motionless looking into the darkness. After that horrifying scream, she did not cry or make any other sound. Sobbing Kathleen threw her arms around her mother but Bridget stayed as cold as a statue. She did not notice her daughter's tears. When her senses came back to her she got up placidly and made her way with Kathleen down to the river to look for Peter. The men were already there searching for him. They thought it best that Kathleen take her mother back to the farmhouse. Bridget had a better idea. She took her daughter to the St. Bridget's Well to pray…and wait.

The sun was up by the time Peter's body was retrieved. Bridget and Kathleen were kneeling praying the rosary when the men carried Peter's body towards them. They placed him on the ground before her. Tears rolled down Bridget's face as she knelt beside him and lifted him into her arms. Tightly she held his face in her bosom. Love that is unable to be given away during life has a way of swelling up and making its force known after death. As if by that one act, it could again bring back the chance to show itself. It was Peter himself who broke through those tears as the weight of his lifeless arm pressed against the little rock she always carried in her apron pocket. The sharp pain from it brought back the memory of that day which now didn't seem so long ago. The day when Peter on this very spot offered to love her forever. The pain marked for Bridget the moment when forever ended and eternity began.

The men carried Peter home. Bridget and the girls followed behind. Friends and neighbors were in the house when they arrived. There was already busyness all around her but she was unaware. Numbness was her only feeling. As she passed them, each one tried to offer words of comfort but their voices were distorted. This moment felt like a dream more than any other nightmare she had ever had. Bridget walked into the kitchen and took from the cupboard the bottle from which first her father and then her husband drank. She poured herself half a glass.

She sipped the whiskey. It burned as it touched her lips. Its fiery taste was no more scorching than her husband's last words. Words she would always remember.

"Women are you daft? Why didn't you come right away when I sent Dog to fetch you?" The hot whiskey burned her throat as she swallowed it but its heat could not end the suffering she felt in her heart. A heart now seared and blistered from Peter's final words.

Bridget finished the rest of the glass in one large gulp. No longer could she stay in this place. No longer could she find happiness here. Her beloved land, river and blessed well would forever remind her of her pain. She knew what she must do.

"We'll go to America and there you'll have a chance for a happy life," she told her daughters.

~ Chapter Six ~

Three thousand miles of ocean and land separate Brooklyn from Ireland. However, the deep bonds that connect the Irish spirit knows no boundaries. Bridget's heartfelt correspondence to her brother traveled along with other letters written by friends and neighbors recounting the same tragic event to their loved ones in America.

Jimmy Donahue dreaded waking up. Tomorrow, he knew, would be worse. He dressed for work as he did every morning. He took no comfort in the luxuries that surrounded him in his apartment. Dressed in his herringbone tweed suit, with his derby hat and cane in his hand, he left for work.

His somber mood distracted him from seeing the colorful array of spring flowers in the front yards of the houses he passed as he walked the five city streets towards Flatbush Avenue. It was almost noontime and the avenue already had a wave of people all scurrying about from one place to another.

Donahue's was the finest restaurant in all of Brooklyn. Everyone knew it and everyone wanted to be seen there. Politicians, judges and notables made it their hangout. Babe Ruth, Gene Tunney and Jack Dempsey never missed the opportunity to dine there. Even Lois Delander, the blond 16-year-old newest

Miss America, added her name to the list of the famous patrons. A picture of her wearing her crown, standing in front of the large elegantly carved oak doors and under the name Donahue's etched in the half-round glass transom above, graced the evening papers the day she dined there. This was the place where the common man could rub elbows with the who's who.

Jimmy opened the grand door and walked into the marble foyer. The room was large enough to hold a couch, a few chairs and assorted potted ferns. On the ceiling was a wonderfully detailed amber glass fixture with a decorative frieze trim. It was from here that his patrons had two choices.

To his right were the oval flower etched glass panel doors, entrance to the elegant *Rose* dinning room. Jimmy nodded to the waiters adding the finishing touches by placing small vases of fresh flowers on the many linen clothed tables that filled the room. Burled mahogany panel molding framed the flowery fabric wall coverings. A large, vibrantly colorful stained glass window of a beautiful young woman holding a single white rose was the room's focal point.

The menu was eclectic with good food from simple cooking to fine dinning. Specials were offered daily. All served by friendly waiters that without any notice would break into singing an old Irish melody. The reservation list was long with names of people from New York City to as far away as New Jersey. Nevertheless, there was always room for one more.

Etched into the glass door to his left was a helmet of a knight above a shield that bore an eagle above two wolves. Jimmy was proud of the Donahue family crest, which symbolized perseverance, wisdom and nobility. This was the door he opened. This was entrance to the tea room.

"Good morning, Tommy," Jimmy said.

"Good morning, Jimmy," Tommy replied, continuing to place samplings of food on the bar's counter. The long mahogany bar went the length of the room. It was highly polished and stylishly carved. A long three-panel mirror ran the length behind it. In front of the mirrors were rows of assorted size cups and glasses. A long brass rail ran across the base of the front of the bar and before that stood a line of stools all waiting to be filled. In this lively fun loving place, there was never a shortage of customers waiting for a glass of *lemonade* or *ice tea*. Across the room was a long row of booths for those who wanted a little more privacy.

"I put your mail on the desk. Looks like you got a letter from Bridget. Put that one right on top, I did," Tommy said.

"Thank you," Jimmy said walking into his office. He made no small talk as was his usual custom but Tommy understood.

All of Donahue's was spacious except for Jimmy's office. The desk and a couple of chairs could barely fit in it. Jimmy hung up his hat, coat and cane. He quickly looked through the letters. The one from Bridget he folded and placed in his pocket. There was no suggestion that there would be any urgency in it. He hoped the words he found in there would help to make this day more bearable and thought he would read it with his evening meal.

From a shelf on the wall behind the desk, he took a book. That action caused the wall to slowly move and provide an opening to a much larger hidden room. Jimmy walked in and closed the wall behind him. It was from here that he ran his saloon. He went over to the large desk and picked up a book. In it were the receipts for the weekend sales. Boxes and crates filled with bottles of bootlegged liquor lined one of the walls. On the other were kegs of good beer.

This might be the days of bathtub gin but Jimmy would have none of that. He had friends who supplied him with first rate wines and champagnes from France. It was not for a cheap price but his high society types had no problem with the cost. Of course, the common man could get any kind of hooch he wanted. But Donahue's served only the best quality hooch. Never was it heard that anyone became sick from a drink they had there.

For that matter, even though, so to speak, alcohol was illegal, no one was ever arrested there either. Donahue's was never raided. This was a good testament to the loyalty of its patrons and the honorableness of those who took their bribes.

This Monday as all the rest, he checked his inventory. Jimmy's heart was not in it. Before beginning, he knew he would be leaving early. *The boys can take care of things tonight as well as tomorrow.*

Danny Cooney rushed into the secret storeroom. He stood there trying to catch his breath.

"Danny, what's wrong?" Jimmy questioned. Danny stood without answering. "Danny, is everything all right?" Jimmy questioned further. "Is it your good wife?" Jimmy asked standing next to him. Danny was speechless. This was not what he had expected. He raced all this distance to come to the aide of his closest friend. And it was apparent that Jimmy didn't know.

"Jimmy, everything is fine with me," he answered. The rest of the his words stuck in his throat. How would he begin to tell him the horrible news? Jimmy waited.

"Have you received a letter from Bridget today?" Danny struggled to get the words out.

"I have," Jimmy answered. "It's right here" he said taking the folded envelope from his pocket. Danny's eyes betrayed there was trouble in it.

"What does it say?" Jimmy asked.

"I think you should read it for yourself," Danny answered. It was difficult for Jimmy to open the shaking envelope. "Has something happened to my sister?" Jimmy questioned. "Is it one of my nieces?"

"It's your brother-in-law Peter. My cousin Alice wrote us. But Jimmy, I think you should read it as your dear sister intended," Danny said offering Jimmy a chair to sit on. Tears swelled in Jimmy eyes as he read the letter. He folded it and put it back into his pocket. They left the storeroom and went to the bar.

"Peter was a good man…in the prime of his life. Too good a man to have died so tragically," Jimmy lamented. He took whisky from behind the hidden panel below the counter and poured Danny, Tommy and himself a teacup full. "And my poor sister to have seen such a sight," Jimmy said shaking his head.

"You are so right, Jimmy. It seems to me that the ones that are too good go so tragically and how hard it is on those who love them," knowingly Danny said to his oldest friend.

"To Peter," Jimmy said. They each took a sip.

"What is Bridget going to do?" Danny asked.

"She wants to come here with the girls," Jimmy answered.

"Then it's true. Behind every cloud the sun does shine," Danny said. "It will be grand for you to have them here with you."

Jimmy stood looking into his teacup. This was one of his dreams. One he had given up so many years ago and now it was going to be.

"Yes, Danny it will be grand," Jimmy said. Danny did not have much more to say. He stayed drinking with his friend, offering support by his presence. A stream of friends came one by one to offer their condolences to Jimmy. He thanked each one. Tommy offered to complete the inventory as Jimmy prepared to go home and write Bridget. He barely had the hat on his head when one more person came in to see him.

"Good day to you, Jimmy," Officer Ryan greeted him. Just looking at Jimmy this experienced police officer could tell that Jimmy had heard the news.

"I am sorry for your loss," Officer Ryan said.

"Thank you, I am going home now to write my sister," Jimmy answered.

"That is a fine idea. Did she know her?" asked the officer as he was motioning for Tommy to poor him a wee drink.

"Did she know her?" Jimmy asked, not sure that he heard him correctly. Officer Ryan quickly pick up that there must be something else going on here. He stiffened himself, readying himself as a man who frequently was the bearer of bad news.

"Jimmy, I came here today to tell you about your aunt's death. From the look of you I thought you knew," Officer Ryan said.

"My aunt's death?" Jimmy asked.

"Yes, Jimmy. Your aunt, Emily Murphy, died sometime during the night. I heard about it on report this afternoon. The sergeant contacted your cousin. Sean has made all the arrangements by telephone and he is on his way down here from Boston. The wake will be just the one night and then the funeral mass. Thought you'd want to know about this straight away," Officer Ryan reported. He was accustomed to weekly reporting important information to Jimmy. In exchange, Jimmy would hand him an envelope filled with money that the sergeant would divvy out to all the station. There was always an extra envelope for Officer Ryan.

"Will you be going Jimmy?" Danny asked. Jimmy stood there motionless for a moment. *Will I be going?* he thought. On any other day, this question would not have been asked. On any other day, of course, he would be attending the wake of his aunt. This was the woman in whose home he lived when he first came to America. She had fed him. Cleaned for him as she had done for her own husband and son. But this was the day he dreaded most of all the calendar. This was the one day he could not protect himself from the memories. He could not shield himself from the loss. Yet, he knew he must go and be with Sean. This would not be an easy day for him either.

"I'll be there," Jimmy answered.

He sat in his apartment trying to find the words

to write to his youngest sister. They were not forthcoming. Instead he made the check he enclosed larger.

Jimmy went to bed. Thoughts of all he had to do to make ready for Bridget's coming raced through his mind. For the first time in all these years, he fell asleep on the eve of that unspeakable anniversary.

~ *Chapter Seven* ~

*T*he ladies from Holy Name Church came, donating their time and efforts to clean and arrange Mrs. Murphy's apartment for her wake. The landlady, Mrs. Quinn, a rather short well-fed woman, had no trouble in recruiting any of them for the job.

Actually, there was an air of excitement and anticipation as the troop armed with mops, pails, rags and an assortment of cleansers stood waiting on the steps of the brownstone for Mrs. Quinn to come and unlock the door. Everyone in the neighborhood knew of the recluse old lady Murphy. She was always seen at 9 o'clock mass on Sunday. And once a week she would go to the market and order her groceries. But most of the time, Mrs. Murphy was seen just sitting behind her lace curtains looking out her parlor window. She sat there alone, day after day, rocking back and forth in her black rocking chair and waited. There were the sad stories about her that the old bitties would tell. There were the scary stories the children would whisper as they ran past her windows. Yet, with all these stories, there were still many more unanswered questions about her. She was a mystery to all of them. Even Mrs. Quinn was never invited in. She received the monthly rent check by mail from Sean up in Boston.

Now, these chosen ladies were hoping to find the answers to all their questions hidden in the dust and dirt as they cleaned her apartment. The voices of the young women quieted as Mrs. Quinn opened the door. William Carter and his men could not have entered the tomb of Tutankhamen for the first time with more of a thrill.

The heavy velvety materials that draped the parlor windows were drawn closed. What little morning sunlight able to peak in through the sides revealed the large amount of dust particles floating in the stale air. Mrs. Murphy's Brooklyn brownstone apartment was frozen in time. The outside roar of the twenties did not penetrate this solid oak door. Nor, was the jazz and ragtime music of the day able to slip in past the sliding iron keyhole cover. The only music to be heard was from the bells from Holy Name Church. The rhythmic ticking of the mantel clock was the only sign of life. What a sharp contrast this Victorian apartment made to the modern art deco outside world of 1927.

Mrs. Murphy had kept it a shrine to the memory of her husband who had died twelve years earlier. A monument to a time long ago, for no longer could one call this a home, as this widow's life had died along with her husband's. Nothing in it was changed or rearranged. Everything down to the smallest detail was in its exact place. Every item in its precise place it was the day her husband, sitting in his favorite Sleepy Hollow chair before the fireplace, took his last breath. His slippers now covered with dust were still there. His reading glasses and the *Brooklyn Herald* were still on the end table. As if, she was waiting for him to come home and finish reading it.

The once exquisite carved mahogany Victorian parlor furniture, which she so cherished and cared for, was now worn and faded. Now the oak dinning room furniture with its ornate carvings of pineapples and scrolls was dry and cracked. Where once these exquisite woods had a fine rich patina now they were dull and covered by dust.

"Idle hands are the Devil's workshop," Emily Murphy said during her daily ritual of dusting and cleaning all her fine things that made up a comfortable life. She kept her mind busy, putting all of her nurturing into the care of her house, as there was no family anymore for her to hold dear. Once her husband died, there was no longer a reason to keep up the house. Why should she? No one ever visited.

She had to face the loneliness. God had taken three of her children. One by one, her babies were taken and now she was left with only one thankless uncaring son. Sean had aimlessly drifted from one job to another. Harsh words were always exchanged in this house between father and son.

Finally, Sean obtained a promising job that he loved. For a short time, everything looked bright while he worked as a security officer on the Brooklyn Bridge. Then on the evening of May 31, 1883, it all changed. The exchange of words between father and son that night where no more brutal.

Nevertheless, Sean left amidst them, over forty years ago, never to return. Three months had passed without a word from him, until finally she received a note.

the 7th of September, 1883

My Dear Mother,

I am well and will now be living at Mrs. Moore's rooming house on Church Ave. Boston MA. I have found good employment at Hayes & Dwyer. You may depose of everything that I left behind as you see fit. I will not be in need of anything.

Your son,

Sean

Mrs. Murphy wrote long letters pleading to her son to come home. She went to church and lit candles before the altar to ask for God's help. Her pleas were ignored. She made novenas to her beloved saints. She continued to write begging her son to come home. On and on her life continued like this.

Eventually, she tired as her heart became hardened to the reality. Her son was not coming home. She stopped writing to him. Finally accepting it, she stopped praying about it. After all, there was no use. He was as stubborn a man as his father was.

Moreover, neither of them would give in for her sake. She had Father O'Connor get a message to him by telephone to inform him of his father's death. She kept her son's Western Union telegram reply.

8:45 P.M. THURSDAY APRIL 25, 1915 MOTHER. STOP. RECEIVED YOUR MESSAGE. STOP. UNABLE TO ATTEND. STOP. WIRING

SUFFICIENT FUNDS TO COVER EXPENSES.
STOP. PLEASE ADVISE IF ANYTHING ELSE
REQUIRED. STOP.

SEAN MURPHY. STOP.

Old habits are hard to break. Alone in the
loneliness of her memories, she would sit in her
rocking chair gazing out the front window for hours.
Occasionally, a gentleman would pass by and tip his
hat to her, but always she mumbled a grunting noise
as she turned her face away.

When children would play outside her window,
she would knock on the glass and chase the
hooligans away, lest the sounds of their laughter and
joy would magnify the sadness of her apartment.
Mrs. Murphy no longer found solace in the weekly
Sunday mass she attended.

Convinced she was the subject of conversation
of everyone she passed, she stopped talking to them.
No one would have realized she had died, except that
the night patrol officer walking his beat saw her
slumped over in her rocking chair in the window at
two-thirty in the morning.

Mrs. Quinn was in her glory walking around the
apartment. With each new item she saw her tongue
was sharper and her voice louder.

"This place is a pig sty. I'm going to lose money
with all the time it will take me to get it ready to rent
out again. Can you just imagine what it is going to
cost me to have all this junk removed?" she said
making sure that everyone heard her. In her heart,
she already knew that Sean Murphy had agreed to

pay her for her time and all her trouble to clean the apartment and to get rid of all the junk there. He wanted none of it.

The ladies from Holy Name Church, with the same quiet solemn manner as they used cleaning the altar continued their work. A task they delighted in as they went through Mrs. Murphy's private things. Not one of them wanted to speak ill of the dead.

The oak woodwork and sliding oak doors, which divided the parlor from the dinning room, were cleaned and then polished with lemon oil bringing out their rich finish. Every inch of the apartment was scrubbed, dusted and polished. Many of the old unneeded items were thrown away.

The living room furniture was rearranged making room for the coffin that would later be placed between the two front parlor windows. Scarves were laundered and placed over the worn-out arms and on the back of the Victorian couch. Only Mrs. Quinn dared touch the items of Mr. Murphy. The paisley shawl covering the piano was shaken and aired out. All the framed pictures of unknown people that were on top of it were cleaned and polished.

In the secretary, they found an old cigar box that held the letters and telegrams that Mrs. Murphy had saved. The good ladies read each and every one of them out loud.

"I'll make sure Sean gets this box," Mrs. Quinn said adding, "I think a son as horrible as himself should feel some torment. Don't you agree?"

"Don't you think," one of the women suggested.

"It would be more fitting if some of these notes and telegrams were placed around for the reading by those who come to pay their respects?"

"Here's one I particularly like," another said offering it for the group to read.

the 7th of June, 1883

My Dear Emily,

I could not end this day if first I did not take a moment to thank you for your kind and caring words to me this afternoon over the tragic loss of my beloved daughter, Mary Rose.

My dear cousin, your love and friendship has been a comfort to me for so many years. But over this week it has been my only strength. I sincerely wish I could find the words to ease the burden you carry worrying about young Sean. We will both pray over this. He will come to his senses and return to his home and loved ones.

Emily, you have been such a good mother. He will not turn his back on you for long.

With love and affection,

Helen

The apartment was finally ready for the wake. The undertaker had prepared Mrs. Murphy's body. She looked peaceful. All the whiskers that sprouted out of her face had been removed. Her hair was neatly fixed and makeup had been applied to her. With the lights in the dinning room turned down low and only the light from the candles lighting the parlor, the room looked beautiful. Mrs. Quinn, now herself neatly dressed, was quite pleased with the way the apartment looked.

"I might still be able to get the $37.50 a month rent without doing much work on it," she told her husband.

There was a large crowd of visitors. Some were neighbors, some were relatives and some were just curious, but not one of them had been a visitor in this apartment for many years.

Jimmy and Sean stood as giants in the room with their six foot three inch frames. In their younger days, they looked and acted like brothers. There were still remnants of their young good looks. Sean was now portly and overweight. His ruddy face was partially hidden behind a graying beard and mustache. Nevertheless, it could not hide the flush redness of his cheeks and nose, which gave evidence of his drinking.

Jimmy looked more distinguished now than in his youth. His hair was darker and his face freshly shaved. His well-tailored suit, derby hat and fancy cane were a testament to his restaurant Donahue's financial success. There was dullness to his eyes and a sense of pain in his tone of speech. The warmth between them, as the two men spoke of long ago times, was visible. They both stood as strangers in the house they shared in their youth.

Mrs. Quinn intruded in on their private conversation. After a few uncomfortable words of thanks to her, Sean went to talk to the others. Jimmy took this opportunity to speak with Mrs. Quinn about the apartment.

"Do you have someone in mind to be renting this apartment?" he asked.

"Well Jimmy, there's quite a few people who

have approached me. Do you have need for the apartment?" she asked him.

My sister Bridget and her daughters are coming from Ireland and I thought this to be a good location for them," he answered.

"You're right, it's a very good location," Mrs. Quinn quickly added. "That's why it is such a desirable apartment. It is close to the park. Close to church and shopping and close to transportation. How would your dear sister and her daughters be paying the rent?"

"I'll be covering all of their expenses," Jimmy said plainly enough.

"Jimmy, you're a good Irishmen to be taking such care of your family. I heard about Bridget's misfortune. Such a tragic shame, it was. Let me help. I'll give you the apartment for $42.50 a month. That's quite a bargain, you know. Let me see, today is May 31. Sean has paid the rent until June 14th. You can have it from then on. Will she be needing furniture and household items?" Mrs. Quinn asked slyly.

"Yes, she will," he answered.

"I can give you a good deal on all of these fine furnishings and linens and such. Do any of the girls play the piano?" Mrs. Quinn was quite the businesswoman.

"I don't know," he answered. The price of the piano was now being added to the list. Of course, the price of Mrs. Quinn giving the family piano lessens was also figured in.

"Well, that will be grand now won't it? It will be nice to have some life back in this apartment. Jimmy, we have to take care of our own. I'll do the figures and tell you the total price when you come to give me the first month's rent and a month's security for the apartment. Bridget is a lucky woman to be coming here and with all this waiting for her." Jimmy nodded and agreed with Mrs. Quinn.

It was set then. This would be the new home for Bridget Kelly and her girls. Mrs. Quinn was well pleased with herself. Telling all her friends what a fine Irish woman she was for coming to the aide of that poor Bridget Kelly in her hour of need. Wasn't it convenient that she had all these fine furnishings to get the Kelly family started? A convenience that was well worth the raise in rent and the price she would charge for all of Mrs. Murphy's old items. Mrs. Quinn went and told her husband that later he needed to go back out into the garbage and make sure that nothing had been thrown away earlier that she could now sell to them.

Jimmy reminiscently looked around the apartment.

"Bridget will like it," he told one of the women there. It had two good-sized bedrooms. The larger bedroom that he had shared with Sean still held the same bed he slept in. There was room enough for all three of his nieces. All he needed was an extra twin bed for one of them.

Of course, Mrs. Quinn knew where she could get one for him at a savings. The other bedroom was small, but it would be large enough for Bridget. It was surely larger than the bedroom she had back in their childhood home in Ireland. This apartment would be modern to them. They are going to love it. *Love…* He had not used that word in his thoughts for all these years.

Being back in this apartment brought forth memories he had safeguarded himself from. Unexpectedly, warmth started to spread throughout him. Warmth he had not felt for over forty years. *Yes, they will love it.* *It will be grand to have Bridget and the girls here*, he felt it in his heart.

~ Chapter Eight ~

Kathleen was sixteen when the Kellys made the voyage to America. That crossing remained always as one of the highlights of her life. For Elizabeth, who was twenty, and Margaret, who was eighteen, it opened for them an unknown world. Some might say they opened up Pandora's Box.

The two older sisters already felt confined by their life in Ireland. It didn't appear that the death of their father affected either of them as hard as it did Kathleen and their mother, Bridget. This might partly be explained, as neither of them was there to hear their father's last words or the sounds of his body falling to the river below.

Kathleen's mind was plagued with visions of her father's battered body. Nothing eased the pain. Each night the terrifying dream was the same. Always the nightmare began innocent enough. There she was, sitting at the table having a cup of tea with her father. She was listening intently to what he was saying. As he spoke, Kathleen studied his face, almost tracing each line on it into her memory. Something about his red shirt began to glow breaking her concentration. As she looked at the shirt, yet, before she could make the item out, the loving kitchen scene transformed into the unbearable one of seeing her poor father in that same red shirt. Now it was bloody and dirty as his lifeless body was in her mother's arms. Trembling, she would wake. After the dream, she could not remember his words or the sound of his voice He was gone and she would never remember. Staying curled in her bed, afraid to sleep, she cried.

Eventually, the nightmare began invading her daytime hours. Anything with the color red in it began to trigger memories of that cursed night. Kathleen kept the dreadful feelings and fear to herself. No one noticed her odd behavior.

When Bridget announced they were going to America her daughters gave her no argument. No one had any reason to want to stay in Ireland. Actually, each one was looking forward to the opportunity of a new beginning. Time and care was given to what they would pack.

There was no need to make a decision about Peter's dog. He never came back home. He continued to walk to the tavern each evening and there the men would bring him out a saucer of stout and a handout of food. Mostly, Dog was seen at Peter's grave. The priest and the grounds keeper promised to care for the poor creature. The Kellys left much behind. Yet, all their emotional scars and memories they brought with them.

They were all impeccably dressed as they boarded the train. Elizabeth and Margaret were fine seamstresses. Both girls enjoyed looking through all the fashion magazines and dress pattern books and for ideas to make their own clothing and hats. They not only made these items for the Kelly family but they had been making a little money making them for the neighbors. They had been on the train many times before going to the bigger cities to bring back materials for their little business. Elizabeth and Margaret excitedly talked to everyone during the train ride. They had secretly dreamed of going to America together but thought in reality it would never happen.

On the train, they talked with another young woman who was going to be on the same boat. Plans were made to see her on it.

Kathleen and their mother, Bridget, sat quietly, each deep in her own private thoughts. With the steady somniferous movements of the train, it was hard for Kathleen not to be lulled into a daydream. All the scenery went by so quickly outside the train window that it was not too long before what was familiar was now gone.

Arrangements for their overnight stay in Dublin at the Shelbourne had been made by Jimmy. It was a superb first-rate hotel. Elegant Victorian style furniture and decorations, satin materials, bright colored wallpaper patterns, rich woods and beautiful silver filled the rooms.

There was a little extra time after arriving at the hotel. The girls wanted to see and shop in Clery's on O'Connell Street. However, on the other side of St. Stephen's Green was Our Lady of Wisdom church. Bridget Kelly would never be within walking distance of a church and not be going in for a little visit. And to Bridget Kelly almost everywhere was within walking distance.

The sky was thick with clouds all through the next day's train ride. However, the clouds at Cobh station could not keep Bridget from seeing the steeple of St. Colman's Cathedral.

"There'd be time enough for a little visit," she said. Up a narrow winding road they walked. Passed rows of beautiful colorful houses they went. There on top of a steep slope stood the cathedral. Magnificently, it reached to heaven in such splendor and grace. They walked in. It was grand. It took them a few moments to adjust their eyes to the darkness. After making the Sign of the Cross with holy water they slowly, reverently walked to the front altar. The family knelt in the first pew. Privately, they said their prayers.

Finished, Bridget got up and started walking throughout the great church. The girls walked with her. Bridget wanted to take in every detail. She read every plaque. The construction of it started in 1868. *How much of it had Jimmy seen*, she wondered. *Had he stopped in for a visit?* She looked at every carving. Each one telling part of Church of Ireland's story from the time of St. Patrick. Walking around the great cathedral Bridget obtained the best views of each stained glass window. It didn't take long before Elizabeth and Margaret grew tired of walking around the church so slowly. They sat in a back pew and impatiently waited.

Kathleen went by herself to pray at the Blessed Virgin's altar. Bridget found the statue of her beloved St. Bridget and there she knelt and prayed for the safety of her family. She had no way of knowing if she would be able to find the same peaceful feeling in a foreign church the way she found it here in her homeland. Bridget knelt in prayer as long as possible. This would be her last visit here. As she moved on the kneeler to get into a more comfortable position, the rock she carried in her pocket stabbed her. She had thought of leaving it at Peter's grave when she went to visit him and said goodbye.

"Peter, the day the Good Lord called you home, the sun disappeared from the sky. It has not shown here for me since. I'll be taking the girls to America to be with me brother Jimmy." Bridget had said kneeling at his gravesite. The little rock clutched in her hand. She loosened her grip to place it on the hallowed ground. The feel of it...the look of it...the memories it held swept over her. Bridget thought it best to put the little rock back into her pocket and to keep it with her as she had done for all these years. Grateful now she had done so.

There was so much to examine and absorb at the Cathedral; it would be difficult to remember it all. Nevertheless, Bridget tried to do so as she walked towards the vestibule. *What a fitting site as the last of Ireland she would be seeing,* she contemplated. *What a wonderful site for those blessed to be seeing in Ireland for the first time,* she also thought.

Before they left, there was one more thing to do. It was their custom to make three wishes the first time they visited a church. Mother and daughters knelt in the last pew and fervently made them.

As they exited the great cathedral, the thickness of the clouds thinned. Downhill towards the harbor, a hint of a red hue could be seen. A sense of panic developed in the pit of Kathleen's stomach. How ardently she had prayed and offered all her wishes to leave this horrendous fear behind her here in Ireland.

Elizabeth and Margaret began yelling. There in the harbor below were the red smokestacks of the

Cunard line's *Franconia*. Kathleen's dreadful feeling of doom soon transformed into anticipation. The sight was spectacular. The *Franconia* was gigantic. Elizabeth and Margaret jumped up and down in a frenzy. Kathleen and Bridget could not keep themselves from catching the excitement. The first of the Cathedral's carillon of forty-seven bells rang out. From the largest to the smallest, each one unhurriedly struck. After the chain of the toll, the bells all chimed out together. The sheer volume of their sound added an element of joy and solemnity befitting a great feast, as God himself blessed the moment. Ave Maria rung out as they made their way down the hill.

Wearing their finest attire, they boarded the tender. The girls were each wearing cloches that Elizabeth and Margaret had made. Bridget was more comfortable wearing a small brimmed hat, which better flattered her features. Questions about the immense ship's ability to float filled their conversation. With the helping hand from a ship's crewmate, they each boarded the *Franconia*.

With these steps, they walked towards the New World and into a new life. These steps took each of them into a world and a life that their experiences up until now had ill prepared them.

~ *Chapter Nine* ~

The Franconia was magnificent. Elegance and opulence they had never seen before. The awaiting officers and members of the crew all in full dress uniforms welcome them as they boarded the ship. An impeccably dressed matronly woman named Mrs. Madeline Raynor stood in line to greet them. She wore a light blue linen suit, the cut of which flattered her. Her makeup was perfect. Not one piece of her graying brown hair was out of place. She wore just the right pieces of jewelry to accent her look. There was a sense of annoyance about her but she was keeping it under control. She had expected them to board the ship much earlier. The train was on time. All the Kelly's luggage had been delivered straight away. Mrs. Raynor had no way of knowing they would not have come to the ship directly.

Jimmy had hired her through the Cunard lines New York City's office to assist them on their trip. Many other women in first class had their personal maids with them but that was not her role. The Kellys were a proud group of women. Jimmy knew it would hurt them deeply if they felt out of place. It was going to be Mrs. Raynor's job to quickly prepare them adequately enough to fit in with the high society types they would be meeting on the ship.

Jimmy so wanted them to enjoy the voyage. Mrs. Raynor would be more of a teacher, advisor or mentor. Luckily, Mrs. Raynor with the expertise of a diplomat was the right woman for the job. The steward accompanied by Mrs. Raynor led the way to their cabin. They walked through the meticulously cleaned, polished and painted corridors. Bridget realized, for the time, how well her brother had done for himself. Elizabeth asked if they could tour the ship.

"You never get a second chance to make a first impression," Mrs. Raynor snapped back. She did not want them to be seen until she felt it was the proper time. Moreover, the Kellys were already off her schedule.

They stood awestruck in the cabin. Gaily-colored formalized floral motif paper covered the walls. At their feet, a valuable Persian carpet lay on the floor. A beveled full-length mirror stood beside real beds. One cabinet had ebony and ivory inlay. Another one was made of gilt wood, bronze and leather. Swags of drapery hung over the porthole windows. Their cabin had more comforts than they had ever known. However, it was the extravagance of it all that amazed them. On each of the beds, new items of clothing had been neatly laid out.

Mrs. Raynor had taken the liberty of picking out dinner dresses she thought they would like. It was amazing that not knowing these girls and only having approximate sizes from what information Jimmy provided, how well she picked out outfits for all of them, including picking out a beautiful classic black dress for the widow Kelly.

Mrs. Raynor was very sensitive to Bridget's

feelings and wishes. She told the group that provisions were made at the boutique on board the ship for them. At a later time, they would go there to pick out other items for themselves. She was ever so pleased with Elizabeth and Margaret's knowledge of the latest styles.

The girls would have kept talking all night on the subject but Mrs. Raynor stopped them. They were already off her timetable. Arrangements had been made at the salon to have their hair and nails done. It was obvious to all that Mrs. Raynor was a woman of schedules and punctuality. Bridget was uncomfortable but the girls easily talked her into going. They did not see the ship leave port nor did they wave goodbye to their homeland. They were not finished in the salon.

"One's future is so much more important than one's past. Don't you agree?" Mrs. Raynor's commented, not waiting for an answer.

The smile on Mrs. Raynor's face made her pleasure visible when they were finally ready. She took them back to the room.

"I am sad to say that not everyone aboard this ship is going to be nice. There is a different type of personality on board," she said sounding like a teacher. "There are two classes of people in first class. The first is old money. They are people who come from money. Money has been in their families for generations. I do not expect any problem with any of these. As they are much too refined to cause us any embarrassment. But the second is new money," her voiced changed as she began to explained the threat. "They walk around behind a façade and they can be snobs. These are people who have just come into money. They know they're not so far away from the farm that the foul smell of manure is still in their noses. I think that's why they walk around with their noses so up in the air." The girls giggled.

"They don't want to be reminded of their past," she seriously warned. "If they get an inkling you're greenhorns, they'll have no sympathy for you. They will distance themselves from you in words and actions. They will not want to be seen with you as this might give them away." Mrs. Raynor paused for a moment for all her words to settle in. "This is going to be a new and exciting experience for all of you and I know it," she continued. "But, you can't act that way. You'll be making a lasting first impression on these people. I'll be taking you around to acquaint you with the ship. As we walk around do not stare at anything Just give it a passing glance like this," Mrs. Raynor slowly moved her head from side to side as an example.

"Do not show any outward excitement. Save any and all of your questions until we are alone again in private. And, if any situation arises that you are unfamiliar with just follow my example. Are there any questions?" she finished by asking. There was none.

"Oh, just one more thing then before we're off," she added. She still had their full attention. "This is also good advice for New York City. As you know, a good start makes for a good ending."

They left the cabin and began their tour. The *Franconia* was breathtaking, 624 feet overall. She was enchanting with the look and feel of a luxurious hotel. They had walked into an extravagant fantasy.

They viewed a room that was two decks high. The decorators styled it after the fifteenth-century residence of El Greco. Mrs. Raynor pointed discreetly to the silver plate, on which the words SMOKING ROOM were inscribed. Later they saw a large oak paneled room that had a charming brick inglenook fireplace. This smoking room was less impressive. This she later told them was a reproduction of an English Inn.

On the upper deck were twin garden lounges filled with exquisite plants and ferns. There was a verandah café with garlands of flowers and a sun deck. The Lounge on the boat deck decorated in graceful simple shapes was modern and sophisticated. It was here, at any hour day or night, one could go for coffee, tea or light refreshments. They could breathe in the delicious aroma from the *Franconia's* Chocolate Shop well before it was visible.

"It is going to be easy to forget the smell of manure here," Margaret whispered to Elizabeth.

"Yes, it will be and I don't want to remember that smell either," Elizabeth replied while she put her nose up in the air. Mrs. Raynor acted as though she had not heard a word that either of them said. She continued on giving a lecture about the gymnasium, health center and the racquetball court, which they would see tomorrow. Now it was time to go to dinner.

They went into a private room just outside the main dinning room. There was a table formally set for five. There were enough assorted sizes and shapes of crystal glasses, goblets, dishes and silverware to serve a family of twelve. Mrs. Raynor was very careful with her choice of words and tone of voice not wanting to offend anyone.

"In the high society of New York as in Europe there is a proper style of dinning," she said in general to the group. Mrs. Raynor turned then to speak directly to Bridget. "Your brother knows it is unnecessary but wanted me to demonstrate this to the girls." As soon as Bridget nodded her acceptance, the lesson began.

There were different forks to use in eating everything from oysters, salad, meat and fish to dessert. Using the knives would be no easier. There was one for spreading butter to others for fish, meat and cheese. The same complicated rules applied for an array of different sized plates and glasses. Diligently the girls tried to memorize each one. Bridget's mind not being so expandable easily became overwhelmed.

"Mrs. Kelly," Mrs. Raynor softly said. "You have a variety of choices for dinner to choose from. The easiest would be to order room service and to dine comfortably in the cabin."

"That would be fine," Bridget answered relieved by the suggestion. Her daughters were not so happy about the prospects of doing so.

"We could dine by ourselves in the café," Mrs. Raynor added. Reluctantly, Bridget thought on this.

"Mrs. Kelly," Mrs. Raynor said, gaining back control of the situation. "I must strongly emphasize to you what a wonderful experience it would be for the girls to eat with and meet people in the main dinning room." The girls voiced their agreement.

"If you have any doubts on what to do, you only need to watch me and do as I do," Mrs. Raynor added giving extra encouragement.

"If you want to try it, then I'll give it a go," Bridget answered.

The Main Dinning room was spectacular. The magnificent grand staircase was its impressive focal point. An enormous, exquisitely cut crystal chandelier hung in the central space above it. On both sides were ferns and formal flower arrangements. The types of flower and colors from those arrangements were copied into smaller versions placed in the center of each of the room's tables.

The *Franconia* was a modern ship. She no longer had large long tables for her guests to dine on. Instead, she was one of the first to have smaller round tables holding eight to ten seated comfortably in padded, swivel back leather chairs. The brocade wall coverings were a spectrum of vivid intense colors. Exquisite draffpes adorned the windows and archways with an abundance of material. There was crystal and gold gilding everywhere. The service was white glove. Each evening the menu for the eight-course meal was a gastronomical delight fit for a connoisseur. During these meals, the girls enjoyed tasting everything from turtle soup and caviar to elaborate desserts and fine wines. Bridget was not so adventurous.

The maître d' brought them to table eleven. The Roberts' family was already seated. The elegant looking Mr. Eugene Roberts stood. The slightly graying temples of his jet-black hair accentuated his distinguished appearance. The family came from the Midwest. He was fourth generation of a large family retail business and proud of it. Mr. Roberts was all the happier to be seated at a table filled with beautiful women. He frequently boasted he dined at the best table on the ship.

The trip had been partly for business and partly for vacationing. Mrs. Roberts, Annie, had a quiet, more gentle way. Even though there was no visible gray in her hair, she was close in age to Bridget. Hearing that Bridget had recently become a widow upset her.

Annie was stunning. The elegant pink evening dress she wore complimented her. Her gorgeous jewelry set her above everyone else in the room. Each night she wore a different setting more unique and beautiful than the one before. The color of her hazel eyes appeared to change depending on the color of her clothing.

Kathleen noticed that her left eye drooped a little. No one else in the family could see it. Kathleen had a way of always observing little things about everyone with whom she spoke. Mr. Roberts' hands were the first man's hands she ever saw that didn't have calluses on them. Even the priest and the doctor hands back home had calluses.

Annie Roberts worked in the Roberts' family store when she met Eugene. It was a fairy tale life for them ever since. That was as Mr. Roberts told it. Annie just smiled at everything he said. She asked Bridget questions about Ireland and her growing up there.

Annie Roberts had traveled extensively all through Ireland many times over the years with her husband as he acquired imports for his stores. She loved the Irish countryside. In reality, she had seen much more of it than Bridget ever did. Nevertheless, Annie treated Bridget as the most interesting person at the table.

Bridget's mouth became dry from all her talking and being left-handed she drank from the wrong glass. She had taken Margaret's water glass. Margaret in turn took a sip from Elizabeth's water glass. Kathleen watched the event unfolding and wondered what they should do next. She looked over to Mrs. Raynor for direction in correcting the situation when Mrs. Roberts took a sip from her husband's water glass. From that moment on, every evening everyone at their table drank from the wrong glasses. Not one word was said about it. Mrs. Raynor never corrected them. Kathleen understood what Mrs. Raynor meant by old money and presumed they felt sorry for a poor widow traveling to a foreign shore with her three daughters.

Mr. and Mrs. Roberts had one daughter. Victoria was twenty-two and beautiful. To look upon her was to see a magazine cover come to life. Her dark brown hair was short and waved with little curls around her face. Her eyebrows were plucked and penciled into thin arches. She had her father's blue eyes but her most remarkable feature was her lips.

These she painted bright red. She could use her mouth to make facial expressions to get what ever she wanted. She had an arsenal of these expressions from the pout she used around her father and the coy or teasing look she used around the young men.

Her dress for that evening was made from embroidered red silk. Seated at the table they could see it was beautiful. However, it was not until later in the evening that they could get the full view of it to really appreciate how exquisite it was.

After dinner each evening they all went together

to the Grand Ballroom for an evening of music and dancing. Mr. Roberts enjoyed the honor of being all of their escorts.

The Grand Ballroom was as spectacular as the Main Dinning room. Already it was starting to fill with handsome men and glamorous women all wonderfully dressed in formal attire. The women wore dresses of luxurious fabrics: silks, chiffon and taffetas. All of which were made to move while dancing. Some were embroidered while others were embellished with elaborate beadwork. It was here that the beauty of the women could really be appreciated.

The cut of Victoria's dress showed off the shape of her body to its best advantage. And just as she knew how to make the most of the movements of her lips, she took full advantage of the movements of her hips. The embroidered red silk swayed and moved with each step she took. It was perfect. As were her matching pump shoes which had the daintiest of straps across the ankle to hold them on better for dancing.

The girls learned first hand that night the meaning of making a lasting first impression. Mrs. Raynor had previously picked out attire for the Kellys. They too looked marvelous. All the young single men were drawn to Victoria, Elizabeth and Margaret as moths to a flame.

Bridget, Mrs. Raynor and Kathleen left the first night early. They continued that pattern all through the voyage. Elizabeth and Margaret would stay on much later with Victoria. The sisters enjoyed music and dancing. Naively, Bridget thought not too much harm could be found on the ship.

A troupe of thespians sat at a table by the piano. A ring of cigarette smoke encircled them. Raucous laughter, ribald jokes and clinking of ice cubes in fancy mixed drinks emanated from their location. The others in the room tolerated the behavior. The rowdy group accepted Victoria into their circle without any hesitation. Elizabeth was ecstatic that they were welcomed also. Margaret, ill at ease interacting with them, nonetheless followed in her sister's footsteps.

Victoria taught them a lot more than new dance steps during these nights. Elizabeth had a fabulous time drinking, smoking and dancing her way across to America. Margaret coughed, vomited and woke up with hangovers but otherwise enjoyed the passage.

While the sounds and rhythms of ragtime, jazz and waltzes set the pace as the ship raced through the star lit nights. It was the steady rhythmic movements of the water splashing against the ship's hull which set the pace during the day voyage.

The *Franconia* had three spacious promenade areas, providing adequate space for sitting, walking, and most of the daytime activities. There were fun-filled three-legged races, egg and spoon races as well as shuffleboard. The girls also enjoyed going to the gymnasium with Victoria.

Bridget sat in the same comfortable deck chair amidships on the starboard side of the Promenade deck reading, thinking and praying during most of her daytime voyage across the Atlantic. Kathleen enjoyed partaking in some of the games. She found the girls around her age to be too silly. Although there were plenty enough young men around her sisters, enough in fact, that she was always asked to dance in the Grand Ballroom no one particularly grabbed her attention either. None of the Kellys ever saw on the ship the young woman they met on the train to Dublin as first class passengers stayed apart from the others in second and third class.

On the first morning of the voyage, Annie Roberts sat reading next to Bridget Kelly and Mrs. Raynor. Elizabeth and Margaret were off with Victoria in the gymnasium. Their mother saw no use in it.

"A woman gets plenty enough exercise from a good day's work," was Bridget's statement on that.

Kathleen enjoyed walking on the Promenade deck. There were times she would stop and just stand looking out over the ocean. Watching the water's movements and its changes in colors all gave her such delight and peace. She could have not been in a better state of mind when she went to check on her mother. Politely she asked Mrs. Roberts what she was reading.

"I have just finished the most important book I have ever read," Mrs. Roberts informed her. Kathleen was intrigued.

"This is *The Story of a Soul*, it is the autobiography of St. Theresa of Lisieux," Mrs. Roberts said holding up the little book for her to see. Reverently she continued, "She was a Carmelite nun who became a saint by doing little things with great love." Kathleen took the book and skimmed through it.

"Kathleen, would you like to borrow it? I would love to have someone to discuss it with," Mrs. Roberts asked. Kathleen could not believe her ears. Mrs. Roberts wanted to discuss a book with her.

"Yes," she answered quickly before Mrs. Roberts could change her mind.

Kathleen traveled across the vast ocean reading the story of a young nun who died fourteen years before she was born.

The book itself was the shortest and easiest one she had ever read. The words were simple enough but she found herself thinking about things differently. There was nothing in her life that was anything at all like St. Therese. The saint's mother had died when she was four and her older sisters and a very loving father raised her.

Kathleen found herself not so much thinking about the loss of her father anymore but more of how grateful she was to have been raised by a loving mother. Kathleen loved her sisters but they were always together and apart from her. She found herself trying to imitate St. Therese's *little way*. She enjoyed talking with Mrs. Roberts. Moreover, Mrs. Roberts seemed very interested in what she had to say. Mrs. Roberts drinking from the wrong water glass held a new meaning to her. Kathleen never mentioned it to Mrs. Roberts, not wanting to take away from the act.

Mrs. Roberts gave the book to Kathleen to keep. Being polite, Kathleen at first refused it.

However, it didn't take much effort for Mrs. Roberts to talk her into accepting it.

Elizabeth and Margaret were also given a gift. As it became their habit each day in the afternoon at two o'clock, they would go to the *Chocolate Shop*. First, they enjoyed the enticing aroma. Then they enjoyed tasting all the free samples. Finally, after much deliberation they would make a purchase.

One afternoon, Elizabeth stood besides the most breathtakingly beautiful woman she had ever seen. Her complexion was flawless. Her features were soft and delicate. The woman, who the counter girl called Miss Fortesque, turned to Elizabeth.

"Darling, you must try this one. It is simply decadent," she said. After Elizabeth tasted it, the look on her face showed her agreement.

"Aren't you the two beautiful creatures I saw boarding the ship in those gorgeous cloches? I just loved the both of them. Yours had some pleated design on it, didn't it?" Miss Fortesque kept eating her chocolate during the conversation. Elizabeth nodded yes. Margaret stood there speechless.

"Where did you ever find them?" Miss Fortesque asked.

"We made them ourselves," Margaret spoke up now, as Elizabeth stood dumbfounded.

"Do you have your own shop? Can I purchase one?" Miss Fortesque questioned sounding so very interested in them. Margaret had first found the words to answer. However, it was not to long before Elizabeth joined in telling Miss Fortesque all about their home business.

"Darlings, I have a dear friend who owns a millinery shop on 47th street in New York City. It would be my pleasure to give you a letter of introduction to him," Miss Fortesque said. "I am sure you two could find wonderful employment there working for him."

"Thank you. Thank you so much," Elizabeth responded. "I want to give you my hat as our way of showing our appreciation."

"Much too gracious a gift. I will be pleased to

accept it but only if you allow me to pay for it," Miss Fortesque replied. "Dear," she said to the counter girl, "Please give me a piece of stationery." On it she wrote,

Thursday the 23rd of June 1927
Somewhere in the Atlantic

Maurice,

You will undoubtedly thank me later for sending these two talented women to you. I myself have bought and will be wearing one of their creations. I'll be by your showroom on the last Tuesday in July.

With fond regards,

Mabel N.

Elizabeth and Margaret excitedly shared the news of their good fortune with their mother and Kathleen. There was something oddly familiar about this woman. Elizabeth felt she had seen her before. However, she was sure that if she had ever met her previous to today she would have remembered the meeting. She was an angel sent from heaven. The girls knew it. Their mother and Kathleen agreed.

Later, when they told Victoria and their new friends, they were barraged with unbelieving questions.

"Didn't you recognize her? You really don't

know who she is, do you?" one of the group asked. "Miss Fortesque, is Mabel Normand," another from the group began explaining. Elizabeth and Margaret were not comprehending what was being said. "Muriel Fortesque is a name she uses when she wants to be incognito," the thespian continued. "She is traveling on the ship trying to get a well-earned and needed rest."

How could they not have recognized her? They questioned themselves. Here she was a famous movie star and they hadn't recognized her. They had seen her face in magazine ads hundreds of times. They had seen her larger than life on the movie screen. They had this once in a lifetime opportunity to talk with her and all they talked about was themselves.

From that moment on, Elizabeth became Mabel's biggest fan. She was sure to buy any magazine with any mention of Mabel in it. If Mabel indorsed a product, Elizabeth used it. Elizabeth drank Coca-Cola, used Ingram's Milkweed Cream as part of her beauty ritual, and cooked using Carnation evaporated milk. Furthermore, her favorite expression became, "It is simply decadent."

Even the usually composed Mrs. Raynor became excited when Elizabeth and Margaret told her, their mother and Kathleen that it was Mabel Normand. She advised them on the etiquette for properly handling the situation.

"If Miss Normand does not want anyone to recognize her than you must respect her wishes," she instructed them. They sent the cloche along with a simple note in a package with the room steward.

Bill of Sale
June 23, 1927
One cloche one dollar
Elizabeth and Margaret Kelly

Miss Fortesque responding by sending them two dollars and a note.

Friday the 24[h] of June 1927
From my cabin

Darlings,

First rule of business:
Higher Prices = Higher Profits.

And at two dollars I still thank you for the discount. It looks wonderful on me!

Best Wishes,

Mabel N.

~ Chapter Ten ~

Sunday the twenty-sixth was the last evening of their crossing. It was filled with a mixture of emotions for all of the Kelly clan. They exchanged address with their newfound friends and promises were made to keep in touch. As was their routine, Bridget and Kathleen along with Mrs. Raynor left the evening's entertainment early.

Bridget could not fall asleep. Back home to insure a good night's sleep all she needed to do was to step outside into the cool evening breeze for just a little while. She dressed quietly, so as not to wake Kathleen from her sleep. Bridget went by herself up to the Promenade deck. There in the shadows, she stood by the ship's rail. Her eyes wet with tears. Protecting herself from the wind, she wrapped her shawl tightly around her shoulders. She was powerless in the face of the memories that were overtaking her. *How is it that remembering such wonderful events and happy times in our lives can bring with it such pain?* she contemplated.

"And, darling Bridget, do you want to be going to America to be with your good brother Jimmy?" she could hear Peter's sweet voice asking her. He asked that same question after they finished reading each of her brother's letters. As didn't Jimmy end each of them with that invitation.

"For sure, Peter, if the good Lord wants me to be going to America, he'll have to make the sun disappear from the sky to show me." She remembered her quick standard answer to that question each and every time asked.

"'Tis that day we'll be going? Ah, so then, it is. The day the sun disappears from the sky will be the day we'll be going to America," as well she remembered Peter's teasing response. Deep in the privacy of her own thoughts, she did not notice a man walking out onto the deck. He stood only a few feet away from her and lit his cigarette without noticing her. He turned to study the clear night sky when he saw her serene silhouette. His inspection broke through her trance. She turned and looked at him. He took a few steps closer and introduced himself. As he drew nearer to her, she recognized having seen him before.

"Pardon me for this intrusion. I had no idea that you were standing there. It was not my intention to interrupt you. I have just come out for a breath of fresh air and a cigarette," he said offering her one. He stared into her glistening eyes. She shook her head no

"I am Professor George Addington," he said suavely offering her his hand. He was alluringly handsome. However, he wore much too much cologne. Even outside on the deck, it was overpowering.

"I am Mrs. Bridget Kelly," she answered and gave a small smile.

"So sad our cruise is ending tomorrow," he remarked. He took another drag from his cigarette. "But it is certainly a brilliant night, don't you agree?"

he asked looking at the stars above them.

"'Tis a beautiful sight for sure with all the stars and all," the map of Ireland was heard in each word she uttered.

"Yes indeed, the celestial bodies are radiant," he answered, smiling at her. Professor Addington looked at his wristwatch. "I dare say if we were in your homeland at this very moment we would be watching an extraordinary event taking place. Almost, my dear Mrs. Bridget Kelly, as remarkable as my meeting you," brazenly he spoke to her. Uncomfortable by his words, Bridget responded by taking a step away from him.

"I can tell by the manner of your speech that Ireland is the place of your birth," he charmingly uttered. "The sun is beginning to rise above the Emerald Isle. But today, at this very moment, the sun will disappear from the sky." The blood stopped pumping through Bridget's body and she felt faint.

"My dear Mrs. Kelly, I did not mean to scare you in any way," he said stepping forward to help steady her. "It is simply a scientific fact. Right now a solar eclipse is happening during their sunrise." Bridget's body revealed her fear as she uncontrollably trembled.

"I can assure you that it will cause no harm. No one will be hurt," Professor Addington patronizingly said trying to comfort this simple woman. "It is simply an alignment of the planets, sun and moon. There is nothing to fear. By now, it is over."

Bridget regained her composure. Tears continued freely running down her face but the horrible shaking had stopped. Pleased with his ability to find the words to soothe her, the Professor had just one more piece of interesting information to tell her.

"We won't be able to see the solar eclipse here in America it was only in the British Isles," he informed her in a scholarly tone.

"The British Isles!" Bridget snapped back with the sound of Irish wrath in her voice.

"Good night," she said and left. *How a learned man such as himself could be calling Ireland part of the British Isles?* She gave it only a momentary thought. There were much more important thoughts to be dwelling on.

Bridget rested her head on her pillow. *Ah, so then, it is*, she heard Peter's voice. *The day the sun disappears from the sky will be the day we'll be going to America.* She closed her eyes thanking him for the loving sign. She fell asleep comforted knowing she had his blessings and that of God himself on her decision.

But Peter Kelly's work was not yet done. Kathleen overly excited about docking in New York City in the morning took Mrs. Raynor advice. She went to bed early so as not to be too tired for the next day's adventures. As with her mother, all sorts of notions raced around her mind as she started to fall asleep. There was St. Theresa of Lisieux holding in her arms a crucifix nestled in a bouquet of red roses. Fragments of conversations with Mrs. Roberts faded in and out. Sounds of laughter...pictures of people...echoes of music...pieces of puzzles... all materialized than vanished.

In a hypnagogic state, vague thoughts and images of Mr. Roberts emerged. Clearing they became visions of her own father. Scenes from the many times they laughed together flashed before her.

Forgotten memories from all the times they sat and talked, ate and drank tea together began revealing themselves. She watched as they played out as a movie before her. Then suddenly, she was sitting again talking with her father in the kitchen. Intently she studied his wonderful face. She memorized every line that life had written onto it. Happily, they talked as his favorite well-worn red shirt began to glow. Kathleen was not afraid.

"The roses are in bloom at St. Bridget's Well," her father said. The timbre of his tender voice warmed her. Comforted by the lovingness of its tone she did not pay much attention while his glowing shirt became bloody and then from the center of his chest came a rose.

"Here, I've brought you one," Peter said handing her a perfect red rose. Once she touched the flower, her father instantly became luminous. Looking peaceful and angelic, the signs of a hard life no longer carved into face. He stood up and leaned down, kissing her gently on her forehead. His fatherly kiss, kissed the spot it had always blessed. Kathleen watched as her father slowly dissolved into a grand white light coming from a cloud that appeared above him. Kathleen woke fully with the sound of her father's voice echoing in her ears. She awoke no longer trembling or crying. Her father was in heaven. She again said her night prayers to the good God above. Kathleen did not open her eyes. She felt the soft petals of the red rose in her clenched hand.

"I will spend my heaven doing good on earth. I will let fall a shower of roses," she heard St. Therese whisper her promise.

"Thank you... Thank you," were the only words Kathleen could find to say to her. She lay there falling asleep, savoring the sound of her father's voice and the touch of his lips gently kissing her forehead.

"Daddy, I love you," she kept repeating as she drifted off to sleep.

~ Chapter Eleven ~

The weather was ideal the morning of their arrival. All of the other passengers were on deck by the time the ship was pulling into New York harbor but Mrs. Raynor had had them get up much earlier to be on deck to see the sunrise. The sky was clear as the sun began its journey upward. This was to be the first sunrise for the Kellys' here in New York and it was fantastic. God did not skimp on his use of his full palette of colors creating his masterpiece for them. It was amazing that back home in Ireland only a few hours earlier this inspiring site was hidden from their countrymen's eyes.

Here, off these shores, God made up for that loss. On their starboard side, they first passed Long Island, then Brooklyn. As they entered the Narrows, New Jersey was on their port. By this time, all the fellow passengers filled the decks. The harbor was full with an array of tugboats, barges, fishing boats, sailing ships and the like. All were alive and bright with flags and masts. Each tooted their horns in welcome.

"She is a sight you will never forget," Mrs. Raynor said adding, "this is certain to be the highlight of the trip." By the mood of the crowd, it was obvious to them that Mrs. Raynor was going to be right.

There in the harbor on Bedloe's Island she stood. So grand. So serene.

"Ah, there she is," cried out a fellow passenger from below. There she stood wrapped in a flowing robe. A book was in her left hand. The rays of the sun illuminated the flaming torch she held high in her right hand lighting the way for them. Many of the passengers were shouting and waving at her. Many more stood in wonder at the sight. Bridget wondered how many prayed as they saw her. *Did Lady Liberty answer their prayers as her beloved St. Bridget did?* Tears were in everyone eyes as Mrs. Raynor recited from memory the inscription that was on the Statue of Liberty's base:

"Not like the brazen giant of Greek fame,
with conquering limbs astride from land to land:
Here at our sea-washed, sunset gates shall stand
A mighty woman with a torch, whose flame is the
imprisoned lightning, and her name
Mother of Exiles.
From her beacon-hand glows worldwide
welcome; her mild eyes command the air-bridged
harbor that twin cities frame.
"Keep, ancient lands, your storied pomp!"
cries she with silent lips.
"Give me your tired, your poor, your huddled
masses yearning to breathe free, the wretched refuse
of your teeming shore. Send these, the homeless,
tempest-tost to me,
I lift my lamp beside the golden door!"

Mrs. Raynor, her own eyes now wet, told them that a woman, Emma Lazarus, whose parents were immigrants themselves, had written this poem.

The Kellys stood in awe watching as the sun reverberated off this Mother of Exiles. Moreover, if seeing this was not enough to satisfy everyone's eyes, beyond her was the colossal Manhattan skyline. Great excitement and anticipation filled their hearts. Mrs. Raynor was right. This was a magnificent sight more than they had even seen.

Manhattan stood as a true testament to the abilities of man. Each edifice built in competition with the others. Each one different, each one more elaborate, each one more enormous as it raced to be the highest one in God's heaven. The sun played with them as it danced and glistened on the sides and tops of these quiet giants. These skyscrapers reached elevations that the Kellys dared to think were ever possible. At this moment, the grand *Franconia* paled in comparison. Now these women who question the ability of the enormous ship to float questioned the ability of these skyscrapers to stay erect and not fall over.

They watched in wonder as the little tug boats towed the ship safely into the dock. They observed the crewmen securely tying up the mooring ropes.

Once done, other crewmembers lowered the gangplank allowing for the unloading of the luggage and the bringing on of supplies. While waiting for the announcement to disembark, children threw pieces of bread onto the wharf below. Only with the promise of an easy meal did the waiting pigeons leave the comfort of the corners in the overhang on the adjoining buildings.

Mrs. Raynor's words uncharacteristically choked up as she tried to say goodbye. Tears filled her eyes. Elizabeth threw her arms around her and thanked her for all her guidance. Margaret next followed by Kathleen. It was when Bridget did so that Mrs. Raynor openly cried.

"Please write down for me an address for our correspondence. I would like very much for us to keep in touch," Bridget said. Mrs. Raynor wrote an address where she could be contacted and handed it to her.

"Please come and visit us in Brooklyn when you have an opportunity to," Bridget earnestly invited her.

"I would love to," Mrs. Raynor responded. Leading them down to the lower deck she went over all the lessons the girls should remember.

"This is a wonderful time to be a woman in America. I wish you good fortune!" Mrs. Raynor called to them as they walked down the gangway.

Freezing dampness pierced their bodies as they stepped onto the pier. The dilapidated buildings lining the waterfront prevented any sunlight from penetrating through. Foul-mouthed stevedores screamed to one another. The previously throng of ships passengers now deftly darted between the longshore men's trucks and carts as they made their way to the customs house.

Bridget's first steps onto this new land were not as she had envisioned. To her, America was a fruitful land, a land of abundance. Here standing on this slippery cobblestone pavement, she was unsure of what to do next.

"There, over there is where we have to go,"

Elizabeth confidently said. She hurriedly led them towards a closed door. Elizabeth comfortably took her rightful place as leader. Quickly, Margaret went after her. Never in complete agreement with Elizabeth's impetuous nature, Bridget cautiously lingered behind. Dutifully, Kathleen stayed at her mother's side.

Elizabeth had indeed taken them to the place where Mrs. Raynor had instructed her earlier. Uncomfortably, Bridget answered all the personal questions that the inspectors impersonally asked. Gathering all their papers up she turned to see Jimmy on the other side of the counter.

Bridget's galloping heat skipped a beat when she saw his face. It had been all of forty-seven years since they last laid eyes on each other. Yet, easily they could still pick each other out. The years had been kind to his good looks and he was dashing at sixty-six. However, she hadn't remembered how much he resembled their sister Meg.

Jimmy, himself, was surprised how beautiful a woman his younger sister was at fifty-two. In her face, he also saw Meg's resemblance. There were tears and laughter as the family hugged and kissed. Jimmy and Bridget held each other with a tightness making it visible they would never let each other go away again. Jimmy stood back and inspected each of the girls very carefully.

"Bridget, you must be right proud of these beautiful young women," he said. He then began to comment further on each one's unique feature.

"Elizabeth, you have your mother's eyes. They have the smudge of God's thumbprint on them," he affectionately said.

"Margaret, you have your mother's smile. With that funny little curve on the side, I could have picked you out anywhere," he assuredly emphasized. He turned his gaze unto the youngest daughter.

"Now Kathleen, you certainly have a face as fair and pretty as your sisters but where, my dear child, did you ever get such large feet?" he laughingly questioned.

"Uncle Jimmy, I have long pondered on that myself," seriously she said. "As my father told me, they're so the winds of trouble can't knock me down," she contentedly answered.

"Then they'll come to good use one day. Those winds blow on every one of us at sometime," he knowingly stated. "I hope I have not offended you on our first meeting by my observation," he sincerely asked.

"I am not. It was a good observation and a fair question," Kathleen answered. "I think I deserve to ask a question of my own."

"Fair enough, go ahead with the question," he welcomingly answered.

"Uncle Jimmy, I have observed you using your cane to help you walk. What is wrong with your leg?" she inquired.

"Kathleen has found me out," he announced loudly. "Sure," he spoke now in a whispering tone, "I'd be walking around with this here limp so I could carry my stash of hooch right here under the eyes of any prohibition officer without him ever knowing." Uncle Jimmy pointed to the exact spot in his cane were the illegally prized beverage was hidden. Seriously, he put his index finger to his lips. He looked each one in the eye. The Kellys all nodded acknowledging they each would keep his secret.

"Excuse me, Mr. Donahue," Steve O'Brien interrupted. Jimmy had a car and driver for the day. It was at this time the handsome uniformed driver came up to them. Standing straight and tall, with his cap under his arm, he spoke with the utmost respect. "I have their grips and luggage all tucked away. Sir, the car is ready."

The family walked towards the waiting Lincoln passenger car. Proudly O'Brien's face beamed as the Kelly women admired it. And well they should, for it was gorgeous. The deep maroon colored exterior was highly polished. The lush velvet seating was luxurious. Its fancy grillwork and chrome trim were regal looking. O'Brien opened the door for them. Each of the Kelly women felt like royalty sitting in it. O'Brien started the car.

"I would like you to meet Steve O'Brien," Jimmy said. "He is a good friend. He offered to bring me here in his car to pick you up." It was not until years later that the Kellys found out what a good friend Jimmy had been to him. Jimmy had co-signed the loan for O'Brien to buy this car and to start up his business. O'Brien, as well as so many others, always remained grateful to Jimmy for his generosity.

"Would you like to see some of New York's sites before we go to Brooklyn," O'Brien asked.

"Is there a church I could make a little visit in?" Bridget hopefully asked.

"Is there a church? My dear Mrs. Kelly, we have St. Patrick's Cathedral!" O'Brien proclaimed. "So that will be our first stop on the tour, that is, if you ladies are up for it?"

Up for it? The Kelly girls were eager for the

experience. And what an experience it was. Pedestrians dressed in such fine fashion walking next to others dressed in rags. O'Brien adroitly maneuvered his car up and down rows of streets and avenues all lined with massive stone and steel buildings. Jimmy went into detail giving not only the structures' names and heights but interesting facts about each one of them.

"The Singer Building was the largest building in the world in 1908. There's an observatory on its 40th floor." Jimmy said. "The Metropolitan Life Insurance Tower became the largest building a year later in 1909. Its clock tower is modeled after the one on St. Mark's Cathedral in Venice...."

On and on Jimmy went recounting all the facts as they passed the New York Public Library, the Morgan Library and Pennsylvania Station all of which were never the largest of anything but were all very impressive, just the same. Jimmy talked about the different kinds of architecture from Gothic, Italian Renaissance to Beaux-Arts. There were buildings with balconies, towers, cornices and clocks. They passed synagogues and churches from all kinds of religions.

The Kelly heads were spinning from the influx of information. They could easily tell that Jimmy was proud of the accomplishments of his fellow New Yorkers in their quest to fill the sky with magnificent buildings. The girls stretched their necks in wonder.

To Bridget the most beautiful building on all of Fifth Avenue was St. Patrick's Cathedral. Its twin spires were majestic. Its grandeur was impressive.

"St. Patrick's is the largest cathedral in all of America," Uncle Jimmy informed them.

"Its spires rise 330 feet," he spouted out all the statistics about its construction. "When we get inside you'll see the Stations of the Cross. They won first prize at the Chicago World's Fair back in 1893. You will also see the baldachin over the main altar. It is made from solid bronze." He knew all the facts.

However, once they went through the grand oak doors, it was Bridget who could name all the statues of saints filling the many side altars. Only a few steps into the vestibule and the outside tumult was gone. St. Patrick's was a solemn place and awe-inspiring. They had just started walking towards the front altar, when Bridget saw St. Bridget's chapel to the left of her. Her heart jumped for joy at this wonderful sight. The family first went to light a candle before the main alter. It was there they knelt to thank Jesus for their safe journey. For the first time in this new land, they made their three wishes. Having completed their obligatory prayers at the main altar, they visited each and every side chapel.

Kathleen found a little chapel to St. Theresa behind the main altar. After lighting a candle, she stayed to pray for a while. Elizabeth lit a candle before Our Blessed Lady. Margaret did the same. Bridget also lit one before Our Lady, but after lighting one before St. Bridget, it was there she spent time in prayer. Refreshed, they left the sanctity of the great church to face the overwhelming city again.

Sounds and smells foreign to their senses assaulted them as they drove through the different neighborhoods. Only the covered over sounds from hooves and wheels from the horse drawn carts reminded them of home

"Aren't there any motor vehicles in your town?"

O'Brien asked.

"Of course there are," Bridget proudly replied. "But I dare say that each of the automobiles has a different sound."

"Mother is right," Elizabeth and Margaret agreed.

"Mother is indeed right," Kathleen answered looking at O'Brien in the rear view mirror.

"Long before we can see the vehicle coming up the road by its motor's sound we can tell if it the priest, the doctor or the police."

"They have you there," Jimmy laughed.

Here in New York there was no gentle sound from the hundreds of motor cars. They roared with their horns honking. Crowds of people whether on foot, in cars, hansom cabs or trolleys were all hurrying to get to some unknown place. From the water, New York appeared quiet but from this vantage point, it was anything but. And, if all that wasn't enough to be unsettling, coming from behind them then racing past was a fire engine wildly clanking its bell with a police car and an ambulance speeding closely behind with their sirens blaring. Bridget's heart could not beat any faster. They past the Park Row house, which had been the largest in 1889 and then Jimmy had O'Brien stop in front of the Woolworth Building.

"This here is the largest building in the world," he told them. Even with stretching their necks, they could not see the top of it from the street. Jimmy lectured about the great steel skeleton which held her up. He had only one more statement to say about this impressive building before they left the site.

"The Woolworth Building is called the

Cathedral of Commerce," he announced proudly. Bridget could now put her finger on it.

"This is an unnatural place. Not at all as the good Lord intended," she said in her soapbox voice.

She began making an impromptu speech.

"Where is the good earth in which a man can plant his own roots?" she rhetorically asked. There was no stopping her. The girls knew it and Uncle Jimmy could read it on their faces.

"Here in this land the soil is covered with all sorts of man-made products. Trees should be free to grow where the good Lord wants them. Here evenly spaced in neat little squares of soil they line the streets and avenues. Look at their roots buried under slabs of slate and rows of cobblestones. Flowers do not grow freely. Here, in this man-made city, they are potted and when it seems appropriate, put on windowsills," the strength in her voice escalated as the passion of her opinions exposed itself.

"And, if that was not bad enough," she added, "here in this God unholy place, man thinks he is so superior to the Creator that he raises buildings to go higher in God's own heaven than the steeples that belong there." She was done. She expected no one to give a proper rebuttal to her words of enlightenment. There was silence for a few moments as her words settled upon them. Jimmy smiled as he had listened to her.

"Brooklyn, my dear Bridget, is called the City of Churches and, I dare to say, you will find it and its people much more to your liking," he respectfully answered her. By the look on his nieces' faces, he could tell they were not in total agreement with their mother. On the contrary, traveling throughout this imposing city filled each of the girls with excitement and wonder.

They remember Mrs. Raynor's words, "This is a wonderful time to be a woman in America." Here a woman could do or be anything she wanted. They were eager to fit in this new city among the granddaughters of the Victorian women and the daughters of the Gibson girls.

Here in this new city were the women of the twenties: the daredevils, the free spirits and the flappers. The Kelly girls were eagerly looking forward to their lives here.

"O'Brien, it's to Brooklyn now we'll be going," Jimmy request.

"Thanks be to God," Bridget replied.

~ Chapter Twelve ~

The grand gateway to Brooklyn was by way of the Brooklyn Bridge. Long before any of the Kellys laid eyes on the bridge, they each thought they knew what to expect. After all, a picture of the bridge had always hung in a place of honor in their home. Having grown up hearing all the adventurous stories of its construction, they knew all the facts by heart. In his letters, Jimmy reenacted the scenes of the gigantic spools of wires rolling back and forth laying the strands of steel from one side of 1,595-foot bridge to the other. He depicted how he attached those strands of steel together as he sat high up in the cables in his boatswain's chair.

As a young man, Jimmy had sent a lithograph back home to his mother. Mary Donahue was mighty proud the day she hung the picture of the world's first cable-wire steel suspension bridge in the parlor. As this, of course, being the best representation of the bridge that her son built with his bare hands.

"Only an Irishman could take those strong threads of steal and with his hands weave them into something so glorious," Mary Donahue said each and every time she looked at the picture.

The Kellys thought they knew what to expect but approaching it and seeing its grandeur first hand was another thing altogether. One never really thinks of a bridge as beautiful but this one, with its magnificent arch towers and its grand steel lacework spanning it, is remarkably so.

As they came near to the entrance, Kathleen was the first to see the pedestrian walkway sign.

"Can we walk over it?" she asked. Before Jimmy could answer, her sisters were joining in with the request.

"If Bridget is up to it, I see no reason not too," Jimmy replied.

"Sure, and it will be grand to be stepping on the very bridge that me dear brother, himself, built with his own two hands. And will you be showing us the exact spots you worked on?" Bridget optimistically asked. O'Brien pulled the car over and told Jimmy where he would be waiting for them on the other side.

They started the crossing in silence. The sun was full in the sky. The water below was calm. Neither Bridget nor any of her daughters had ever been up as high as this before. It was awe-inspiring. Below them, they watched as the ships with flags and masts unfurled sailed by. Cars drove underneath them on the lower deck.

"You can whisper in God's ear right in this very spot, I'm sure," Bridget said. They stood still by the gothic archways admiring them and the surrounding scenery. As Bridget stood on the bridge in the picture she had dusted so many times, her body relaxed. Seeing the sea of church steeples ahead of her in Brooklyn was a welcoming sight. Brooklyn would not be like home. There she knew everyone and all their families. Here in this place of strangers, where she herself was a stranger, strange how this new bridge was an old friend.

Ill at ease, Margaret stood clenching onto the brickwork of the arches. The strength of the steel felt flimsy under her feet standing high above the East River. Alternating, Elizabeth and Kathleen took this opportunity to unmercifully tease her.

Jimmy was quiet. No longer was he rattling off statistics as he had vociferously done earlier. His reluctant stride gave voice to an inner somber mood as he walked on this consecrated ground. When asked, he did point out where he had added his contributions to the bridge.

"Yes, right over there. I would have picked it right out meself," Bridget proudly said. "And isn't it the grandest part?" Elizabeth and Kathleen agreed with her completely.

Margaret could not speak. Afraid to look neither up nor down her eyes were squinted almost closed as she tried to make her way across the vast bridge. O'Brien was waiting for them on the other side to drive them towards their final destination, their new apartment. But first, he drove along Flatbush Avenue right past Donahue's. Jimmy waved him on and told him not to stop there just yet.

"Tomorrow evening will be soon enough for you to see it," Jimmy said. "I have planned a party for you and the girls then," Jimmy announced. "That will give you time to get settled in a little bit before you see everyone." Jimmy listed the names of all the invited guests. Bridget smiled as hearing their names brought back sweet memories. Eagerly the girls began planning what they would wear.

O'Brien drove them past rows and rows of

impressive buildings as in New York City.

Here in Brooklyn, many of them were made of brownstone, some of brick and others from wood. In front, stood exquisitely made wrought iron fences and lamps, electric lampposts and cascading staircases all cordially inviting their visitors. Moreover, in Brooklyn everything was much more in a manageable size. O'Brien had the good sense to drive along side Prospect Park. Although the city park did not have all the hundred shades of green as Ireland, it was comforting nonetheless.

"Such a grand place. Sure, there is no finer place in all America than Brooklyn," Bridget approvingly proclaimed.

As they drove along Ninth Avenue, Jimmy wisely named all the different parishes they drove through. Bridget would have at least six different churches within easy walking distance from her new home. At the end of the park, Jimmy informed the Kellys that Holy Name would be their parish church.

"Down there, one block," he said pointing "is where your new home is."

"Mrs. Kelly, would you like to visit Holy Name before I take you to the apartment?" O'Brien asked.

"I would," she replied. O'Brien parked the car directly in front.

"Across the street is where you'll be doing your shopping," Jimmy said beginning again to point out locations. The girls stretched their heads to see them as he called out their names.

"So many to choose from," Elizabeth said.

"Brooklyn it appears is a place of choices," Bridget answered.

"America is the land of freedom of choices,"

Jimmy stated. All at once, the girls started asking their uncle which stores he recommended.

"There's plenty of time for you to find out which ones suit you best," he answered.

"Oh, she's a grand church," Bridget whispered to her brother as they entered it. He waited in the vestibule as the group made their way to the altar.

The oak walls surrounding the altar were ornately carved. In the center, four kneeling angels, one in each corner, raised up the marble altar. To the left was the side altar to St. Joseph. To the right was the side altar to the Blessed Mother. It was here they lit their candles. As they turned to walk to the back of the church below the choir loft hung, to Kathleen great pleasure, a picture of St. Theresa.

Unfortunately, for Bridget they could not find a statue or picture of her beloved saint. Having made their three wishes they left.

"With so many churches, St. Bridget is bound to be in one of them," Bridget confidently said aloud as they drove down Sixteen Street.

"I'm sure she is," Jimmy agreed.

"Would you be so kind and write down the directions to each of the churches for me, Jimmy. As I'll be mighty pleased to make a pilgrimage to each one until I find her. I would." Bridget stated one of her first tasks in her new homeland to them.

"Bridget, I'd be happy to do that for you," Jimmy responded. "However, it would be easier if I call each rectory and ask. That would save you the time and trouble of going to each one."

"Time? St. Bridget has always had time enough to listen to me. And it'd be no trouble for me to go and find her. But, what a wonderful thing for you to do for me, Jimmy. I could go straight away to that one fine church first to say me prayers," Bridget happily told him. "Oh, Brooklyn is grand."

Etched into the transom over the oak doorway of their new home on Eight Avenue was the address *Six Eighteen.* Its three stories of windows were all sparkling clean. As they approached the steps, Mrs. Quinn opened the door.

"Welcome…Welcome to your new home," she hospitably said. As they stood in the foyer talking the Kellys could see what a fine building it was. Only the slightest scent was noticeable from the freshly painted tin ceiling. There were no signs of wear on the brightly patterned carpet going up the steps towards Mrs. Quinn's apartment. Matching carved brass wall sconces were at top and bottom of the staircase. On its newel post was a brass statue of a woman dressed in a flowing piece of cloth holding up a Carnival glass flame.

"This is so pretty," Margaret commented. Beaming with pride, Mrs. Quinn turned on the light.

"She looks like the Lady in the harbor," Elizabeth added. Everyone agreed she reminded them of the beautiful statue they had seen so long ago this morning.

"I felt the same way the first time I saw Lady Liberty," Mrs. Quinn agreed. "From the street corner I watched as they reassembled her under drapes in the harbor. Wasn't it thrilling when they unveiled her, Jimmy?" Mrs. Quinn asked.

"Yes, indeed it was a marvelous sight to watch. All those on the American Committee have a right to be proud. Even though they had difficulties they were able to raise enough money for her pedestal,"

Jimmy said.

"Well Jimmy from what I heard you helped contribute substantially to the project," Mrs. Quinn added.

"It wouldn't have been right now, for us, would it, if we didn't come up with the money for the base. The people of France had given us a wonderful gift," Jimmy said. "Much of the money was raised when her 30-foot arm was on display at Madison Square Park."

"Best money I ever spent," Mrs. Quinn announced, "me and my husband gave a quarter and walked right up we did."

Mrs. Quinn unlocked their apartment door and handed Bridget the key.

"Let me show you around," she said. Bridget and the girls stood in the center of the furnished parlor. They could not get over the beauty and artwork put into everything. The cast iron radiators were ornate. There was even a fancy grating coming off one of them, where you could place your feet on it to warm them while you were sitting in a chair. The plaster parlor ceiling had an elaborate relief work all around the ceiling fixture. All the old gas fixtures were now electrified. To the right of the doorway was a piano covered with a paisley print scarf. On top of it was an assortment of pictures from Mrs. Murphy. The furniture looked wonderful to the Kellys. There was so much of it. Mrs. Quinn pushed open the pocket doors and revealed the dinning room and the rest of the apartment.

"You can entertain and have divine dinners in this spacious room," Mrs. Quinn said. Entertain, the sound of that word rolled around in the girls minds.

Walking through the dinning room they passed by both bedroom doors. Mrs. Quinn opened each for their inspection. Elizabeth immediately picked out which bed she wanted. Margaret took the one that Kathleen didn't.

Mrs. Quinn opened the kitchen door. The icebox and cabinets were stocked full with food and staples. Of course, this was Jimmy's request and with his money. The room was beyond their belief containing all the new and up-to-date conveniences. Seeing them thrilled the girls and scared Bridget.

"There is a surprise I made you for dinner in the box," Mrs. Quinn told them.

Off the kitchen was the bathroom, which housed a small tub and indoor plumbing. The Kellys' were in heaven. They would never be able to go back. Their enthusiasm about their new home pleased Jimmy. There was one more door in the kitchen.

"What a sad sight," Bridget said looking at the long narrow backyard overgrown with weeds. She bent down to feel the soil. "Such good land going to waste. It would make a fine place for me flowers. And over here what a glorious spot for me vegetables and medicinals," Bridget added walking around evaluating the space. Jimmy walked by her side.

"Would you like me to ask Mrs. Quinn if you could have use of the space?" he asked her.

"I have never given use of it to anyone before," Mrs. Quinn replied. "I don't know if I should be doing it or not. I'll have to discuss this with Mr. Quinn and then I will let you know our decision."

"I understand," he patiently answered her. Mrs. Quinn's face scrunched up as she stood quietly thinking.

"Jimmy, seeing it is for your sister I think I should do it and I'll tell Mr. Quinn later," she said. "Of course, there would be a little extra charge in the rent."

"Of course, Mrs. Quinn," Jimmy replied. Bridget Kelly was within earshot of their conversation.

"A little extra in the rent, I think not!" Bridget snapped. "It will be me own hard work the cleaning, the planting and the tending to it." All eyes fixed on her. "Of course, Mrs. Quinn," regaining her composure Bridget continued, "as you are the owner of the land, I am willing for you to make use of the harvest. They'll be plenty enough to go around for the Kellys and Quinns and then some."

"What do you say to that, Mrs. Quinn?" Jimmy asked. Unfamiliar with being in this sort of situation the landlady stood there dumbfounded.

"Now, that I am thinking about it," Bridget asserted, "I'm thinking that with all the work I'll be putting in, perhaps there should be a little lowering of the rent?" The seriousness of Bridget's face underscored the significance of her question.

"That is an interesting point," Jimmy responded.

"What do you think about it then?" Bridget asked. Before he could answer Mrs. Quinn interrupted.

"Oh, my goodness," she said looking at her watch. "I hadn't realized the hour. I have intruded much too long on your time with this being your first day here. As I see it, Mrs. Kelly, you would be working on my land and your offer to share the harvest is agreeable with me. I look forward to tasting our first yield." Without replying to the crazy notion of lowering the rent, Mrs. Quinn was out the door.

"From now on Bridget shall be in charge of all dealing with Mrs. Quinn," Jimmy proclaimed. In celebration, they dinned on the chicken that she had prepared for them.

Jimmy enjoyed hearing every detail of the trip from Bridget and his nieces.

"What a wonderful opportunity," he told Elizabeth and Margaret. "One thing I have learned in this great country is that when you get such an opportunity you must act on it at once." The girls nodded in agreement. "I will have someone here by ten in the morning to escort you to Maurice's. I'm not sure who," he uncomfortably mumbled as Elizabeth and Margaret were hugging and kissing him. "But I'll have someone here."

"What are your plans?" he asked Kathleen.

"I have always wanted to work in an office," she answered.

"I have a friend who might be able to help get you into the Washington Business School," Jimmy said.

"I would love that, Uncle Jimmy." The smile on her face showed how much.

"Just give me a few days to work on it," he asked. Jimmy was a man for whom there was always a friend to help. The girls spent the evening dreaming aloud their plans for their future. Jimmy made them believe here everything is possible. They laughed as they shared stories of the old country and he of the new. However, the best laugh was over Mrs. Quinn ever thinking she could have pulled anything over on Bridget Donahue Kelly.

~ Chapter Thirteen ~

Tuesday the 28th of June 1927 was a proper day for a beginning. Bridget and Kathleen spent the day becoming acquainted with their wonderful new neighborhood. It was easy for them to find their way around in Brooklyn. The streets went in order from south to north, Sixteen, Fifteen and Fourteen .... The avenues went from east to west in the same way, Eight, Seventh, and Sixth....

They walked west down Sixteen, past the open-air trolley running across the intersection on Seventh Avenue, making their way to the shopping extravaganza awaiting them along Fifth Avenue.

"What a wonderful means of transportation that is," Bridget acknowledged. Kathleen heartily agreed.

Fifth Avenue was home to every type of store imaginable. Unfortunately, for them elevated trains screeched passed over their heads.

"What a God awful idea that one was," Bridget screamed trying to be heard over the roar. She feared for their safety of their lives under it.

"That bloody thing is going to fall off and kill us for sure," upsettingly Bridget told her daughter. Kathleen was somewhat in agreement. This experience was not turning out as they planned. They traveled further along Fifth Avenue to Ninth Street, shopping in each of the shops they passed along the way.

"Uncle Jimmy said this is as far as we need to go," Kathleen announced standing in front of the twenty-four hour pharmacy on the corner. "He said we should turn here." They walked up towards Sixth Avenue, passing three movie houses and two different halls where live theatre was performed.

"So many books," Bridget whispered in the Public Library they stopped in before walking further up on Ninth Street to the entrance of Prospect Park. There they found the respite from the hustle and bustle of city life which they needed.

"It makes one wonder, why do they need so much here in Brooklyn? We went into four churches, not one having a statue of St. Bridget. I lost count of how many groceries, butchers and fish markets there are. Do you remember?" Bridget tiredly asked, leaning back on the wood bench.

"There were four groceries but I think you liked the one on Thirteen Street or was it on Fourteen? I don't remember," Kathleen exhaustedly answered.

"I think it best we do our shopping across from Holy Name," Bridget said.

"I agree," Kathleen quickly answered. "There is far too much madness down there."

"It's pleasant here. Don't you think?" Bridget asked enjoying the fragrance of the freshly cut grass and the music from the singing birds.

"Yes it is nice here," Kathleen answered resting with her eyes closed.

"There is only one more place we have to stop at. Then we can go home," Bridget said having regained her strength.

"I know," Kathleen answered.

"Father, me and me family are new to the parish," Bridget told the young priest who answered the rectory's doorbell.

"You must be Mrs. Kelly," Father Fannon said ushering them into his office.

"I am Father," Bridget said. "But how would you be knowing that?"

"It's the talk of Brooklyn, your coming here with your daughters," The priest said, relaying the gossip he heard. "So sorry to hear of the tragic death of your husband. May God grant him eternal peace." Father made the sign of the cross as he spoke.

"Amen," Bridget and Kathleen answered bowing their heads.

"Thank you, Father," Bridget said. "Yes, we are the Kellys and we need to register in the parish."

"We are happy to have you. There is much we can offer you and much we need help in," Father said giving Bridget a form to fill in. Once it was completed, he carefully read it over.

"Good. Good. I see you have three daughters. That's nice, indeed. And which of the Kellys are you?" he asked.

"I am Kathleen."

"Well Kathleen, our Rosary Society is in the process of raising funds to buy two new stained glass windows for the church. Can I count on you to be joining them?" Father Fannon inquired.

"Yes, Father, you can," she answered him. Father Fannon blessed them before they left and offered to bless their new home.

"That would be grand, Father," Bridget said. "Would you like to come for dinner on Sunday?"

"I would love a good-home cooked Irish meal," the priest happily answered. "You can tell me what time you want me after Sunday mass."

"Good day, ladies," a man called out to them as they walked up their front steps.

"Good day," they answered turning around to see him graciously tipping his hat to them.

"I am Tony and this here is Sally," he proudly introduced himself and his horse. "We bring you the finest fruits and vegetables to your door everyday. You see, no one have better than Tony. You ask around," he said.

Proud as a peacock, Tony stood before his vegetable wagon, wearing a bright colored shirt and his thumbs around his wide suspenders. His gray mare, flamboyantly wore a wide brimmed straw hat with colorful flowers stuck all over it. As Tony spoke, Sally became impatient and started nibbling at his back. Tony turned and in a gentle tone spoke a language filled with vowels to her. He went to the wagon and gave her a carrot to eat. Watching the man break from his business to lovingly tend to his horse reminded Bridget of Peter. *How he loved Gypsy Dancer*, she thought.

"Eat, for this is the finest grass in all the world," Peter would tell Gypsy Dancer as she grazed. There would be no sweet grass for Sally to eat here in Brooklyn.

"Would you like to try something," Tony asked pointing to all the items in his wagon.

His question brought Bridget back into the present. Bridget and Kathleen surveyed the wagon.

Everything on it looked tempting. There were

items there she knew nothing about. Tony gave her their names and instructions for cooking. He told them which ones he thought they would like and others he was not yet sure of. This was the beginning of their friendship. Tony did have the best produce. And eventually, he began saving what he felt were the best of his best for her.

Elizabeth and Margaret also began a friendship that day as their Uncle Jimmy, being true to his word, sent someone to take them into New York City.

~ Chapter Fourteen ~

At nine forty-five in the morning, a rather good-looking young man came to their door.

"I'm Billy O'Brien, Steven O'Brien's cousin," he gallantly introduced himself. Every inch of his hair all slicked down in place and him being dressed in his finest suit. Elizabeth coyly smiled and then showed him into the parlor. After introducing himself to Mrs. Kelly, he began rambling on.

"As luck would have it, today is my day off," he smilingly said. "Mrs. Kelly, I'm a New York City fireman," he pompously announced. Even through the fit of his suit, the girls could tell he had the strong muscular body of a twenty-two year old. They had no difficulty in envisioning him carrying a woman to safety in those arms.

"I'll be happy to take the girls into the city for their job interview," he offered his services. His irresistible charm did not affect Bridget. She was reluctant to let her daughters go with this man unattended.

"Here is a note from Jimmy," he said confidently handing it to her. Bridget read the note of introduction and the explanations of the new ways here.

Having been born in Brooklyn, Billy knew of no

other ways. He was street smart and used to a different kind of girl. The girls in his life were more hip and brazen. Bridget going against her inclination gave in under her brother's influence.

"These are the Kelly girls. There's a party for them at Donahue's tonight," Billy said to all the young men who gave the girls a once over as the trio walked by.

"Don't be looking up at all those buildings," Billy laughingly ordered. "You'll look like a couple of rubes." He strutted between Elizabeth and Margaret while taking every opportunity to put his arms around their waists as he led them towards their destination.

"I think it best if I hold your letter of introduction until we get there," Billy advised them.

"You do. Seems like your holding onto everything else!" Elizabeth snapped back.

"Don't get your knickers in a knot!" he answered.

"Get my... you really do think we are a couple of rubes. I have been safely holding onto this letter since before we landed," arrogantly Elizabeth answered him.

"Can't take a little teasing, can you? Won't do here in Brooklyn. Plenty of teasing going on around these parts," he amusingly said.

"Calm down Elizabeth," Margaret chimed in, "he's just fooling with you."

"I must admit, I'm a little nervous about going there," Elizabeth warily confessed.

"It is a little nerve racking," Margaret added.

"If these here fancy hats you're wearing are any indication of your work you two are a shoe in," Billy convincingly told them. As they walked towards Forty-Seventh Street, he eagerly built up their confidence.

Maurice, La Maison Des Chapeaux Exquis. There it was. They stood across the street and looked at the unimpressive storefront.

"Go ahead girls, you're ready for it! I'll wait for you over there in the coffee shop. Take your time and get those jobs!" Billy said as he pushed them towards the street.

Elizabeth opened the door and walked in first. Margaret followed. Once inside the large open room they were surrounded by head shaped forms all supporting hats of every style imaginable. This was paradise.

"May I help you?" the receptionist asked.

"I am Elizabeth Kelly. This is my sister Margaret," Elizabeth announced.

"Yes, Miss Kelly, are you interested in buying one of our hats?" the young woman asked. "This is not a retail store. You can find our items in all the best stores." Before she could continue any further Elizabeth interrupted her.

"Oh no, I am sorry," she said. "I have not made myself clear. Miss Mabel Normand sent us." Becoming interested in them the woman got up from her seat behind the desk.

"I am Sybil," shaking their hands she told them. "Miss Normand is a long time friend of Maurice's. He lets her pick out what she likes as a courtesy. But I am sure if you are good friends of hers he will do the same for you."

"Again, I am sorry. Sybil. We are not friends of Miss Normand. I wish we were," Elizabeth confessed. "We met her on our way over here from Ireland. She loved our hats and she gave us this letter of introduction and recommended that we come here to apply for employment."

"Why didn't you just say so? May I see the letter?" Sybil asked. Elizabeth handed it over to her. Sybil quickly read the note.

"If you will excuse me for a moment, I will show this to Maurice," she said before she went out the back door.

"I don't know how you are doing it. I can't say a word, my heart is stuck in my throat," Margaret confided once they were alone. Before Elizabeth could answer, Sybil was back in the room.

"If you don't mind waiting for a few minutes Maurice will be with you shortly," she informed them.

"We don't mind," Elizabeth answered. The girls were commenting on the latest styles when Mr. Maurice came into the office.

"Hello girls," he brusquely said. They had expected an elegant looking Frenchman. Instead who walked in was a rather short disheveled man with an unlit cigar hanging from his mouth. From the tone of his voice, the look of his rolled up sleeves and the sweat upon his brow, they knew he must have been working on a problem somewhere. Their hearts sank as they misinterpreted this.

"This is good," Maurice said waving the letter. "Is Mabel in good health?"

"She appeared so," Elizabeth answered.

Maurice waited for more information.

"She was enjoying chocolate when we last saw her," Elizabeth added.

"Good. Very good. She's in good health then," he nodded as he spoke. "Are these your own creations?" he said pointing to their heads.

"Yes sir, they are," Elizabeth replied.

"Maurice, just Maurice," he said. "Let me see?" he asked taking the hats off their heads inspecting their craftsmanship. "I don't have much time. You tell me quick about your experience."

"Maurice," Elizabeth said, starting out on familiar terms. "For the last two years at home we had a little business where we made hats and dresses. Some, we have done from patterns. Some were our own creations." From her manner of speech, Maurice noted that their home was Ireland and from the letterhead, it was apparent they had met Mabel on their way over. They, on the other hand, were not quite sure of his accent.

"Good. Very good. You said that quick enough." Maurice said without ever taking the cigar out of his mouth. "You don't speak?" he asked Margaret.

"Yes sir, Mr. Maurice, I do speak," she softly answered.

"Maurice, it's Maurice. No one calls me sir. I want to know everything that happens in my place. No one tells a sir, but Maurice you can tell." Knowing she was as green as grass, he tried to gentle his tone. "Normally, I ask for three references. But seeing Mabel believes in you, I will forgo that. So, I am prepared to hire you both today."

"Thank you. Thank you," the girls kept repeating while shaking his hands.

"Let me first tell you my conditions," Maurice began. "There is much more to the hat business than the designing of them." He looked at them for a sign of agreement. Not quite understanding, they nodded.

"If I give you this opportunity I must first know you are up to it. I can teach you everything. But Maurice doesn't waste time. I must see you have a good work ethic. Do you?" he asked.

"We do. We will work hard for you. You will see," Elizabeth answered for both of them.

"And you? You must speak for yourself," he asked Margaret.

"I do very good work and I will work hard for you," Margaret assured him.

"You will work your way through every aspect of the business. And only then will I consider your designs," Maurice said adamantly. "You must know how to work with all different types of materials. We buy them in large quantities. You must know the kinds of problems we can encounter and how to solve them. This way you can prevent them when you design for me. You two are so pretty, you could be models in my shows. But I will start you with sewing. Is this agreeable to you both?"

"Yes sir, it is," they answered him.

"Maurice," he reiterated. "Maurice."

"Maurice, it is agreeable to me," Elizabeth answered.

"Maurice, it is definitely agreeable to me," Margaret quickly followed with her answer.

"When can you start?" he asked. The girls looked at each other.

"Tomorrow?" they answered.

"Good, tomorrow then. Be here by eight," he said. "Sybil can answer any other questions you have." Before any further conversation could continue, he was out the back door.

"Welcome to Maurice's, the home of fine hats," Sybil said.

"Thank you, thank you," Elizabeth and Margaret were excitedly saying.

"That was easier than I thought it would be," Margaret said surprisingly.

"Amazingly so," Elizabeth agreed.

"Oh, Maurice is like that. Right to the point. Doesn't waste a speck of time," Sybil told them. "With a letter from Mabel and those beautiful hats of yours, you two were a shoe in."

"Maurice's, the home of fine hats, is that what the name outside means?" Margaret asked.

"Yes, it does. It's in French," Sybil said as she handed them papers to fill out.

"Is Maurice French?" Elizabeth asked.

"Oh, Maurice isn't French," Sybil laughingly announced. "He's Jewish. Born right here in New York City. His real name is Max Silverheart. It really should have been Goldenheart cause he's a real sweetheart when you get to know him." Sybil made the girls feel right at home as she talked with them. "Of course, every now and then he gets in his moods. But then he blows off some steam and he gets back to himself. Maurice's was the name he chose for the business. He thought it would bring him a classier clientele and he was right. Now everyone calls him Maurice, even his wife." Elizabeth and Margaret left after filling in all the employment papers.

"Gee, that's swell," Billy responded to the good news. "We should go and celebrate and I know just the place." Both girls were hesitant.

"It's on me. I know this great little place only a few blocks from here. You're going to love it," he assured them. His smile was wearing them down.

"Just one drink, what harm could come from that?" he asked.

"Everything went quicker than we thought. We do have time to see the place and have one drink," Elizabeth convincingly said to Margaret.

"If you think mother won't be upset, I guess it would be fine," Margaret consented.

"Don't tell her, no need for her to know if you think it would bother her some," Billy advised them.

"She wouldn't have to know. Really, we need not tell her," Elizabeth urged.

"An event as big as this needs to be celebrated!" Billy added.

"Alright then," Margaret agreed. "Let's go and we won't tell her."

Joyously they walked the two blocks to the speakeasy. There were no markings on the outside of the plain black painted door. Billy rapped his knuckles against the wood in a secret rhythm. A little window slid open.

"Coogan sent me." Billy said to the peering eyes. The door was unlocked and opened to them.

A rush of adrenalin ran through their bodies as they walked down the grungy staircase and into a dimly lit room. All the walls and basement windows were all pained black. Some of the regulars sat at the bar. They could hear the muffled sounds of their laughter over the jazz music coming from the bar's radio. Billy escorted the girls to a corner table. A waiter came over to take their order.

"What will you have?" he asked them.

"The house's best." Billy said. "We are celebrating a special day."

"Then you should come back here after nine. That's when we really come alive," the waiter told them. "We have a jazz trio that makes this place jump. I'll bring you three of our best."

"To our special day," Billy toasted.

"To our special day," Elizabeth and Margaret replied as the trio tapped their glasses together.

"Our special day?" Elizabeth asked Billy.

"For sure, now isn't it my own special day as haven't I met the girl of my dreams," he said as he warmly smiled at Elizabeth. She smiled back then coyly looked away.

Margaret watching them unwillingly forced herself to smile.

As Billy promised, they enjoyed just the one drink. But before leaving, Billy also promised to bring them back again another night after nine.

"Mrs. Kelly, I have brought your daughters home safe and sound from the sinful city," Billy said, thinking he was amusing. "And with new jobs to boot."

"How wonderful!" Kathleen clapping her hands joyously exclaimed.

"'Tis glorious," Bridget said hugging her daughters. "I'll make a pot of tea and you can tell us all about it."

"This is a good time for me to be leaving," Billy announced.

"Thank you for taking care of me daughters," Bridget said.

"Mrs. Kelly, it was my pleasure. I will see all of

you later at Donahue's for the party," Billy told them. "Till tonight, Elizabeth," he whispered in her ear as he passed her.

~ *Chapter Fifteen* ~

"*There is a Chinese restaurant* and a theater on Ninth Street," Kathleen told her sisters between sips of her tea.

"A Chinese restaurant?" Margaret questioned. "What type of food is that?"

"I don't know," Elizabeth answered "but with our first pay checks let's go to eat there and see a vaudeville show afterwards."

"We should take Uncle Jimmy with us," Kathleen suggested and everyone agreed.

"How much will you be paid for working?" Bridget asked. The sisters were silent.

"We don't know. We didn't ask," Margaret sheepishly answered.

"No need to somber up the moment. He sounds as though he is a good man. I am sure he will pay you fairly," motherly Bridget advised them. "You can ask him tomorrow. And see to it that you do fine work for him."

Steve O'Brien pulled his car in front of the brownstone as he brought Uncle Jimmy to pick up the Kellys. The girls and Bridget talked nonstop from the moment they entered it, recounting every event of the day.

"There is no music sweeter than the sounds of

happy women," Jimmy told O'Brien.

"None in the world," O'Brien agreed. "Here we are."

Through the glass windows, they could see the large crowd milling around in the Rose dinning room.

"Oh Jimmy," Bridget alarmingly said. "There are so many people."

"Bridget, you will recognize many of them from home. They have all come to see you and introduce you to their families," Jimmy calmly explained. As they walked into the foyer on the table in the center of the room was a large statue. Bridget's eyes became wet when she saw it.

"I called every church and I could not find her," Jimmy excitedly said. "I have a friend who has a friend and he was able to find her."

"Oh Jimmy, she's the prettiest statue of St. Bridget I have ever seen," Bridget thanked him.

"The bishop himself blessed her this afternoon," he tenderly told her.

Jimmy always had a friend or a friend of a friend who was more than willing to help him. For Donahue's was also known to have another entrance door.

This one in back, just off the alley was the kitchen door. At this door, anyone could enter Donahue's for a good, free meal. These were Jimmy's rules; no one was ever to be turned away and no questions asked. He was also known to help any man or woman in dire straits with financial help. He gave without expecting anything in return but almost everyone he helped paid him back over the years.

The packed house began applauding as Jimmy and the Kellys entered. Jimmy motioned for them to settle down.

"When Irish eyes are smiling...," the waiters began signing. Everyone, including the Kellys, joined in.

"So happy to see you after all these years," a stranger was saying to Bridget.

"So sorry to hear about Peter," another woman interjected.

"Shamus, is that really you? Mary, Mother of God, it is you," Bridget searched faces trying to remember names and stories of people she had long ago forgotten.

Kathleen stayed by her uncle's side. Helping him as he made sure the beer was flowing and that plenty of food was constantly being served.

"It takes a lot of wood to fuel a party," he told her.

Beside the piano player, some of the guest brought their musical instruments from home. To the gregarious, foot stomping music from button boxes, uilleann pipes, tin whistles and the bodhrán drum everyone sang and danced the evening away.

Elizabeth and Margaret's eyes scanned the room looking for Billy. Both their faces lit up when he snuck up behind them.

"Boo," Billy joked. "Told you I would see you tonight," he looked into Elizabeth's hazel eyes as he spoke. "And, Margaret, I brought some of my friends for you to meet."

"Good to see you again," Elizabeth answered.

"My friends are over there," he told the girls.

Throughout the evening, the Kellys met many

new friends and were reacquainted with old ones. In a mixture of laughter and tears, they retold stories from home. Filled with promise they listened to stories of their new homeland.

Only knowing their dreams and not yet knowing what their true future held for them, they enjoyed the wonderful evening. And, they had not yet learned of Jimmy's heartbreaking past.

~ *Chapter Sixteen* ~

"*The weather was warm and balmy* as Elizabeth, Margaret and Billy O'Brien drove to Long Island's Roosevelt Field for the Labor Day air show. The summer had been a thrilling one for the girls as New York shared many of its firsts with them.

The trio rode in one of the first cars to drive through the Lincoln Tunnel to New Jersey. Billy laughed as Elizabeth and Margaret screamed on their unforgettable ride on the newly opened Cyclone roller coaster, in Coney Island.

"You're going to like this guy. He's a lot of fun," Billy eagerly said.

"I haven't seen him in awhile. But I'm sure he's still crazy. Wait till you see him fly."

The girls sat holding onto their hats as Billy raced his car towards the airfield. The road was lined with hundreds of people all walking in the same direction. Above their heads, the exhibition pilots circled, dropping handbills offering an opportunity to soar along with them.

"There he is…Hi, Ace," Billy yelled over to his old friend on the field. Beside the bright yellow biplane in the distance, the daredevil aviator stood waving back to them.

"Hi, Billy. And who do we have here?" Ace

seductively asked, looking at Elizabeth.

"This is my girl, Elizabeth and her sister Margaret Kelly. Girls, this here is Ace Hunter, aviator extraordinaire," Billy enthusiastically introduced them.

"Miss Kelly," Ace nodded as he spoke to Margaret.

"Mr. Hunter," Margaret nodded as she answered back.

"Please to meet Billy's girl," Ace charmingly whispered taking Elizabeth's hand.

"Please to be meeting one of his old friends," Elizabeth answered looking into his dark eyes. As the sleeve of his soft brown leather coat brushed against her arm, shivers ran through her body. She blushed as Ace knowingly smiled at her.

"After the show, I'll take you up for a ride," he told them still staring at her.

"I'd be afraid to go up in that little thing," Elizabeth said.

"Little thing, my sweet lady, this here is a Curtiss Jenny," as Ace spoke the sun reflected off his goggles that fitted over the brow of his leather helmet. Although the helmet was tight and covering all of his curly brown hair, it could not hide his undeniable good looks. Margaret, content with looking at Billy, was unaffected by the electricity that Ace gave off. The daredevil powerfully continued to speak and with each movement he made, the silk scarf around his neck waved fanning the fire that was blazing inside of Elizabeth.

"She is the best plane in all the sky. Even birds are envious of her. And little, not so at all. She is over twenty-seven feet long with a wingspan over forty-three feet," Ace informed her. Billy and Margaret listened intently, for Elizabeth it was all a blur.

"I think it best we leave you to get ready for the show," Billy said. "We'll come by later and catch up with you."

The three made their way over to the blanket at the end of the field that Bridget, Kathleen and Uncle Jimmy were sitting on. They joined the thousands of other spectators sitting on blankets, chairs, in cars and on hanger rooftops watching the exhibition pilots give their best aerobatic performances throughout the day.

Zoom. Zoom. A plane's motor roared as the plane approached them. Its roaring engine deafening them as it flew directly over the crowd heads.

"Good God Almighty he's going to kill us," Bridget feared for their lives.

"It's only part of the show. Don't worry," Jimmy comfortingly said. The impressed crowd gasped as they watched the daring spins and dives as these unconventional flyers soared above them. Wing walkers doing one-upmanship with each other did everything from handstands to grasping on to trapeze bars with only their teeth.

One biplane took to the air and performed a loop-the-loop. As it finished a barrel role maneuver the biplane went into a spin. The pilot desperately tried to pull the plane out of it. Suddenly the plane turned upward and flew higher in heaven. As the engine sputtered, smoke emanated from it. When the biplane leveled off the death-defying flyer bailed out. The terrified crowd screamed.

"Lord, have mercy," Bridget yelled before

covering her face with her hands. All eyes fixed on the falling pilot as he hurled earthward. Miraculously, his parachute opened. The crowd breathed a sigh of relief. And then for some unknown reason the pilot cut himself from his parachute and was again plummeting closer to his death. Elizabeth and Margaret were screaming in horror.

"Look, look, he has another parachute!" Uncle Jimmy said loudly, calming down the hairs that had risen on the back of his neck. The Kellys, along with the other spectators, watched the stunt man come safety to the landing that he planned. The enthralled audience did not notice as a hidden pilot safely landed the plane.

Before the crowd could completely calm down from the scare, overhead with magnesium flares fastened to the wingtips in the show's final performance, Ace's Jenny flew over their heads. Entertainingly, his flares sparked and smoked as he slowly rolled his biplane onto its back and flew upside down. He turned the plane around and lowered its nose. At 60 mph, he aimed his plane directly towards the open doors of a hanger. Atop its roof, people scurried to jump off as Ace flew right through the building and out the previously opened back door. Once again up in the open sky he ended by doing a dippy twist loop as when he reached the top of the roll he did a snag roll. The multitude escaping their commonplace lives cheered in delight at his showmanship and his aerobatic skill.

Elizabeth and Margaret left Bridget and Kathleen to pack up the food basket and blanket They went with Billy zigzagging their way through the horde swarming down onto the airfield. In the mist of an adoring mob of young and old alike, Ace stood with an attractive redhead clinging to one of his arms and a blond on the other. Elizabeth's words were barely audible over all homage being paid to the barnstormer.

"Oh, that was wonderful, just wonderful," she admiringly said to him. Ace haughtily smiled accepting her praise with all the others.

"What do you think of her now?" Ace asked pointing to his Jenny.

"How ever can she fly upside down?" Elizabeth asked as she took his scarf from the redhead's shoulder and placed it rightfully back around Ace's neck. He bowed making it easier for her.

The crowd's attention frenzied as Uncle Jimmy made his way towards Ace with a tall lean young man walking beside him. A wave of applauds and cheers surrounded the handsome young man.

"That was some mighty fine flying," the young man said.

"Thank you. Thank you. Coming from you it means a lot." Ace's attitude changed as he answered him.

"Slim, this is the rest of my family," Jimmy said, introducing the young man.

"Girls, I want you to meet the greatest flyer of all times. This is Charles Lindbergh, the first man to fly solo across the Atlantic Ocean."

"Honored to meet you," Margaret said.

"And so am I," Elizabeth added offering her hand.

"May I shake your hand, sir?" Billy asked respectfully. "I was in the crowd that morning when you left from here."

"Be my pleasure," the famed pilot answered. He graciously shook not only Billy's, Elizabeth's and Margaret's hands but almost everyone that reached out to him.

"We best make our way back to your mother and Kathleen," Uncle Jimmy said after Lucky Lindy left. "I told them I'd bring you back there after I brought Slim over to meet you."

"Don't you want to go up for a ride?" Ace asked.

"Don't think there's time for that today, son. Perhaps another time," Uncle Jimmy answered for Elizabeth.

"Perhaps, then another time," Ace said.

"I hope so," Elizabeth answered.

"I'm sure I'll be able bring the girls out here another time for a ride," Billy responded.

"I don't think their mother would consent to it. The show itself was frightening enough for her. I don't think she could ever stand to think of them up in a plane like that," Uncle Jimmy informed them.

"Well in any event, Elizabeth, I am always at your disposal," Ace captivatingly said to her. Billy was unaware of the look in Elizabeth's eyes as she smiled back.

~ *Chapter Seventeen* ~

From the moment Billy O'Brien first laid eyes on Elizabeth, he knew she was the girl for him. Right from the start, they became quite the item as he made his intentions known. Everywhere he went he took Elizabeth and of course, her sister Margaret.

"Are you sure you want me to come?" Margaret would ask him.

"Of course, I do," he always answered. Each time they went out, he brought another of his friends for her inspection.

"You're bound to get a sweet tooth for Marty, he's a baker," Billy laughingly said. Nevertheless, as with all the other double dates they went on, Margaret stayed glued to Billy's side. And, as with all the other double dates it was Elizabeth who enjoyed the company of her sister's potential suitors.

"He didn't catch your eye?" Billy asked as they sat alone in the speakeasy.

"There's none that can compare to you, Billy O'Brien," Margaret said laughing as if it were a joke, knowing all the while for her it was the truth. "Fair enough, but not to worry I have plenty of friends left for you to meet." He teasingly went down the list of brother firefighters, office workers, an Irish tenor, two inventors and a few fellows who worked in the shipyards that he had already brought for her approval. Billy and Margaret laughed as they reminisced over each of the dates. Elizabeth and the baker danced the night away.

"Ace just telephoned me," Billy delightedly told Elizabeth as she greeted him at the door for Sunday dinner. "He'll be back in town next Saturday."

"Next Saturday!" a flush of excitement rose in Elizabeth's body as she answered him.

"Elinor Smith is planning on flying under all four of New York City's bridges on next Sunday," Billy said. "Ace is planning to celebrate with his friends afterwards but he wants us to meet up with him Saturday evening. He also said he wants us to be the ones standing next to him on the Brooklyn Bridge to watch Elinor fly under it. Won't that be something to see?"

Something to see? Elizabeth had longed to see him again. *Next Saturday…how will I be able to last that long?* His not showing for last month's air show had left her disappointed. But that feeling left and in its place was that hot feeling deep inside her that always swelled up when she thought of his face.

"We're to meet him at that place on Thirty-Ninth Street," Billy informed her. "I'll have to see who I can get to bring for Margaret."

"Don't worry about that. Margaret won't need a date," Elizabeth answered him. "She'll be happy enough to see Ace and I'm sure he'll have other friends there." Billy agreed.

"Best not to tell my mother," Elizabeth advised. "She'll give us a hell of a time for wanting to go."

"Go where?" Margaret asked.

"Talk lower. Don't let mother hear you,"

Elizabeth ordered.

"Do you think it will be safe?" Margaret asked Billy after Elizabeth told her everything.

"I can't believe you're asking that. If you don't want to go you don't have to," Elizabeth snipped. "But for God's sake keep your mouth shut."

"Margaret, it will be safe. You can stand by me," Billy offered.

"I'll go. Didn't say I wouldn't. Just asked a simple question, that's all," Margaret answered.

Elizabeth could think of nothing else throughout dinner. She was of little help as the family sat together working on the puzzle of Leonardo Da Vinci's *Last Supper*.

"Kathleen, how is school going?" Uncle Jimmy asked. With the help of another one of his friends, he had assisted Kathleen in enrolling in the prestigious Washington Business School in New York City. Uncle Jimmy comfortably fit into the shoes left empty by her departed father. His Sunday visits for dinner not only minimized the distance which had developed over the years between him and Bridget but it brought Kathleen and him closer as the family joked putting together the challenging jigsaw puzzles he always brought.

"You are indeed an appropriate candidate for our school. And it is with pleasure that you are accepted into our program," Kathleen had been happy to report the admissions officer said after her intensive interview. "It has become harder than I thought it would be. But I am keeping my grades up. I want to make you proud of me," she answered him.

Uncle Jimmy motioned to Billy not to be looking at the picture on the box for help finding which color goes where in the puzzle.

"No cheating," Jimmy said. "Billy, you don't need to know what it will look like in the end to figure it out. This should be an easy one for you, as I am sure from all your church going you know the picture of the Last Supper in your head," he laughed as he spoke.

"As well as I think you do, Jimmy" Billy quickly responded. Jimmy nodded in agreement.

"I am already proud of you, Kathleen," he replied to her. "Father Fannon stopped by to see me yesterday. He said and I quote, 'Your niece's enthusiasm was a major influence on our collecting enough money to have the two new stained glass windows installed in the church.' Then he invited me to the unveiling."

"Will you come?" Kathleen eagerly asked.

"I wouldn't miss it," Uncle Jimmy said, inserting a large section of pieces he had been working on, into the puzzle before him on the dinning room table.

The week was just about unbearable for Elizabeth as every waking moment her thoughts fixated on Ace Hunter. Every remembrance of him magnified. Ace's thrilling death-defying feats overshadowed Billy's life saving acts of a firefighter. Actually, over this last year Elizabeth thought every one of Billy's friends to be more exciting to be around than Billy himself. How Margaret could listen so intently to every dull word Billy uttered, Elizabeth did not understand. Nor could she comprehend why the more she tried to distance herself from him, the closer Billy tried to get. But no more wasting time with thoughts of Billy. Ace

Hunter was coming back into her life and this time she was going to make him stay.

Billy rhythmically rapped on the Thirty-Ninth Street door and lowly saying, "guests of Ace's," the door magically open for them. The speakeasy was jumping when the trio arrived. The patrons were drinking and dancing with wanton abandonment as they tried to keep tomorrow from coming into their lives.

Ace sat at a large table surrounded by a bevy of seductively dressed women. As soon as he saw Billy escorting Elizabeth and Margaret towards him he acted as thought there was no one else in the room.

"Elizabeth," he cordially said.

"Ace," she responded. The loudness of the music covered her trembling voice but he noticed. He noticed everything about her. She knew it. He looked at her differently than any other man she had ever met.

"The music is great for dancing," Ace said. "Would it be alright with you Billy if I took a spin with your girl?"

"Sure if she wants to," Billy answered.

If I want to... I have dreamed of nothing else, Elizabeth thought. "I would be pleased to," she answered. Her heart skipped a beat as he took her hand into his.

"Then Elizabeth, may I have the pleasure of this dance?" he asked. Ace motioned to the bandleader and the music slowed to a ballad.

"Elizabeth, I have thought of no one else but you since the day we met," Ace said as he had his arm tightly around her.

"Oh, to believe that," Elizabeth answered. "You

must think I'm brainless. Where have you been all this time?"

"Knowing you were Billy's girl, I tried to keep myself away from you," Ace said. "God help me, but I couldn't. I had to see you."

"I thought you were here to see Elinor," Elizabeth questioningly said.

"That was something to tell my friends. It's you I wanted to see. Forgive me, but I had to see you," Ace said pulling her closer to him. "Tell me you haven't thought of me at all and I'll not say another word," he whispered in her ear. Elizabeth could not answer.

"I knew I felt your thoughts on me," he said. "I'd be doing a roll or something and I'd see your angelic face and I knew you were thinking of me. Wanting me as much as I wanted you." Elizabeth believingly listened to every word he said.

How many times had I thought of him flying and wished he was thinking of me, she thought. "I have thought about you many times," she answered. "Why haven't I heard from you before this?"

"You're Billy's girl and I didn't want to come between you. But I want you and I know you want me," he confided.

"We're not serious. Billy just thinks we are," Elizabeth said. "I've tried to tell him but he doesn't listen."

"Thank God, you feel the same way about me," Ace said into her ear as the dance ended.

Drinks slid down as easy as water. And each time a glass was emptied Ace saw to it that is was filled again. Elizabeth could not tell which was intoxicating her more, the alcohol or being around

Ace. Billy and Margaret were singing with some of the regulars. Friends of Ace's took turns coming to the table to talk with him.

All the while, hidden from view, Ace took every opportunity to titillating stroke his hand along Elizabeth's thigh. More drinks... and Elizabeth daringly touched his thigh. Under the unseeing eyes of Billy and Margaret, they took turns seductively playing. As Ace slowly moved his hand up to between her legs Elizabeth's face burned.

"Are you alright?" Margaret asked.

"I think I need a breath of fresh air," Elizabeth answered.

"Why don't we take a walk outside for awhile?" Ace asked.

"You do look flushed. I'll take you," Billy offered.

"No need for you to leave all the fun," Ace said. "I can see these guys anytime."

"You wouldn't mind?" Billy asked.

"Not at all," Ace answered.

"Elizabeth, would you be alright with that?" Billy asked.

"Yes, Ace is right. You shouldn't have to miss all the fun," she answered.

"Do you want me to come with you?" Margaret questioned.

"No... No I'll be fine. Just stay with Billy," Elizabeth told her. Ace courteously stood up and helped Elizabeth up from her chair. They walked down a hallway towards what Elizabeth thought was the back door. Ace took a key from his pocket and unlocked the door.

A dangling ceiling fixture with only one

working bulb barely lit the packed storeroom. In the far corner was an unmade bed. Ace took Elizabeth in his arms.

"I have thought of nothing else since I met you," he said. She could not deny she had thought the same.

"This is the first time for you, isn't it?" Ace asked.

"Yes," Elizabeth fearfully answered.

"I thought that you and Billy..." Ace started to speak.

"No. He never tried. I never wanted to..." Elizabeth said stopping him. "And now?" Ace asked.

"I want to," she answered him.

"I knew you wanted me as much as I wanted you," he spoke softly, looking deep into her eyes. "I can see it...I can hear it." She gasped as he gently touched her nipples through her dress. "And I could smell it," he pulled her body closer to him. He kissed her and when he knew there would be no turning back he took off his shirt. Picking her up in his arms, he held her tightly.

"What a gift you give me," he acknowledged. Slowly he undressed her, seeing for the first time what no man had ever seen before. Kissing her, he laid her on the bed. He took off his pants and revealed his full manhood. He laid upon her naked body and thrust himself into her. Her body tingled and then raged with fire as he moved inside her. He gasped... groaned... and was done. Ace pulled out his now shrunken manhood now covered in blood. He rolled off, over, and stayed beside her for a few minutes without uttering another word. Elizabeth stayed there silently feeling naked and ashamed.

"I think it's time to get dressed and get back to the party," he said putting on his clothes. He watched her again as she uncomfortably dressed before him.

"Think best we never talk about this again," he told her as they walked back to the table.

Nothing in the speakeasy had changed. Everyone was drinking, dancing, singing and having a good time. No one noticed that everything had stopped for Elizabeth. "Good night Elizabeth," Ace said before they left. "Remember, I am always at your disposal." Elizabeth looked away.

~ Chapter Eighteen ~

How could I have done that? How could I have *been so stupid?* Throughout the long night, Elizabeth wrestled with her conscience as it prevented her from sleeping; by morning, she was sick.

"It's time you readied yourself for church," Bridget informed her daughter.

"I'm too sick to get out of bed," Elizabeth moaned.

"You can go back to bed after church," Bridget answered.

There is no way out of it, Elizabeth thought. *How can I receive Holy Communion without going to confession? How can I ever tell this in confession?* Her stomach muscles all twisting into knots as she tried to find a way out of this.

"Maybe, I should try and eat a little something before I go to church?" Elizabeth asked, hoping to buy herself a little time.

"Not at all. You can't eat and receive the Eucharist. Why would you go to Mass and not receive?" Bridget responded.

I am damned to spend eternity in Hell. Elizabeth's body burned with fever as she began facing the consequences of her actions. Cowardly, she stopped on each of the church's fifteen steps.

"Hurry up," Margaret urged, walking up the stairs behind her. "You're holding everyone up."

God is going to strike me dead. I know it, Elizabeth feared. Terror engulfed her as suddenly the organists began his music.

"What is the matter with you?" Margaret snapped as Elizabeth jumped back into her. No one waited for an answer. The family proceeded into the gaily-decorated church. The altar overflowed with flowers. Their perfumed fragrance filled the air, mingled with the scent from burning bee's wax candles. Large white bows marked off the front pews assigned to dignitaries and members of the Stained Glass Window Committee.

I am going to die...I am going to die right here. Elizabeth could feel it in her bones. *Lord, forgive me.*

"Jimmy," an usher called. "There is a pew reserved for Kathleen and your family up front."

Proudly, Uncle Jimmy escorted the Kellys as they followed the usher to the pew that had Kathleen Kelly's name on it. Smiles of approval from the other parishioners followed Kathleen while she walked down the aisle.

Elizabeth followed her sister and mother. The penitent sinner kept her eyes downward, afraid to look directly at the altar.

God, forgive me for daring to come to the front of the church with this mortal sin on my soul, Elizabeth prayed. Each of the woman in the family genuflected as they entered the pew. Uncle Jimmy only slightly bowed his head. Elizabeth sat looking at Jesus hanging on the cross. A cross he hung on because of her sin. And now she would add another mortal sin to her soul for him to pay for.

Forgive me...Forgive me, she uttered as the altar boy rang the bell announcing the start of Mass.

What is going to happen to me? Elizabeth worried.

"*In nomine Patris, et Fílii, et Spíritus Sancti.* Amen," Father Fannon said beginning mass.

Dear God, please...please... forgive me, Elizabeth implored in her own private prayers. *Please help me out of this so I don't have to go up for Communion.* Ardently, she begged for a way out of this situation.

"*Kyrie eléison,*" Father Fannon said. Everyone stood. While the choir sang the Gloria, everything around Elizabeth momentarily darkened and she felt weak. Unfortunately, for her, too soon the blood ran back into her head and the dizziness left.

If only I had fainted, then I could leave the church without having to go to Communion. Why God, didn't you let me faint? she asked. The priest and everyone around her continued on with mass.

"Dóminus vobíscum." Father prayed.

Et cum spíritu tuo," the altar boy responded. Vague sounds from the priest and the servers penetrated her ardent prayers.

"Teacher," Father Fannon read aloud during the gospel. "Which is the greatest commandment in the Law?" Jesus replied: "Love the Lord your God with all your heart and with all your soul and with all your mind. This is the first and greatest commandment. And the second is like it: Love your neighbor as yourself." Elizabeth heard none of it as she continued to beseech God for forgiveness.

The dreaded moment was almost upon her. The altar boy rang the three bells.

"*Sanctus, Sanctus, Sanctus,*" Father Fannon said.

If only I could vomit, then I could not receive, Elizabeth thought. *Raw eggs, slimy, slippery swirling around my mouth.* Desperately, she tried to make her stomach heave up it contents.

The altar boy rang the bells again. Father Fannon genuflected and held the host up.

Rotten eggs mingled with vomit itself, all rolling around in my mouth, Elizabeth tried to visualize her words. *Sulfur, the rancid smell of sulfur.*

"*Hoc est enim Corpus meum,*" Father Fannon said changing the bread into the holy body of Christ.

The bile in her stomach burned. Just a little more concentration on disgusting smells and she would surely vomit.

Oh God, forgive me, again she pleaded. *I've brought the devil in church with me. There'll never be forgiveness for me.* Only the stench from the fire and brimstone from Hell could have been that vile.

Bridget, Kathleen and Margaret stood, Uncle Jimmy stayed seated. Elizabeth made the decision to go up and receive the Holy Eucharist.

Each step she took increased the panic in her. Her hands shook as she reverently had them folded before her. She knelt between her sisters at the altar rail. The altar boy placed the gold paten under her chin. Trembling, Elizabeth opened her mouth. Father Fannon placed the host on her dry tongue. She expected him to have been able to see into her soul and to have denied her the Eucharist. She expected God to make the host jump off her undeserving tongue and onto the cold golden plate. She expected the little wafer to burn as it was placed on the tongue of a whore in mortal sin. But nothing happened. Elizabeth walked back to the pew while the little wafer quickly dissolved in her mouth as it had always done.

How could you have let me defile the host like that? Why didn't you stop me or show me some sign of disapproval? Her stomach muscles relaxed and she calmed down while she reflected on this.

The altar boy rang the final bell signaling the end of the mass. Those fortunate enough to be sitting in the front of the church for mass now followed in procession after the altar boys, Father Fannon and the Bishop towards the back of the church.

The Bishop blessed the flock of worshipers with holy water along the way.

Once the privileged were tightly packed into the vestibule, the Bishop pulled down the drape coverings over new church windows.

"They are magnificent," the Bishop announced. The congregation agreed. The life size stained glass window to the left of the doorway was a spectacular picture of Jesus pointing to his sacred heart. The other stunning life size window to the right was of the Blessed Mother showing her own sacred heart. In perfect position, the sun shown through both these loving hearts as the windows were unveiled. The Bishop began blessing each one of the windows. He sprinkled holy water on Elizabeth as she was standing directly under the Sacred Heart of Jesus window.

Why didn't the holy water hurt me? she asked God. *Where is your power?*

"Will the members of the committee please step forward," Father Fannon asked. Kathleen joined the other women in meeting the Bishop. They kissed his ring and he complemented each one personally for a job well done.

In only a little over a year, Kathleen's frightful fear of anything with the color red in it had left her. And now looking at the afternoon sun shinning through these two loving hearts brought back the memories of her loving father. Uncle Jimmy, standing at her side, squeezed her hand as if he understood.

You can't hurt me. Elizabeth, the sinner said, seeing the light shine through the loving face of Jesus. *Can you?*

~ Chapter Nineteen ~

"*Where do you think your going?*" Margaret angrily questioned.

"What business is it of yours?" Elizabeth irately answered.

"It is very much my business," Margaret snapped, picking up the unfinished cloche from the sewing table. "If you're not here working on this if Maurice stops by, he may fire you and me."

"A girl has a right to go out to lunch, doesn't she?" Elizabeth taunted.

"Elizabeth, you know how important this is. Margaret pleaded. "Mrs. Thornton will be here in the morning to see them."

"Loosen up a little, will you? I'll be right back," Elizabeth answered.

"Please Elizabeth, don't go," Margaret begged.

"We get thirty minutes for lunch. It doesn't take that long for a quick drink," Elizabeth answered. Her hat on her head she walked out the door.

Why is she doing this to me? Margaret thought. *If Mrs. Thornton chooses either of our designs for her daughter's trousseau, Maurice will surely let us create others.* Margaret picked up Elizabeth's design pattern. It had everything Mrs. Thornton's daughter asked for. Elizabeth had taken a long quill feather and dyed it a cardinal red. The only thing left for her to do was to paint velvet dots on it and sew it and a flamboyant ribbon on to finish the hat.

Margaret unpacked her lunch and made herself a cup of tea.

"He'll never use any of our designs," she thought over Elizabeth's constant complaining over the two years that Maurice taught them the art of blocking, wiring, binding, sewing and trimming. Margaret took another bite of her sandwich while she worked.

"It isn't any fun around here," Elizabeth persistently grumbled.

"Can't you see, he wants us to prove ourselves," Margaret reassured her older sister.

"Life is to short for me to be proving myself," was Elizabeth's remark. Now they had their chance.

"I want something a little more quirky that would suit my daughter's exuberant style," Mrs. Thornton told Maurice.

"You give me until next week. I promise you that I will have two such items for you to select from," Maurice guaranteed her.

"Girls, I need from each of you your most modern idea for a hat," Maurice asked them.

Quickly, Elizabeth and Margaret started sketching ideas that were already swimming around in their heads.

"Good. Good," he told them. "You make them perfect for me by next week. Here are Miss Thornton's measurements."

"I am counting on you to capture Miss Thornton as a new client. When she buys from us, so will her friends," he told them when he came one morning to inspect their work.

I won't let him down, Margaret thought continuing to sew on the colorful beaded appliqué she made for the hat she designed.

Elizabeth sauntered the two blocks to the speakeasy. She tapped her own private code on the pealing black painted door.

"Howdy, girl," the bouncer said.

"Hi Rudy, any of the guys here yet?" Elizabeth asked.

"There're a few stragglers sitting at the bar," he laughingly said.

"Hi, all," Elizabeth announced her arrival.

"The usual?" asked the bartender.

"Yeah, and I better make it quick. My sister is giving me hell," Elizabeth informed him.

"Again?" he said as he put the glass in front of her.

"Always," Elizabeth answered.

"Put that on my tab," a voice came from one of the booths.

"Is that you, Georgie?" Elizabeth asked.

"Sure enough. It's been awhile," he said now standing beside her at the bar. "Why don't you come over and…"

"Can only stay for one drink. I have to get back to work," Elizabeth said walking towards the booth with him.

"How is Billy," he asked.

"You know Billy, nothing ever changes with him. Told him for months now that we're nothing more than friends but he never gets it," Elizabeth told him.

Forty-five minutes Margaret said to herself

looking at the clock. *"Where is she?"* She asked herself the same question at sixty, seventy-five and ninety minutes.

"Where have you been?" Margaret was finally able to ask her sister.

"Were you able to cover for me?" Elizabeth asked.

"Maurice hasn't been here yet," Margaret answered.

"I'm here now," Maurice said walking into the room. "Are you looking for me?"

"No. Not at all. We were wondering when we would see you, that's all" Elizabeth responded.

"Are they ready?" he asked.

"They will be before quitting time," Elizabeth happily answered. Maurice looked over both projects carefully.

"Splendid, they are beautiful. Good work, girls," Maurice delightedly approved their work.

"Thank you," Margaret answered.

"I want for you to show these hats to Mrs. Thornton," Maurice told them. "She will have much to say of this, I am certain."

"Where the hell were you?" Margaret asked after Maurice left.

"Look, I ran into a friend I haven't seen for a while" Elizabeth flippantly answered. Margaret did not respond.

"What's the problem?" Elizabeth asked. "Maurice is happy and we'll be done shortly. No harm was done."

"I'm sure it was a male friend," Margaret retorted.

"So what if it was?" Elizabeth dismissively

asked.

"Are you going to sneak out with this guy like the last one you ran into?" sarcastically Margaret retorted.

"Why should you care?" Elizabeth snapped.

"I don't care," Margaret lied. "It's not fair to Billy."

"What I do is my business. Keep out of it," Elizabeth demanded.

"I will," Margaret replied.

"There is no reason for Billy to find out unless someone tells him," leeringly Elizabeth stared at Margaret as she said this.

"I have no intention of telling him," Margaret answered. "But your going to get yourself in trouble."

"I'm not looking for trouble," Elizabeth said angrily.

"No need for you to look for it," Margaret said sarcastically. "I'm sure it's going to find you."

~ Chapter Twenty ~

"*Oh, my God!*" a woman shouted. Billy, along with the walking swarm of people stopped to look up. Horrified they stood frozen, watching the hurling body as it plunged from the Manhattan skyscraper. Their screams muffled the body's thud as it smashed onto the pavement.

What just happened? Billy questioned himself. *Was their anything I could have done? If I had walked a little faster... if I had only gotten here sooner*, Billy reproached himself.

Would I have looked up and seen the man standing on the ledge? Would I have had time to get to him? Would I have known what to say to keep the man from jumping? These questions he never asked.

Never before had Billy stood by helplessly watching death's victory over some poor hopeless soul. Billy O'Brien ran into burning buildings to save lives. Billy O'Brien ran into dangerous situations as others fled. Now uncomfortably Billy O'Brien stood looking at the splattered body and at the man's undistinguishable head as it lay split open like a fallen watermelon on the dirty sidewalk.

If only I had been here sooner. I could have done something, Billy blamed himself.

"I can't get that guy out of my mind," he anxiously told Elizabeth. Billy had barely given Elizabeth enough time to answer the front door before he reported the event to her. "All afternoon, I kept seeing him lying on the street. Why did he do it?" Elizabeth sitting next to Billy on the sofa had no answer.

"He was alone on that ledge," Billy's eyes watered over as he spoke. "Was he always alone or did he have a wife and children? What's going to happen to them? God, Elizabeth, he jumped."

"They said a lot of money was lost today in the stock market," Elizabeth casually answered. "I guess he was one of those who lost their fortunes."

"Elizabeth, he died alone. I don't want to ever be that alone. I don't want you to ever be that alone," he nervously said. She smiled, acknowledging what he said. Billy knelt down before her, taking her delicate hands into his.

"Will you marry me?" he asked. "I know, I don't have a ring right now but we can go and pick out one together. How about it?"

"Billy, get up," Elizabeth ordered pulling her hand from his. "You're upset right now and you don't know what you're saying."

"I am upset but I love you and I want us to spend the rest of our lives together," Billy persisted.

"I'm not ready to marry you," Elizabeth coldly said.

"Not ready?" Billy asked.

"Billy, you're a nice guy and I like you. But we're just friends that's all. I told you that," Elizabeth said.

"We have more than that," he argued.

"I never led you to believe it was ever anymore than that," she insisted.

"Elizabeth, it has been just you and me since we first met. I know you love me as much as I love you," Billy said forcibly grabbing her towards him.

"Let me go," Elizabeth said freeing herself. "Billy, you can't be that stupid. You have to have realized I've been seeing other men." His body stiffened as he stepped back.

"Billy, you don't make my heart go pitter patter. My body doesn't tingle when you're near me," Elizabeth candidly said. His face paled. He was speechless.

"For awhile, we had a good time together. That's all. The rest is all in your head. There isn't anything between us," Elizabeth callously informed him.

"Elizabeth," Billy chocked on his words. "We don't have anything?... I thought we had it all." His shoulders slumped as he turned to leave.

On Black Tuesday, October 29, 1929, the bottom dropped out of the stock market, taking the life of that faceless man crushed into the sidewalk and taking the fortune of countless thousands as the Great Depression began.

On Black Tuesday, Billy's world collapsed. Wrenched from him was his dream of a loving life with Elizabeth. Forced now to face it as a delusion, his own private depression engulfed him.

Great minds joined with President Hoover trying to solve the economic problem of the country. Where did they go wrong? Why hadn't they heeded the warning signs? What could they do now?

Billy asked the same painful questions of

himself. Had he too had a laissez-faire attitude?

Sure, he had noticed the little looks Elizabeth shared with other men, but weren't they just innocent flirtations?

Margaret tried interceding for Billy with her sister.

"You'll never find a better man," she told her.

"I know he's a nice guy. But he's not the one for me," Elizabeth snapped back. "If you like him so much, then you marry him," she flippantly added.

Margaret deftly walked a fine line, never betraying her sister while she comforted Billy.

"How could I have been so blind?" he asked her. Margaret listened. For weeks, she listened. For months, she listened as he talked of nothing else but his undying love for Elizabeth.

Then, almost without their noticing, he no longer discussed her older sister with her.

"Elizabeth, I want to invite Billy over for Sunday dinner," Margaret timidly said. "Would it be alright with you?"

"Sure. I don't care," Elizabeth truthfully stated. Honestly, she could not have cared less about it. He had been an obstacle in what she wanted most …enjoying herself. Now he was no longer in her way.

"Thank you," Margaret gratefully answered.

"Are the two of you serious," Elizabeth asked

"We're just friends. That's all," Margaret replied.

"Be careful with that. You know Billy," Elizabeth amusingly said.

The heightened excitement in the Kelly household was palpable as Bridget and Kathleen made everything ready for his return

"It will be nice to have him coming around again," Kathleen told her mother.

"Yes, it will be. He's such a pleasure to cook for," Bridget answered her. Elizabeth did not join in their enthusiasm. Preferring to keep her thoughts focused on her weekly escape from another Sunday evening of boring jigsaw puzzles and radio shows. Preferring to daydream about her new boy friend, Eddie Sullivan, and more lively entertainment.

"I declare, Mrs. Kelly, your food tastes better each time I eat here," Billy said savoring each mouthful. "Salmon with bacon and cabbage is my favorite. I hope it wasn't too much trouble."

"No trouble at all," Bridget happily answered him.

"Thank you," he said.

"Seeing you enjoy it is thanks enough," Bridget answered him. "I made rice pudding for dessert."

Elizabeth hurriedly helped her sister clear off the dinning room table. Billy's constant talking slowed down the meal.

"Eddie is going to be here any minute. Will the two of you please finish the dishes for me, so I can go when he comes?" she asked her sisters. No sooner had they told her yes that they heard the familiar honk of his horn summoning her.

"I have to run," Elizabeth told the family.

"Why can't your friend ring the bell to get you?" Bridget interrogated.

"Too hard to get a parking spot and we're running late for the show," Elizabeth answered racing out the door.

"Perhaps next time?" Uncle Jimmy called after

her. Apparently, Elizabeth did not hear her uncle, as she gave back no response.

"It's good to have you back here for Sunday dinner," Uncle Jimmy said as the two men sat in the parlor while the Kelly women cleaned up.

"It's good to be back," he answered.

"Here," Kathleen said handing a brown cardboard box to Billy. "You're going to like this puzzle. I bought it especially with you in mind." Billy laughed as he read *Eagle Harbor Lighthouse* on the cover.

"I know how much you love the challenge of pictures with both sky and water in them," Kathleen joked with him.

"I bet I do better then you," Billy confidently dared her.

"You're kidding, aren't you? You know I'll do better," Kathleen smugly answered

"The two of you are assuming that it will be a picture of a lighthouse out in the ocean. What if it is a picture of the stairway inside the lighthouse leading up to the light?" Uncle Jimmy questioned. "Or if it is a family picture of the light keeper's family? In either case, with only a 200 piece puzzle, I'll do better than the two of you put together."

"So it's a test to see who is the best! Ma, you be the judge," Kathleen said.

"No, Kathleen, I want no part in this," Bridget answered.

"I'll do it," Margaret announced. "Don't expect me to show any favoritism." She smiled at Billy while she spoke. "Here are the rules; corner pieces don't count as they are too easy. There will be no arguing with me when I announce my final judgment as to who made the best overall contribution to the puzzles completion. Agreed?"

"Agreed," they each acknowledged.

Kathleen sorted out all the blue pieces, Billy worked on what appeared to be the rocky cliffs and Uncle Jimmy put together the red and white tower. Bridget and Margaret put together the border.

"Why don't you and Billy go out one evening with Elizabeth and her new friend Eddie?" Bridget cautiously asked.

"Elizabeth may not want them to," Uncle Jimmy interjected before either of the couple had a chance to answer.

"You girls always seemed to have such fun when you went out together," Bridget said.

"Are you sure that is the reason?" Uncle Jimmy questioned. "Or could it be you want them to check up on Eddie?"

"He never comes into the house," sadly Bridget said. "I thought if Margaret met him…"

"Ma," Margaret interrupted. "If it is alright with Billy, I'll ask her."

"Mrs. Kelly, I'll check him out for you," Billy said, putting a large chunk of the ragged cliff into the puzzle.

"Thank you, Billy. Next week I'll make you shepherd's pie," Bridget told him.

"You don't have to do that. But I would love for you to make it," Billy answered.

Throughout the evening, the family worked quickly interlocking the cardboard pieces.

"Last piece!" Bridget announced.

"And in record time," Kathleen added.

"Amazing how quickly the three of them did it,"

Margaret said.

"And who, my dear niece, is the best puzzle finisher?" Uncle Jimmy asked.

"I have closely watched each of you and I can say without a shadow of a doubt that you are all equally skilled. So it is a tie between you," Margaret proclaimed.

"We should have seen that one coming," Kathleen said.

"We promised to abide by her decision," Billy said.

"And we will until our next challenge," Kathleen added. "But it will have to be when Elizabeth can be the judge. She won't care about any of our feelings."

~ Chapter Twenty One ~

*F*rom their bedroom, Margaret and Kathleen listened to their mother going through her nightly ritual of rechecking all the doors and windows. The house properly secured, Bridget's day of chores ended. She closed her bedroom door. The little bell hanging from the doorknob jingled as it swayed. Its old familiar sound signaled to the girls that it was safe once again to fall asleep.

How Peter laughed at me the first time he heard it, Bridget thought about the bittersweet memories the bell's music carried.

"To keep away the fairies and tinkers?" Peter roared with laughter, barely able to get the words out that first night they shared her bedroom as husband and wife. Lovingly, she looked at his picture on top of the mahogany dresser.

Such a good man, you were Peter Kelly. You never gave me a day of trouble over any of me ways, she said, holding the silver frame in her hands. Gently, she kissed the glass that covered the face she mourned. Before she took her nightgown from the drawer, she placed the frame back in its rightful place next to their special rock sitting on top of the dresser. Bridget readied herself for bed.

A woman's work is never done, she knew the

old adage to be true. The time of the day she dreaded most was upon her. No busy work to occupy her mind. No diversion to keep her from having to face her fears over Elizabeth. Sitting in bed, she took out her rosaries from under her pillow.

Dear Jesus, she kissed the crucifix as she began her prayers. *Sweet Mother Mary and beloved St. Bridget, please bless me daughters. And it is for Elizabeth I especially pray. In the name of the Father and of the Son...* deftly she meditated on the Joyful Mysteries in Mary's life carefully avoiding any thoughts on her own life.

The Fifth Joyful Mystery: Finding Jesus in the Temple, her heart sank as it did every time she thought on this mystery. How she prayed for years to find her dear sister Meg and now she offered all her prayers for her daughter. *Oh Mother of God, if you were worried about finding your son Jesus, who is the Son of God, than you must know the torment that is in me heart over me daughter Elizabeth. Please protect her from harm. Bring her home safely to me.*

Alone, Bridget allowed her tears to betray her emotions. Crying she finished her prayers. Crying she anxiously stayed awake waiting to hear her prodigal daughter return.

The mantel clock struck eleven, then twelve. Bridget kept her private vigil. A car's engine idled in front of their house. Its door slammed.

"Oh shit," Elizabeth exclaimed over the rattling of falling keys.

She is so like you, Peter, Bridget reflected. *I wish you were here. You'd know what to say to her.* The front door unlocked. Laughing and cursing, Elizabeth noisily stumbled all the way to the bathroom and then to her bedroom.

And, so like me dear father, preferring to spend time with friends, Bridget considered.

Dear God, what am I to do? She clenched her hand around the crucifix as she begged. *Peter, give me a sign. Should I go in right this minute and scold her?... She'll never remember anything I say now. Neither you nor me father ever did.* The tears rolled down her face as she listened to her daughter's clumsy footsteps. *I'll not have the courage tomorrow.*

Dear God, I don't know what to do. I tried. 'It's a different world here,' Elizabeth told me. Is it so different a world here? Are these just me own fears? 'You don't understand,' her words cut through me heart like a knife. Sweet Jesus, I don't understand.

Sobbing, Bridget buried her face in her pillow. *She's right. I don't understand. I never did. I never understood me sister. I didn't understand Dog?*

Oh God, I don't want to say the wrong things to Elizabeth and drive her away from me. Maybe she needs a little time and she'll come to her senses. I couldn't stand to loose her like everyone else .What should I do? Please God, please Mother Mary, St. Bridget, Peter, please help me. Give me a sign...

Crash! The music box on Elizabeth's nightstand fell to the floor.

"Elizabeth, settle down. You're waking up the house," Margaret ordered.

"Sorry," Elizabeth irritatingly answered. Margaret turned away and repositioned herself in her bed.

"You know, I didn't mean to wake you," Elizabeth said. "I...

"Elizabeth," Margaret interrupted. "Just go to sleep. It's late and we have to get up early for work."

"Always, everything is about work," Elizabeth argumentatively retorted.

"Elizabeth, it's one in the morning. It's not always about work. We need our sleep. Let's talk about it tomorrow. All right? For now, just go to sleep," Margaret answered.

They'll talk tomorrow, happily Bridget pulled her covers up and got comfortable. In the quietness of the night, it was easy to eavesdrop on her daughters' conversation.

They'll talk tomorrow. Elizabeth will listen to her. She'll get Elizabeth to bring her boyfriend home. She'll get Elizabeth to watch her drinking. Margaret will know what to say. She's so like Meg was, knowing just how to handle things. Bridget fell asleep knowing all her brood were safely in their beds.

~ Chapter Twenty Two ~

Margaret unlocked the office door. As always, she was one of the first to arrive at the showroom in the morning. Many a night, she was one of the last to leave. Her coat hung up, her hat and gloves put away, she filled the kettle. Sipping on her second cup of tea, she looked over her latest design. The office door swung open.

"I'm here," Elizabeth announced bursting into the room

"You're fifteen minutes late," Margaret answered.

"What's the big deal?" Elizabeth asked hurriedly taking off her stylish coat and hat.

"We're lucky to have jobs in this economy," Margaret informed her.

"Maurice is lucky to have us," Elizabeth answered.

"You're lucky he doesn't fire you," Margaret snapped.

"Get off my back," Elizabeth replied sitting down in her seat across from her sister. "I was just a little late. No big deal."

"Elizabeth, it's more than you being a little late," Margaret said looking at her. "It's everything."

"Please, Margaret," Elizabeth groaned. "Not

now, I have a splitting headache. Stop making everything so damn dramatic." Calmly, Margaret got up and went to pour a cup of tea for her sister.

"Here, this will help your head," Margaret said offering a cup.

"Thanks, but I think I need a *little hair of the dog that bit me*," Elizabeth laughed. Taking a silver flask out of her pocketbook, she poured a little of its contents into the teacup.

"Elizabeth," Margaret apprehensively said. "Your drinking is getting out of control."

"Come on, can't a girl have a little fun?" Elizabeth joked. Margaret did not smile.

"You're not just having a little fun," she seriously said. "It's affecting your life. You're hanging around with the wrong sort of crowd. You're out until all hours…"

"Wait a minute," Elizabeth interrupted. "Who's the older sister here? I don't see anyone else thinking I have a problem. How dare you make a judgment on the crowd I go with?"

"You're breaking Ma's heart. Can't you see it?" Margaret asked.

"What the hell are you talking about?" Elizabeth irately asked. "Listen Margaret, this is neither the time nor place to have this conversation. Let's get back to work." Elizabeth got up from her chair and started to walk out of their office.

"Stop! Elizabeth, come back here. We're going to have it here and now," Margaret yelled to her. "When would be the proper time at home in front of Ma and Kathleen?" Elizabeth looked at Margaret in disbelief.

"I don't care who hears me," Margaret

continued. "I'm not going to lie for you anymore here at work. I'm not lying to Ma and telling her you're working late. If you want to go down that road, I'm not helping you any longer. I just can't stand by and watch you." Margaret broke down and cried. "I love you too much for that."

"Margaret, I'm sorry. I don't drink that much," Elizabeth said. "I have it all under control. I just exaggerate to you a little. It's just to tease you, that's all. Don't' worry," Elizabeth reassuringly said. "You don't have to cover for me. I guess that wasn't fair to ask you to do that. But now that I know, I'll change it. I love you too and I don't want anything to come between us."

"You mean it?" Margaret sobbed.

"Of course, I mean it," Elizabeth answered. "We've been through a lot together. And we have a lot further to go." Elizabeth hugged her sister. "I want us to stay close."

"So do I," Margaret agreed. "Do you think me and Billy could double date with you and Eddie sometime?"

"Why not? It will be like old times. You and Billy were always together and I was with your date. Remember?" Elizabeth joked.

"Of course I do," Margaret answered. "I'd like to meet Eddie. I know Ma would like to meet him too."

"I didn't mean anything by not bringing him around. He's just not the kind of guy who likes to meet your mother. You know what I mean?" Elizabeth asked.

"I understand. But we'd like to meet him. I know Ma feels bad about it," Margaret told her.

"She said that to you?" Elizabeth asked.

"Not in so many words. You know Ma," Margaret answered.

"I'll see if I can talk him into it," Elizabeth considered.

"I bet you can talk him into it," Margaret joked.

"You're right. I'll be able to talk him into it," Elizabeth confidently said. "So let's make it definite for this Saturday night. You and Billy. Me and Eddie. And I'll have him come and pick the three of us up and then he'll meet Ma."

"That would be wonderful," Margaret gratefully answered.

"Come on now and go and fix up your face," Elizabeth suggested. "We better get to work or we'll both be fired."

~ *Chapter Twenty Three* ~

The cold wind nipped at Billy's face as he left his Brooklyn apartment. In these hard economic times, the threat of an impending blizzard could not keep the storeowners from opening with only two more days until Christmas.

Billy pulled the collar of his coat up, as he turned the corner, bracing himself against the ferocious wind. His thoughts of Margaret keeping him warm. The snow crunched beneath his feet. Nothing could keep him from picking up Margaret's Christmas gift. Nothing could keep him from making the last payment on her engagement ring. The cold air carried sounds of Christmas carols coming from store radios and the enticing fragrances of roasting chestnuts and pine trees. Men and boys stood on corners trying to sell Christmas trees to those with money enough to spare. One man stood selling pencils as his children with empty stomach looked at windows filled with toys. Billy reached into his pocket and paid the man for some but he didn't take them with him.

"Thank you, sir," the man said.

"You're welcome," Billy answered him. *I am so blessed. I've a job and a good woman who loves me.* Billy thought as he continued towards the jewelry store. *I'm the richest man alive. Wow,* he amazed himself. *Last Christmas, after Elizabeth turned me down, I thought my world ended. Funny how sometimes God answers our prayers best by saying no.* Billy shook his head. *Elizabeth would never have been any good for me. I can't believe how stupid I was. Why was I so blind to her actions? No need wasting any more time thinking about her. Margaret is the girl for me. Thank God, I finally saw what was right before my eyes all the time. Now, I am going to ask for her hand in marriage. But first things first; to talk with her Uncle Jimmy and tell him my intentions and ask for his blessing but first...*

"I'm here to pick up the ring," Billy announced opening the jewelry store door.

"It's ready for you," the proprietor said. Billy opened the ivory colored ring box. The diamond in its lavishly detailed platinum setting sat majestically on a bed of blue velvet.

"It's beautiful," Billy said. "More beautiful, than I imaged."

"I must say this is one of my best designs," the shop owner beamed with pride as he spoke. "Your young woman will approve."

"I know she'll love it," Billy agreed.

Billy was standing in Donahue's foyer, shaking off the snow as Uncle Jimmy came by walking on his way from the kitchen back to his office.

"Billy," Uncle Jimmy happily exclaimed.

"Mr. Donahue," Billy extended his frozen hand.

"Mr. Donahue, is it?" Uncle Jimmy said. "And to what do I owe the pleasure of this visit?"

"I need a moment of your time to talk to you,"

Billy anxiously said.

"Come follow me into my office, we'll have some privacy there," Uncle Jimmy said leading the way. "Sounds to me we'll need a drink for this conversation," he said pulling out his private bottle from the bottom drawer of his desk.

"Mr. Donahue," Billy began nervously. Uncle Jimmy poured two glasses of straight whiskey. He handed one to Billy.

"Take a sip, son. It will help you stop shaking," Uncle Jimmy said. Billy took a swig.

"Mr. Donahue, I've come to ask you for Margaret's hand in marriage," he blurted out. Uncle Jimmy took a sip of his drink.

"Margaret's hand in marriage?" Uncle Jimmy slowly asked. "What do you think her answer will be?" Asking as if it wasn't obvious to him and everyone else how much she cared about Billy.

"We love each other. I'm sure she will say yes. Sir, I wanted to have your blessing as the head of the household first," he answered.

"Billy, I have watched the two of you together. I knew this day would come. I am happy to give you my blessing. When are you going to ask her?" Uncle Jimmy asked.

"Tomorrow, after midnight mass. I plan on asking her then," Billy answered.

"That will be a nice time. Do you have a ring?" Uncle Jimmy questioned. Billy took the box out of his pocket.

"Billy, that had to set you back a good penny," Uncle Jimmy approvingly said, looking at it.

"To my soon-to-be nephew," Uncle Jimmy raised his glass to toast him as he spoke.

"Thank you," Billy said and emptied his glass. Uncle Jimmy gulped his whisky, swallowing back the unwanted emotions the sight of the engagement ring bought back to him.

~ Chapter Twenty Four ~

"*Elizabeth, do you have any* of that red satin ribbon left?" Margaret called into the bedroom.

"Any left?" Elizabeth chuckled. "I didn't wrap any of these gifts myself. I had the counter girl at Macy's do all of them for me," Elizabeth pompously replied.

"There is something like it in the basket next to me sewing," Bridget shouted from the kitchen. Finding just what she was looking for, Margaret continued wrapping the rest of the family's gifts.

The scent from freshly baked apple pies and sweet treats permeated the Christmas Eve's air as Bridget and Kathleen prepared the midnight meal.

"The pies are cool enough. I'll pack them up," Kathleen said.

"Good. I'll get me coat and we'll bring them over to the church," Bridget answered.

"Do you need my help?" Margaret asked as they started picking up the boxes.

"We'll be fine. You finish the wrapping. There is still more work to be done when we get home," Bridget said. "Elizabeth," she called. "Do you want to take the walk to church?"

"No, Ma," she said walking into the parlor. "If you don't need me, I have some things to finish up."

"We'll be fine. The two of you finish what you have to do. We'll be back shortly," Bridget answered.

"That present came out nicely," Elizabeth commented.

"I think so too," Margaret agreed. "It's the scarf I knitted for Billy."

"He's going to like it," Elizabeth assured her.

"I hope so," Margaret wished.

Bridget and Kathleen made their way through the narrow shoveled pathways. The sun warmed not only the two of them, but also the dirt and soot-covered snow mounds that lined their route. Large, stagnant puddles of dirty water sat in the street gutters.

"When the weather is better, you should come in with Uncle Jimmy and see the wonderful building I work in," Kathleen said.

"I'll ask him," Bridget replied. "That would be grand."

"The building is grand. It has thirty-two floors. It's called the Barclay-Vesey Building. Mama," Kathleen animatedly informed her. "The lobby goes right through it, from one street clear over to the other. That's how the building got its name from the two streets it takes up."

"You sound like your uncle, giving us all the facts the day we arrived," Bridget laughed.

"Mama, I can't help it," Kathleen continued. "You should see the entrance. Painted on the ceiling is the history of communication. Each day I walk in, I stand under it for five minutes and stare at it. I keep finding something new in the picture every time I look. Mrs. Raynor would never approve but I can't help it."

"I think you're wrong, Kathleen," Bridget said. "I think Mrs. Raynor would approve. You're not a greenhorn there. It is your building. You hold an important position there."

"Yes, Mama," Kathleen agreed. "Mr. Reynold heads an important department for the telephone company. Working as one of his secretary is a big responsibility.

"Such an important job me daughter has," Bridget acknowledged.

"I was lucky Uncle Jimmy was able to help me find it," Kathleen confided.

"Uncle Jimmy said that having graduated top in your class you would have not had any difficulties in gaining employment." Bridget assured her.

"Mama, these are hard times. There are thousands out of work," Kathleen answered.

"I know, child. Don't think I do not see the hardships all around us. God has blessed us here. Your sisters are doing well at Maurice's. He hasn't had to lay one person off. Uncle Jimmy, the good man that he is, is doing more than his share of feeding the hungry at Donahue's kitchen door."

"Mama," Kathleen interrupted. "I see what you are doing. Never has a man knocked on our door and asked for work in exchange for food that you haven't fed him. And look at these pies you baked for the church to give out tomorrow for the needy."

"Child, our family has known hunger. It is up to us who have, to help those who don't. There's no telling how long this Depression is going to last."

Billy, dressed in his best outfit, came early to escort the Kelly women and Uncle Jimmy to midnight mass. The family along with friends and neighbors navigated their way on the ice to Holy Name Church. Smoke carried their words from their mouths as they spoke but Billy didn't hear any of it.

Margaret. Yes, I'll start with that. But what should I say next? Billy wrestled with the question. Throughout the mass, each of the Kellys sat with their own thoughts. Margaret watched unsuspectingly at Billy's nervous fidgeting. Kathleen followed the mass in her missal. Bridget said her rosary while Elizabeth sat comfortably thinking about Eddie. No longer feeling the anxiety she once had at being a sinner. Now secure in the knowledge that there really is no God to get her as she had been taught.

"Jimmy, would you mind if we followed behind?" Billy asked when the mass was over.

"Of course not, you take as long as you like. We'll see the two of you back at the house," he answered. "I'll tell you on the way home," he whispered to Bridget.

"Margaret," Billy asked. "I'd like to go and see the manger one more time before we leave. If it would be alright with you?"

"Sure, I'd like to see the baby Jesus, too," she answered. Billy and Margaret waited in the aisle as other parishioners came to pay homage to the newly born babe. They were the last to stand before him. Except for the altar boys and the organist, the church was empty. Billy turned to her.

"Margaret, I know I didn't realize it at first, but I know it now," he said and he knelt down before her. The organist stopped straightening up the choir loft as she watched them.

"Margaret, I love you and I want you to be my

wife. Will you marry me?" he asked taking the ring out of his pocket and sliding it onto her finger. Through her watery eyes, Margaret admired it.

"Yes.. Yes.. Yes," she eagerly answered, throwing her arms around him. The organist began playing a sweet melody for them as they kissed. The altar boy continued putting out the candles.

"We're engaged! We're engaged," Margaret excitedly yelled as they entered the parlor. "We know. We know," Kathleen jumped up and rushed over to see the ring. "Uncle Jimmy told us. Oh, it's beautiful."

"I couldn't keep the news to myself," Uncle Jimmy embarrassingly confessed.

"It is. Isn't it?" Margaret said admiring it herself.

"Mrs. Kelly, I hope you approve?" Billy questioned.

"My dear boy, I certainly do. I've been waiting to add a son to this family," she answered. "I don't believe in long engagements."

"I agree," Billy answered. "What do you say, Margaret? How about… June?"

"June?" Margaret said slowly. "Billy, that's a perfect month for a wedding."

"June it is. Is that a respectable length of time for an engagement?" he asked Bridget.

"Yes, I do say it is," she happily answered him.

"I'd be pleased to throw the two of you a mighty fine wedding reception at my place," Uncle Jimmy offered.

"I can't think of a finer place, can you?" Billy asked Margaret.

"Thank you, Uncle Jimmy. There is no other

place I'd rather have it," Margaret answered as she kissed her uncle.

"Congratulations," Eddie said, shaking Billy's hand. "I can't beat that Christmas gift with what I brought."

"You don't have to worry about that," Elizabeth promised. "I'm going to love whatever you bought for me. Don't you worry."

"Congratulations to the two of you," Elizabeth toasted with her eggnog. "Billy, it will be nice having you as a brother-in-law," she said kissing him on his cheek.

"Elizabeth, see my ring," Margaret asked. Elizabeth took Margaret's hand and looked at the ring. As they ate the ham and pies that Bridget baked, Elizabeth stole glances of the happy couple and watched the light reflected off the diamond that graced her sister's finger.

"I can't believe that Margaret's going to get married," Kathleen said.

"You knew this day would come." Bridget answered.

"Yes," Kathleen replied. "But I always thought Elizabeth would be the first to marry."

"Her day will be here soon enough," Bridget guaranteed.

"I'm getting a little uncomfortable," Eddie said loosening his collar.

"Calm down," Elizabeth joked. "I'm not ready to settle down. And by the way, Eddie, who's to say that when I am, it will be with you?"

"Isn't it beautiful?" Margaret again asked as the girls put on their nightgowns.

"Yes it is. It is very pretty. He picked a style that suits you," Elizabeth coldly answered.

"Elizabeth, are you alright with this?" Margaret asked.

"Of course, I am. I want the two of you to be happy," Elizabeth answered. "Like you said, he's a nice guy. I'm glad you got him." The silver bell on Bridget's bedroom door jingled...Safe now for every one to fall asleep.

"Thanks, Elizabeth," Margaret said. "That means a lot to me."

~ Chapter Twenty Five ~

"*When will this freezing weather* let up?" Elizabeth asked looking out through the frosted windowpane.

"Don't worry. It can't last forever," Margaret tried to reassure her.

"It's only the middle of February. We have all of March to go," Elizabeth moaned.

"And then it will be spring," Margaret answered.

"That's easy for you to say. You don't give a damn about being stuck in this house. You're content to sit here and rot," Elizabeth said, confronting her sister.

"No need for you to start in with me. I didn't make the weather," Margaret argued back.

"I'm sure your Billy will make it here to see you tonight," Elizabeth sarcastically remarked.

"I know he's going to try," Margaret answered. "I'm sure Eddie will try and see you also."

"I'm not so sure. I haven't seen him in two weeks," Elizabeth despondently revealed.

"But, it's Valentines Day, I'm sure if he can't make it, he'll call," Margaret tried cheering up her sister. Elizabeth's stomach twisted and knotted at the thought of talking to him on the telephone.

Yesterday, she called Eddie's apartment, only to hear the voice of a strange woman answer it. She dialed the number again to make sure she had done it right and then only heard a busy sound. His apartment was within easy walking distance, but she knew he wouldn't show up.

He's seeing someone else. I know it, Elizabeth perceptively thought. *I always knew the type of guy he is. Why did I ever ask him 'Have you ever thought of settling down?'*

"I'm not that kind of guy. I wouldn't make any woman a good husband," Eddie honestly answered me. *"I'm not trainable."* Those were the last words he said to me. I knew he wouldn't be true to only me for too long. But I thought I'd have him just a little longer.* Elizabeth had trouble admitting this to herself, no less talk about it to anyone else.

"Want to work on the puzzle?" Kathleen said bringing in the box.

"Great. Another boring Saturday night in the Kelly household and the three of us gaily putting together stupid pieces of nothing together," Elizabeth angrily expressed.

The winter storms of January and February brought March in like a lion. By midmonth, the days warmed and March heralded a beautiful spring.

Crocuses were the first to push their way upward and burst forth from the frozen ground.

Margaret delighted over seeing the first signs of spring. *June is not too far off*, she thought. Not so for Elizabeth, with the sight of nature bringing forth new birth, her sullenness worsened.

"Eddie, we have to talk," Elizabeth said. For

two hours, she waited outside his apartment door. Afraid… he'd be bringing someone home with him. More afraid…not to tell him.

"Hi, I was just thinking about you the other day," Eddie answered. He opened his door and led her into his unkempt apartment.

"Excuse the mess," he said moving clothing off the couch, making room for her to sit.

"I always did," she replied. "You were thinking about me?" she hopefully asked.

"Yes, I was. And Margaret and Billy," Eddie casually answered.

"We had a nice time together didn't we?" reminiscently Elizabeth answered.

"We did," Eddie continued. "But I was thinking about Billy because I heard what happened to that friend of his, Bobby Ulrich."

"Bobby Ulrich? I don't think I ever heard his name mentioned," Elizabeth said, settling into his comfortable couch.

"Sure, I know you met him. Oh, that's right. You'd know him by his performance name," Eddie laughed. "Ace Hunter."

"What's so funny?" Elizabeth asked.

"His performance name…get it?" he joked. Elizabeth looked questioningly at him.

"His real name is, or should I say was, Bobby Ulrich," Eddie started. "He had the nickname of Cherry Hunter for always getting to be the first guy to break a girl's cherry."

"You said *was* his name," Elizabeth replied as the word finally struck her.

"Yeah, well once he started flying couldn't call him Cherry Hunter any more so he changed it to Ace.

Well, down in Alabama he was in an air show and he hooked up with this pretty young thing. He lived up to his reputation but this southern bell wasn't like the girls up here in the North. No sir. The morning after, she lost it. She took her daddy's rifle. Walked right out onto the airstrip. She called and he turned around. 'Remember, I am always at your disposal' she coldly said to him. He looked at her and she shot him south of his belt buckle if you get my meaning. Witnesses said she left him there bleeding to death crying for help. She went home and gave the police no trouble when they came to arrest her."

"I think she'll get off," Elizabeth said feeling sorry for that poor girl. *Feeling sorry for herself.*

"You're probably right. They ain't going to like some Yankee doing that to one of their ladies," Eddie agreed.

"Eddie, there is something I have to tell you," Elizabeth apprehensively said.

"Sure, go ahead," he answered.

"Eddie, I'm pregnant," she nervously told him.

"Pregnant? I used protection," he answered.

"I'm pregnant," she affirmed.

"You're sure?" Eddie disbelievingly asked.

"I've been to a doctor. Due in October," Elizabeth reported.

"How much do you need to get rid of it?" he replied.

"I can't do that," she answered, hurt by the offer.

"Are you going to give it up?" he asked.

"Eddie, this is our baby. I just couldn't... I am going to keep it," she stood up as she spoke. "You don't have to do anything. I'm not asking you for any help. Just thought you'd want to know."

"Waite a minute, Elizabeth. Don't leave. I didn't expect this," he said grabbing her arm. "You've had time to think this over. This is the first time I'm hearing it." Elizabeth sat back down as Eddie paced the room.

"This is my baby," he said aloud.

"Yes," she answered.

"I didn't mean for you to answer," he acknowledged. "I know you haven't been with anyone else." She kept her eyes down at the floor as he spoke.

"Elizabeth I don't want any kid of mine to be a bastard. Life is hard enough," he stood before her calmly speaking. Elizabeth looked up at him and agreed.

"Why don't we get married?" he asked. "We'll give it a go. Leastways, he'll have a name."

"He'll?" Elizabeth laughed.

"Or she. I don't care," Eddie jubilantly answered. "I'm going to be a father. How about it Elizabeth, let's give it a go?"

"Why not?" she answered him.

"Does your family know?" he asked.

"You're the first person who knows. I haven't had the courage to tell anyone else," she shamefully answered.

"I'll talk with your uncle," Eddie decisively answered "And then I'll tell your mother."

"We can do it together. Come over for Easter Dinner. We'll tell them then," Elizabeth answered.

"It would be best if I went and talked man-to-man with your uncle then we can tell your mother together," he suggested. Elizabeth agreed.

"You're finally in a better mood," Margaret said to her. Actually everyone even acquaintances at work started noticing a glow about her.

"Eddie's coming to Easter dinner," she answered.

"Glad he's back in your life," Margaret told her.

"So am I," she cheerfully replied.

"A baby, now won't that be grand," Uncle Jimmy supportively said to Eddie when he told him. Unfortunately, for them Bridget Kelly's response was less amenable.

"The shame of it! I will be humiliated in front of all me friends," Bridget yelled. "How could you have brought such disgrace upon our family?" Elizabeth sat in the dining room chair unable to speak…unable to defend herself.

"Mrs. Kelly," Eddie started.

"Don't you be saying me name," Bridget snapped at him. "What nerve to be here sitting at me table. You've no respect for me nor me daughter. I think it best for you to leave. This is the first day that I am happy me poor husband is dead, for this would have surely struck him down dead."

"Bridget, calm down," Uncle Jimmy interjected.

"Calm down! The hell I will," Bridget said slamming her fist on the table. "I want him out of me house. Now!"

"Do you?" Uncle Jimmy calmly questioned. "Sit back down, Eddie," he continued. "Bridget, they plan on getting married. They are going to have this child with or without your blessing. Do you want Elizabeth to be out of your life?"

"She's disgraced our family," Bridget answered disgustedly.

"Bridget, don't be so naïve. This is not the first time that this situation has happened in our family," Uncle Jimmy informed her. His words pierced her heart.

Bridget had never asked him. She didn't even know if he knew. They had never mentioned Meg's name. Ever since her own bout of morning sickness during her first pregnancy, she suspected. Now in the mist of such shame would she be finding out what happened to Meg? Bridget calmed herself to listen.

"Our dear Uncle James, to whom our family owes much, was forced by this same circumstance to marry," Uncle Jimmy started the story.

Still after all these years, never a mention of Meg, Bridget thought.

"Their situation made worse because our Aunt Emily was the daughter of his good friend William Lynch. And our Uncle James was thirty six and she a child of sixteen," Uncle Jimmy waited a moment as those facts settled on their ears. "Her family disowned her," he said looking at Bridget. "She was forced to live with the shame of it. Our cousin Sean is that child. And now no one asks what came first, the marriage or the conception. It was only when they moved away was there any peace for them. Do you want that for Elizabeth and her child...your grandchild?"

"What do we say to the neighbors?" Bridget asked.

"Don't worry about what the neighbors have to say. We'll think of something," Uncle Jimmy said.

"We'll say they eloped and the baby is premature, that will work," Margaret joined in squeezing her older sister's hand.

"That might work," Bridget answered.

"Will you give them your blessing to marry?" Uncle Jimmy asked.

"I see that I have no other choice," Bridget answered. "But don't you be thinking I'll ever be happy about it."

"Thank you, Mama," Elizabeth answered.

"When is the baby due?" Margaret asked.

"In October," Elizabeth told her sisters.

"Good God, do we have to be telling the whole world?" Bridget asked.

"No we don't, Mama," Margaret answered.

"When are you getting married?" Kathleen asked.

"Next Friday," Eddie answered.

"I was right, Elizabeth will be the first to marry," Kathleen boasted. "We should have some sort of celebration."

"It's so close to Margaret's day. I don't want to take away from it for her," Elizabeth said.

"Why don't we tell everyone you eloped and on June 4th we'll all four share the wedding reception?" Margaret asked. "That is, if it would be alright with you, Billy?"

"What ever you want, sweetheart. It's your day," Billy answered.

"What do you say, Elizabeth?" Margaret urged.

"Are you sure?" Elizabeth asked.

"Why not? We have always shared our important days together. Haven't we? It will be fun," Margaret added. "And now I'm going to be an aunt."

"And a godmother," Elizabeth quickly added.

~ Chapter Twenty Six ~

May flowers perfumed the air. Tulip petals gently fell upon the ground as rose bushes began blooming. Wisteria, lilacs and giant rhododendrons intertwined creating a canopy above them. White, pink and violet cymbidium orchids lined the romantic walkways as the engaged couple strolled through the Brooklyn Botanical Gardens.

"No wife of mine is going to work, either," Billy said stubbornly.

"But Billy, so many are loosing their jobs, don't you think I should keep mine for as long as I can?" Margaret asked.

"No. I will provide for my wife," he said resolutely. Lovingly she looked up at him. Nothing was as important as his happiness.

"I'll tell Maurice tomorrow," she answered.

"Margaret, they'll be plenty enough to keep you busy. I want to start a family right away," he announced. Hand in hand, they entered the greenhouse. No thorns would touch their undying love and devotion to each other.

The beginning married life of the Sullivan's was not so flowery. Theirs had more the stench of stale beer and cigarettes. As planned on last the Friday in

April, Elizabeth and Eddie were married in City Hall. Margaret and one of his friends, were their witnesses. Uncle Jimmy provided a wonderful lunch at Donahue's for the occasion.

Eddie's friends planned a celebration party that began that evening and went straight through until Sunday. Monday morning, Eddie dressed and went to work.

"Please… I can't…I'm to sick," Elizabeth begged, talking into the telephone.

"You have to tell him yourself," Margaret ordered.

"Margaret, don't yell. I can't stay out of the bathroom long enough to talk to him," Elizabeth answered.

"Just tell him that my husband said for me to quit," Elizabeth pleaded. "I'm sick. I have to hang up now."

"Alright, I'll do it," Margaret consented.

"It saves me the trouble of firing her," Maurice infuriatedly answered her. "I know you have been doing her work for some time now. You, I would be sorry to see go."

~ *Chapter Twenty Seven* ~

"*I wish your father could see you today,*" Bridget tenderly said.

"I can feel him watching from Heaven," Margaret answered standing in the back of the church.

"Mrs. Kelly, may I show you to your seat?" an usher offered.

"Yes, young man, you may," she accepted. But first she gave Margaret one more kiss. "Kathleen, don't walk too fast," she added before she went to take her seat.

"I'll walk just the way we practiced with Father Fannon," Kathleen calmly answered her. "It's a shame Elizabeth was sick this morning and couldn't be here. I know how important it would have been for you to have her as your matron of honor."

"Kathleen, it's going the way it's meant to be. I'm happy you're my maid of honor. Thank you for willingly standing in," she said hugging her sister. The organist began the entrance hymn.

"Are you ready?" Uncle Jimmy asked.

"As ready as I'll ever be." Margaret answered. He offered his arm. Kathleen took a deep breath, smiled and slowly led the way down the aisle. Everyone's eyes were on Margaret as she radiantly entered the church, accompanied by her uncle. Bridget's eyes watered. Billy smiled as he watched his angel coming towards him. Uncle Jimmy raised Margaret's veil and kissed her.

"Take good care of our girl," he said to Billy.

"I will sir," Billy answered looking into Margaret's eyes.

"I can't believe it!" Elizabeth ranted.

"It doesn't look that bad," Eddie comfortingly said.

"That bad. There is no way I can wear that dress. Overnight.. just look at me... my body looks disgusting," Elizabeth began crying.

"No, not at all. You can hardly tell," Eddie hesitantly answered.

"Hardly tell," Elizabeth yelled. "I've blown up. I can't show my face at the reception."

"Yes, you can. Don't you have something else to wear that will hide it?" he asked.

"Hide it? How can I hide this? I'm not going," she answered.

"You have to. People are going to be expecting us. It's our party too," he encouraged.

"I never should have agreed to share a party with Margaret. Today is her day and we should have had one of our own. Always my life has been the same. I have had to work hard for everything I get and Margaret benefits. She's always had an easy go of it," Elizabeth complained.

"That very well may be, but it is also our party. My friends and family are going to be there. Isn't there anything in your closet that will do?" he looked lovingly at her. "Please, do it for me?"

"I do have a dress that I might be able to make do," she responded.

"Then what are you waiting for. There's a party waiting for us," he encouraged.

The organist played her final piece of music. Bombarded by a hail of rice, Margaret and Billy excitedly ran to the waiting car. Their faces aglow. Off to Donahue's for the reception, but first one short stop. The sun shown on the happy couple as they made their way to Prospect Park Lake for pictures. Elizabeth and Eddie were already sitting on a bench waiting for the wedding party's arrival.

"You look beautiful," Elizabeth said. "Sorry, I just couldn't make it to the mass."

"I understand. It's best you take care of my niece or nephew, or should I just say godchild," Margaret joked. "By the way, you look great."

"I don't know what happened. It's as if over night I blew up. Can you tell?" Elizabeth asked as the photographer posed the wedding party before the serene lake.

"No. Not really," Margaret answered as a pair of trumpeter swans paddled into the background.

For Margaret, the wedding reception was perfect. She danced with Billy. She danced with Uncle Jimmy. She danced with Maurice who promised to always have a position waiting for her if she wanted to return to work. Only the wonderful expression of their lovemaking their first night together as husband and wife could have topped off her day.

For Elizabeth, the drinks went down easily but the heat and her condition conspired against her preventing her from enjoying the party. Drunk and being rowdy, Elizabeth and Eddie made their way home.

Among the cards and gifts of money they woke up, fully dressed the following morning, unable to remember half the night nor how they got home.

~ Chapter Twenty Eight ~

"*Damn it, Elizabeth!* This place looks like a pig sty," Eddie yelled tripping over a pile of magazines left strewn about on the living room floor. Waddling over to the kitchen table, she responded by slamming down his dinner plate. The peas and carrots abandoned his dish. Eddie walked into the kitchen

"Good God, you're still in that dirty nightgown," he angrily said. "I thought you were going to clean the apartment today." Elizabeth picked up the cowardice vegetables off the table with her fingers and put them back on his plate. She had every intention of cleaning up the apartment.

Once the heat of the summer is over, you'll feel better, her doctor told her. Nevertheless, the cool October weather did not bring the promised relief. A rash, which had began under her enlarging breasts and in her groin in July, now met as it covered all her abdomen. Leaving the raw flesh to burn and bleed. The scorching heat of August did nothing to warm the Sullivan's relationship that distanced as the baby grew inside her.

No matter where their outings were, drinking was the only activity the couple shared. New stains of blood and serous liquid emerged as her nightgown rubbed against her excoriated skin.

"Why didn't you get one of your girlfriends to clean up before they left?" she snapped.

"You're still mad?" he asked shaking his head in disbelief.

"Don't look at me that way," she ordered. "I'm not crazy. I know what I saw."

"Elizabeth, nothing is going on," he reassured her. "They're all our friends. You said you'd be back to yourself after the summer. What's the matter with you?"

"What's the matter with me? You're what's the matter with me. I saw you flirting. Don't think I'm blind," she screamed.

"We were having a little fun. That's all. Time was when you were fun," he hollered back.

"Fun enough for you to knock up," she bellowed in retaliation. Eddie's body stiffened in defense of her bitter words as they made their way out the open windows for the neighbors to hear.

"That's it. I'm not up for another go around. I'm out of here," he answered turning to make his way out of the apartment.

"Don't go. I don't know what I'm saying. It's not me. It's the pregnancy," Elizabeth grabbed at his arm trying to stop him. Callously, he freed himself from her hold.

"We've been through this before," he said pulling away from her. "We'll just continue arguing. I don't want either of us to say anything we'll regret."

"I don't want to be alone tonight," she pleaded.

"I need to get out for awhile. Do you want me to drop you off at Margaret's or your mother's?" he

asked.

"Neither," Elizabeth stubbornly answered. "I'll stay home alone."

"Then will you please clean up this place? It really stinks in here," Eddie criticized walking out of the apartment.

It stinks in here? His words echoing in her head as she ran out into the hallway after him. The baby growing inside her kicked, as she leaned over the railing.

"Life stinks! You could have taken out the garbage yourself," she screamed down the staircase. She watched him walk out of the apartment house door without answering her.

Shuffling herself back to their apartment, she rubbed the small of her back. Every inch of her body ached. Her abdomen now so swollen she could no longer see her feet. Her belly button so stretched she feared it would tear open if this child was not born soon. A refreshing breeze blew in through the open hallway window carrying with it the aroma of the next-door neighbor's Italian sauce. Elizabeth walked into her apartment. The stench of stale alcohol and cigarettes met her at the door. Her stomach wrenched.

Where to start? Elizabeth considered the endless possibilities. She wrapped up Eddie's untouched plate. Her unborn baby continued its acrobatics. *Only one way to quiet it down and get some peace.* Elizabeth poured her second drink of the day. The first one she had nursed since lunch. Propping up every pillow she owned, she finally managed positioning herself on the couch. She savored her drink and waited for the baby to settle down.

God damn it! Elizabeth said to herself just becoming comfortable when the uncontrollable urge to urinate came over her. Struggling, she managed to get herself up. But not before the urine started dripping from her.

I'll clean it up later, I'm not up to it now, she promised herself. *What is happening to me? I can't even hold my own water.* Elizabeth stood horrified as she caught site of her reflection in the bathroom mirror.

I'm so disgusting. Look at me in this filthy rag… No wonder Eddie doesn't want to stay home with me. I wouldn't want to. She poured herself a stronger drink to numb her pain. The baby inside her stretched. *For God's sake, can't you calm down? You don't give me a minute's peace*, Elizabeth complained to her unborn child. *If it weren't for you, I'd be out with my husband where I should be… Instead I'm here alone talking to you.* The baby kicked in response. *You thankless child… I'm losing Eddie over you…*The baby continued kicking and stretching, making itself comfortable.

Elizabeth swayed her way back towards the kitchen. *Oh God, I'm losing Eddie over you… I hope you're worth it*, she contemplated her words while she poured yet another drink for herself. *Nothing will ever be worth losing Eddie.* The ice clinked against the side of the glass as she drank. The unborn child inside her finally quieted down.

I wish you'd settle down for ever…forever…I don't need this in my life right now. All I need is Eddie. He's going to come home with the smell of some bitch all over him…I know it… What can I offer him with this repulsive belly?… Can't blame him…

It's all your fault! You've taken my husband away. You're the one keeping him away from me… We can't even snuggle at night. You make it impossible for me to get comfortable. You're the one who's put a wedge between us. You have no right to do this to me. No one ever wants to see me happy. Not even my own child, Elizabeth sobbed. Only the urgency of urination stopped her crying.

Composed, once again she began trying to straighten up the apartment. Overcome by the stench as she opened up the garbage pail, she vomited all over herself. *Damn him, he doesn't do a thing around here. Bet he won't so much as change a single diaper. I'm going to be stuck with you alone. I can see the pieces of my life before me right now.* Gagging and retching, she carried the garbage bag out of her apartment.

"Shit," Elizabeth slurred aloud as she almost tripped by the top step of the staircase. *For God sakes, I nearly killed myself.* One lucid thought made its way across her mind. *That would have been the end of all my problems. So easy…One step…All this would be over…I would get Eddie back… No one would know.* Holding her breath, she held the garbage bag tightly in her arms. *There would be plenty of time for other babies. Not just now…* She threw herself off the top step. Her tumbling body plunged down the flight of stairs, forcibly hitting each step as she passed. The garbage bag ripped from her arms leaving nothing to cushion her landing.

"Oh my God!" the janitor's wife screamed. "Call the police! Get an ambulance!" she ordered her husband. "Elizabeth!" she called running towards the lifeless body. Every tenant in the building responded to the commotion.

"Don't move her," one man advised.

"Is she dead?" a woman asked.

"No, look you can see she's still breathing," another person answered.

"What about the baby?" the janitor's wife asked.

"I don't know," he answered. The nearing sound of sirens was the apartment house residents' only hope as they stood helplessly watching the enlarging puddle of liquid coming from under Elizabeth's nightgown.

"Make way. Make way," a police officer ordered the growing crowd of spectators congregating outside the Twelfth Street apartment building.

"Seventy over fifty," the younger ambulance attendant said taking the stethoscope out of his ears. "Pulse thready. Mrs. Sullivan, can you hear me? We're going to put you on the stretcher and take you to the hospital."

"When is the baby due?" the older attendant in charge asked the janitor's wife, who was giving as much information to the police officer as she could.

"The baby's due in two weeks?" anxiously, she answered. "Will it be all right?"

"Can't say for certain yet. We have to get her to the hospital," he answered. "Do you know where her husband is?"

"No," she answered.

"She has a sister who lives close to here," the janitor interjected. "I have her name and address in my apartment."

"Sir, please get that information for me," the

police officer asked. The two attendants rolled Elizabeth unto the stretcher. Her breath reeked of alcohol, as she moaned.

"Mrs. Sullivan, how much did you drink today?" the younger ambulance attendant loudly asked.

"Just… one," she mumbled.

"More likely one bottle," he said to his partner as they carried the stretcher to the waiting ambulance. "You couldn't tell there's prohibition in this country by this neighborhood," he continued. Once they anchored the stretcher in place, the young attendant sped the ambulance towards the hospital. Elizabeth's eyes opened briefly at times. The wetness between her legs was becoming cold.

"Mrs. Sullivan, try to stay awake," the older attendant told her as he continued monitoring her vital signs. Doctors and nurses bombarded Elizabeth with other orders and questions as they took her from the ambulance. None of which could she comprehend.

"Rush her to Delivery Room 5. They'll prep her upstairs," the ER doctor ordered.

"Should we type and cross match?" a nurse asked.

"Yes and get a complete blood work up," he answered.

Frantically, a chain of telephone calls went from one friend to another as all of Brooklyn was looking for Eddie. The moment Margaret answered her apartment door, the police officer knew someone had already informed her of her sister's condition.

"Will you take me to the hospital to see her?" she asked him. "My husband is at work."

"Yes, Mrs. O'Brien, I'll drive you up there. Is there anyone that can come with us and stay with you?" he asked.

"She's that bad?" Margaret asked tearfully.

"Not being a medical person myself, I can't say for certain. But, times like this, it's best you're not alone," he answered.

"Is it possible for us to stop and pick up my mother and sister?" Margaret asked. "I'll call and tell them we're on our way."

"It might be best if you tell your mother in person. That's pretty unsettling news to hear over the telephone," he advised.

"That might be best," she agreed.

"Mrs. O'Brien," the officer said. "I don't know what your neighbors told you, but you should know that your sister reeked of alcohol when they found her."

"Thank you for your honesty," Margaret answered refusing her first impulse to say that was impossible. "I need to leave a note for my husband then I'll be ready to go with you." Margaret thought it best not to tell her mother or Kathleen this added bit of information until they were alone in the stark white hospital waiting room.

"She couldn't tolerate the drink being pregnant," Bridget loudly informed her daughter.

"Ma, it has nothing to do with the pregnancy. She drinks too much. I've told you that before," Margaret corrected her.

"He had no right to say such a thing. She was taking down the garbage. I'm sure that is where the stink came from. Don't mention this ever again to anyone," Bridget ordered. "Do you hear me!"

"Let it go," Kathleen said before Margaret could say another word. "Now's not the time."

"When will be the time?" Margaret asked sarcastically.

"It has been a difficult pregnancy. You don't understand all the changes a woman goes through. Once the baby comes, you'll see, Elizabeth will get herself together," Bridget said sounding as though she believed what she was saying. "We should be saying our prayers for the two of them right now." Bridget took the rosary beads from her pocketbook.

"Where's the blood I ordered?" the doctor apprehensively asked. "There's a problem." The scrub nurse dutifully reached in between Elizabeth's legs. She wiped the beads of sweat developing on the doctor's forehead as he vigilantly tried to dislodge the tightly wrapped cord around the baby's neck.

Without warning the next contraction came. The baby thrust forward and into the world as Elizabeth had wished...dead. A nurse took the lifeless baby to a corner of the room. There she tearfully poured water over its head.

"I baptize thee, Mildred..." she said, after her recently deceased mother.

Excitement filled the somber Delivery Room when the doctor next spoke.

"What do we have here?" he asked. "I think we have a foot," The contractions continued and within minutes, a second girl was born. "Rush her to the nursery. You can baptize her in there. She's going to have a hard time of it," he advised the nurse.

"Want an IV in her, first?" the nurse asked.

"Yes. From the looks of the mother, this baby

should be going through withdrawal. I'd say within four to six hours at best," he answered.

Eddie anxiously ran into the waiting room minutes before the delivery room doctor walked in.

"Mr. Sullivan?" he asked.

"Yes, Doctor," he answered.

"You have a baby daughter," he seriously announced.

"A daughter. Thank you, doctor. Thank you." Eddie joyously said shaking the physician's hand. "A daughter, what do you think about that?" A look of relief covered Eddie's face but it was not mirrored back by the physician's.

"Is she alright?" Eddie asked seeing the look in the doctor's eyes. The answer was not quick in coming. "How is my wife?" Eddie asked fearing the worse.

"Your daughter is stable for the time being. We will know more about her condition in a few hours. We have given your wife a blood transfusion. She has no major injuries and nothing is broken," he spoke routinely.

"Oh, thank God," Bridget said but she and the family could tell there was something the doctor was not saying.

"Mr. Sullivan, I need to talk with you in private," the doctor said.

"Doctor," Eddie answered. "This is Elizabeth's mother and these are her sisters. Whatever you have to tell me, I am going to have to tell them. So, you might as well just tell us all together."

"Alright, but we should have this talk in private," he led them towards a room next to the waiting room. Uncle Jimmy rushed into the waiting room just in time to follow behind them.

"This is her uncle," Eddie informed the doctor.

"Is my niece alright? Is there a problem with the baby?" Uncle Jimmy fearfully asked.

"They are both stable at this time. As I already told your family. Elizabeth lost some blood from the fall. We've given her a transfusion… Nothing's broken… No major injuries. She will be sore for quite some time," his tone changed as he continued. "I am concerned about the amount of alcohol in her blood tonight."

"My wife's been through a lot lately with that rash. She couldn't sleep or get comfortable…" Eddie was explaining.

"Wasn't sure if she needed to have some treatment for it, that's why I'm bringing it up," the doctor said looking for some indication from the family.

"No Doctor, this was an extenuating circumstance, that's all," Eddie answered.

"The pregnancy was very difficult on me daughter," Bridget added before Eddie was finished speaking. "Right from the beginning, she swelled up. Had difficulty walking … getting around… doing ordinary chores."

"She couldn't catch her breath," Kathleen said. Margaret stood shaking her head.

"I'm not surprised," the doctor agreed. "carrying twins."

"Twins?" they all questioned.

"Yes, twins. Didn't you know?" he asked.

"No, Doctor, we didn't," Eddie answered.

"We were not able to save the first one because

of the trauma of the accident. The cord was around the first girl's neck."

"Another girl," Bridget said sadly.

"I am sorry for your loss," the doctor said putting his hand on Eddie's shoulder. "One of our nurses baptized her." Tears filled the family's eyes. "The hospital can make all of the necessary arrangements for disposing of the body. Eventually, this will be a day of celebration. You shouldn't be putting flowers on the grave of one child while your other child is blowing out candles on her birthday cake."

"Whatever you think, Doctor," Eddie answered for the family. "I'm sure you know what is best."

"Does me daughter know?" Bridget asked.

"No, she's been out of it for some time," he answered. "Has a name been picked out for the baby?"

"No, Elizabeth hasn't decided on one yet," Eddie answered.

"Your wife can name her when she's up to it." Looking uncomfortable, the doctor took a deep breath before he continued.

What worse could he tell us? Bridget thought.

"I need for all of you to understand that the next few days are going to be difficult for the baby. Right now, she is lethargic from the alcohol Elizabeth consumed during her pregnancy. I expect in four to six hours the baby will start going through withdrawal. The amount and duration of Elizabeth's drinking will determine the length and severity of the baby's withdrawal." No further excuses were offered by the family. Only the sounds of the ticking of the wall clock broke the silence in the room. "Do you have any questions?" the doctor continued.

"Could you please have her baptized too?" Bridget replied.

"She already has been," the doctor answered.

"Doctor, is there anything you need for the baby?" Uncle Jimmy asked.

"If there is, we will let you know," the doctor answered.

"Can I see my wife? Eddie nervously asked.

"For only a few minutes tonight," the doctor replied. "She's quiet and sleeping it off now. You can visit her tomorrow."

"Can we see the baby?" Eddie asked.

"They were starting an IV in her when I left. As soon as the nurses have her ready they will come down and bring you up to the nursery," the doctor answered.

"Doctor," Margaret found the courage to ask, "Could the baby die?"

"She's only four-pounds two-ounces," he awkwardly answered. "It's going to be a hard fight for her. There is always the possibility that we might lose her too. For now, let's take it one step at a time."

~ Chapter Twenty Nine ~

In a far off, darkened corner of the hospital's nursery, the unnamed baby girl Sullivan lay in a crib.

"She's comfortable for the time being," said the nurse. "Keep your voices low. We want to keep the stimuli around her to a minimum." Each family member tentatively followed the nurse when it was their turn to see their family's newest addition.

"Which one of you is going to stay here tonight?" she questioned them.

"I will," Bridget, Margaret and Kathleen answered simultaneously.

"I don't know how you are going to work it out. But only one person can come in to see the baby for five minutes every hour," the nurse sternly instructed them.

"Don't worry, they'll work it out," Uncle Jimmy replied.

"I'm not leaving here," Bridget announced.

"You shouldn't." Kathleen said. "I don't think any of us should. We'll take turns."

The family settled into a routine of checking on the baby.

"She's still sleeping… she's sweaty… she's fussing and crying,.. she's having trouble sucking…"

they reported their observations to each other.

Neither Bridget's prayers nor the staff's knowledgeable and caring actions could protect the infant from the frenzy her body was going through as she hungered for alcohol. Shrilling cries, apnea, convulsions ... each hour brought a new horror to the smallest member of the family fighting her mother's addiction.

Eddie worriedly paced every inch of the waiting room until without a word he left to see his wife.

"Now is not a good time," a nurse told him.

"You don't understand what I'm going through. I just want to see her for one minute," his body shaking as he talked.

Eddie watched as Elizabeth tossed and turned trying to get herself comfortable in the bed.

"Oh, thank God, it's you," she said realizing he was there. "Eddie, every inch of me hurts. Get me a little something to drink and get me out of this hellhole. There's a horrible smell in this room. Can you find it?" Elizabeth rambled. "I can't stand it. Find that God damn smell won't you!" she ordered.

"Elizabeth, I don't smell anything," Eddie answered.

"You're as bad as the nurses. They said it's in my head," Elizabeth snapped at him. "Take me home," Elizabeth said trying to get out of the bed.

"Elizabeth, you need to stay here for a couple of days to get some rest. That was a bad fall you took," Eddie said. "I need a drink, get me something," Elizabeth said anxiously rubbing her bruised arms.

"They won't let me bring anything in here," Eddie uncomfortably answered.

"Good God, Eddie, when did you start following

rules?" Elizabeth asked annoyed. "One drink to settle my nerves. Please... Please... I need something to get me over this hump. I'd do it for you. Please Eddie."

"How could I get it in?" he asked.

"There's a small flask on the top shelf of the closet. You don't know how much pain I'm in. This rotten smell is bringing me over the edge. Damn it Eddie! Get me something. I can't take it," she pleaded.

"Alright Elizabeth, I'll get you something," Eddie answered, understanding the need for one drink. He walked out of the hospital telling no one where he was going. Once home he took the flask down from the shelf. He poured the bathtub gin into it. Calming his own shaking hands, he poured himself a glass. Then Eddie Sullivan, loving husband, new father, poured himself another and another....

For twenty-four hours, the family kept watch over the infant as high fever and diarrhea robbed her of essential electrolytes, racing her tiny heart...bringing her to the brink of death. For twenty-four hours, the family kept watch over Elizabeth as she shook, sweated and infuriately cursed screaming profanities at each of them. Except for Eddie, who hadn't come back to the hospital.

"Don't worry about him," Uncle Jimmy told them. "He can take care of himself." Margaret was placing a cool compress on her sister's forehead trying to relieve her headache when Eddie walked into the room.

No sense in asking him where he was, Margaret thought. *He's here now. For how long?* "I'll go and check on the baby," Margaret tiredly told him.

"Eddie, you got to get me out of here," Elizabeth asked.

"Elizabeth, I got something to make the pain go away," he told her. "Here Elizabeth, take a little." Lovingly, Eddie helped Elizabeth take the flask to her lips. "Slow...Slow down. Don't drip it," he ordered.

"God, Eddie... it's been hell here," she said.

"Baby, you'll start to feel better," Eddie smiled.

"Do you have more?" she asked.

"Right here baby," Eddie grinned from ear to ear. "I brought you this perfume bottle and it's full to the top. Not a soul is going to notice a thing."

For three more long days and nights, the family comforted the unnamed infant as she slowly dried out, unaware that Elizabeth eased her discomfort by taking sips from her perfume bottle.

Ninety-two hours and the child had severed the cord that bound her to her mother's addiction.

"She's fine now. By next week, she'll be ready to go home from the hospital. You should all go home now and get yourselves some sleep," the doctor advised them.

Ninety-two hours and the same doctor said that Elizabeth was steady enough to see and hold her daughter for the first time... tomorrow.

"Please take me to see my baby," Elizabeth pleaded with the night nurse as soon as her eyes opened after sunrise.

"I guess it will be alright," the nurse answered. "The doctor said you could go and see her today. He didn't say what time. But it will be kind of nice for me to see you see her for the first time. You know, I was working the night she was born and I would have been the one bringing her for you to see. Give me a few minutes to finish my work. You wash and I'll come back to bring you up stairs."

Elizabeth changed from the hospital gown into a new one that Bridget had bought for her. The rash on her abdomen was healing. No more oozing... No more itchiness. Her body was again her own. She washed her face. *To see my daughter. Hold my daughter.* She brushed her teeth. *My daughter.* Elizabeth opened the perfume bottle to get herself ready for the important meeting.

The nurse held Elizabeth's arm and led her to the nursery upstairs. Slowly they walked down the long hallway. They watched as the elevator stopped at every floor before it stopped on theirs. Elizabeth's heart raced as she walked down the nursery hallway towards the glass door that stood between them and her daughter.

"God has blessed you with one daughter," Bridget had motherly told her the day the doctor gave her the horrific news about her other baby. "Don't think about that one," her mother advised. She didn't... Now much of her pregnancy was a blur.

"There she is over in the corner," the nurse pointed in the direction as she spoke. Elizabeth read the pink sign on the crib as they took the finale steps towards her daughter. Girl Sullivan, weight 4 lbs. 2 oz, born October 7, 8:45 p.m.

"She's beautiful," Elizabeth said.

"Yes, she is," the nurse agreed. "You can touch her hand." Hesitantly, Elizabeth stroked the tiny arm without the IV in it.

"She's so little," she said. "I was so fat that I thought she'd be bigger."

"That's because you were carrying twins," the nurse caught herself before going on to much further. "I'm sorry."

"That's alright. Were you there when I delivered?" Elizabeth asked.

"I was the nurse who baptized both your daughters," the nurse answered.

"Thank you for doing that. It meant a lot to my mother. Did you give them names?" Elizabeth asked.

"I named your first daughter, Mildred, after my mother who just died. I asked her to watch over your daughter in heaven," the nurse had difficulty answering.

"That was nice of you. Did you name this one?" Elizabeth asked.

"No, I knew you would want to," she answered.

"Yes, I do," Elizabeth said touching the baby's cheek. "She's so delicate. Such a small head and look at her turned up nose… Doesn't seem to have any jaw at all… What a full head of hair you have." She turned to look at the nurse. "Last year Mabel Norman's beauty was taken away from the world when she died. I think it just came back. I'm going to name her Mabel."

"You can hold Mabel in your arms, if you like." the nurse said. Elizabeth sat down. Gently, the nurse put Mabel in her mother's waiting arms. Elizabeth rubbed her fingers on her daughter's tiny hand. Mabel startled, her body jerked and she grasped on to Elizabeth finger.

"How does she know to hold on so tightly?" Elizabeth asked.

"Because you're her mother," the nurse answered.

Mother... Elizabeth heard said for the first time.

"What did my other daughter look like?' she asked.

"She was a mirror image of this one," she answered putting her hand on Elizabeth's shoulder.

God would never have let there be that much beauty in the world, Elizabeth's eyes swelled up, as she tasted a bitter fact of life.

"Let me leave the two of you alone to get acquainted," the nurse said.

Elizabeth stroked softly Mabel's silky hair. She counted her fingers and toes. She smelled the newness of the baby's skin. Tenderly, she kissed Mabel's forehead. The baby's small blue eyes opened.

"Mabel," she whispered. "I don't know how to be a mother. But I promise you that I'll give you my best."

~ *Chapter Thirty* ~

In the weeks, months and eventually years that followed Bridget desperately tried to keep her family close. The clan continued interlocking together odd shaped cardboard pieces atop her dinning room table after their ritual bimonthly Sunday dinners. However, each daughter was eagerly ready to go back to her own life when the puzzle was completed.

"I got the promotion! They told me Friday," Kathleen announced while she and her mother were serving the vegetables.

"Congratulations. Let's make a toast to Kathleen," Uncle Jimmy was the first to respond.

"You'd think they're making you president of the company," Elizabeth sarcastically said, chewing on her chicken.

"It is a big deal," Margaret retorted. "1933's still hard times. She has every right to be proud of getting the promotion."

"Not too hard a time. Finally an end to Prohibition," Uncle Jimmy joyously proclaimed.

"Monday, I'll have my own office next to Mr. Reynold's. Come one day for lunch and see it," Kathleen invited her.

"Once you're settled in, I will," Margaret answered.

"See, she didn't invite me," Elizabeth mumbled loud enough for all at the table to hear.

"With Mabel, I thought it would be too hard for you," Kathleen responded.

"Margaret or Mom could baby sit," Elizabeth argued. "I could work something out but you'd never think to invite me," Elizabeth was fired up and eagerly awaiting a fight. Kathleen did not respond. She never craved excitement as her older sister did. Now that Elizabeth was married and had Mabel to raise the only excitement she could find was in the arguments she had with everyone.

"You don't understand how difficult a baby Mabel is," Bridget would tell her.

"Ma, I'm sure Elizabeth is a difficult mother," Kathleen answered her one day.

"Don't be saying anything bad about your sister until you've walked in her shoes. That's the end of it," Bridget demanded.

Elizabeth's temperamental outburst frightened Kathleen. She thought it best to ignore her. She also found it best to visit with her niece either here at home when they came to visit or at Margaret's when she was baby sitting. Being around the drinking and arguing at Elizabeth's was too unsettling for her.

"Kathleen! I'm talking to you," Elizabeth screamed. Mabel began crying. "Now see what you've done." Bridget went to check on the child.

"I have some more news I'd like to share with you, if I may?" Kathleen genteelly asked.

"Sure, kid, go ahead," Billy said.

"I've invited a friend for dinner next Sunday," Kathleen smiled as she spoke.

"A friend?" Margaret teased her.

"Yes, mother said it would be alright. His name is Tom. Tom Walsh,"

"Where did you meet him?" Uncle Jimmy asked.

"He works on the seventeenth floor of my building," she proudly answered.

"You met him on the seventeenth floor then?" Billy asked.

"No, don't be silly, I met him in the elevator," Kathleen quickly answered.

"Oh, that's a better place to meet someone," Eddie laughed.

"Do you know anything about him?" Elizabeth questioned.

"I met him on the elevator when I was riding up with Evelyn. He's her cousin. We've been sharing the same elevator now for a few weeks," Kathleen answered. "I'd like everyone to meet him. He wants to take me to a movie so I thought we could go after supper next week."

"That's a relationship starting off with a lot of ups and downs," Eddie joked.

"I don't know why you'd want him to meet us," Elizabeth answered as she hit Eddie's arm.

"Must be someone important," Margaret said raising her eyebrows. "We'd love to meet him. I promise these two will behave when he's here. We won't let them scare him off."

Kathleen had worked her way up in the telephone company. Not needing the excitement that Elizabeth craved, she easily settled into a routine, balanced life between work, family and church. She grew closer to her mother and her Uncle Jimmy. The real passion in her life was the secretaries' theater club.

Once a month, the small group would go to a play. Kathleen read every review and comment before seeing each play. She read articles written about the directors and actors. She savored reading every page of the *Playbill*. That was until she met Tom Walsh. Before him, she never brought another man home. Before him, she had not even mentioned one name.

Tom Walsh's easily overlooked lanky appearance went unnoticed by Kathleen as he watched her for over two weeks. He first caught a glimpse of her running towards the closing elevator doors. The door shut before she entered.

Nevertheless, that did not stop his heart from racing as the vision of her beautiful face and bouncing hair flashed through his mind. He practiced the words he'd say when he had the chance to meet her. Each day he arrived early to work, waiting in the lobby for her to enter. He walked slightly behind her and stood next to her until the elevator door opens. Each day was the same. His heart pounding as the elevator rose. Moving closer to her, every chance he had to smell her perfume as the elevator filled with occupants. Then politely he moved aside as the elevator emptied.

"Seventeen," the operator announced.

"Excuse me," Tom said. Kathleen, without looking up, without an answer, simply stepped aside.

"What is going on?" the elevator operator abruptly asked Tom one day as he was standing under the mural in the lobby.

"What do you mean?" Tom answered.

"Don't think I haven't been keeping an eye on

you? What are you doing with that young woman?" the operator uncomfortably continued his interrogation.

"She's the girl I'm going to marry," Tom informed him.

"I didn't realize," the operator apologized. "Couldn't tell you even knew each other," he smiled and relaxed as he spoke. "Doing a good job of keeping it private."

"Oh, she doesn't know it yet," Tom answered. "I haven't found the right way to meet her."

"Well, young man," the operator curtly continued. "You'd better do it fast. I don't want you hanging around. If I see you again in my elevator with her, I'm going to report this."

Kathleen entered the lobby. Beads of sweat rolled down Tom's forehead as he brought forth the courage to approach her.

"Kathleen!" a female voiced called. Kathleen turned. Tom watched another attractive young woman walking towards her.

"Evelyn," he shouted. But the word was only in his head. His feet frozen he watched as they entered the elevator.

"Evelyn," his shouted. His loud voice echoed throughout the caverns of the lobby startling not only the passersby and the two young women but stopping the operator from closing the doors.

"Evelyn," he spoke more calmly entering it. "What are you doing here?"

"Hi Tom," Evelyn answered. "I've been working here for about six months. Thought you knew?" Tom smilingly looked at Kathleen.

"Kathleen, this is my cousin Tom Walsh," she

introduced them. "Tom, this is my friend Kathleen Kelly."

"Pleasure to meet you, Kathleen," Tom told her. He nervously blathered on during the entire ride up in the elevator. "Maybe, I'll run into you again tomorrow," he said passing the operator as he exited onto the seventeenth floor.

"Perhaps," Kathleen answered.

From their first meeting the Kelly women approved of Tom Walsh's quiet manner, seeing him as the perfect match for Kathleen. Over the eight months that Kathleen and Tom dated, the men in the family grew to accept his mild-mannered ways.

"Well, look at what the winds blew in." Uncle Jimmy said greeting Tom at Donahue's.

"It's a pleasure to see you."

"I was in the area, sir and I thought I'd take you up on your invitation," Tom said tensely.

"I'm glad you did. You've been seeing my niece for some time now," Uncle Jimmy commented. "It's time we get to know one another a little better." Uncle Jimmy motioned to the bartender. "And I know of no way to know a man's true character than to share a drink or two."

Nervously, Tom gulped down his whisky. They talked of the unseasonably cool October weather. They talked of the repeal of the Volstead Act. Abruptly Tom left. For four weeks, Tom went to Donahue's and drank with Uncle Jimmy and each time he timidly talked about nothing of any consequence and would abruptly leave.

"Tom, seems to me," Uncle Jimmy kindly said, wanting to put an end to Tom's misery. "There seems to be something on your mind." Tom picked up his glass and took another gulp.

"Mr. Donahue," he blurted out, "The truth is, I want to ask your permission, as the head of the family, for Kathleen's hand in marriage." Tom took another quick swig of his whiskey.

"What does Kathleen think about all this?" Uncle Jimmy asked.

"I haven't mentioned it to her yet," Tom answered.

"You haven't?" Uncle Jimmy questioned. A flood of patriarchal questions washed over him. Tom stood beside him, beads of sweat developing on his forehead, his hands shaking.

"Tom," fatherly he said. "Son, you have my permission to marry my niece."

Tom planned every detail for the occasion. Tickets to the opening of *Roberta*, which rumor had it, was going to be the best musical to ever hit Broadway. But first, dinner by candlelight at the swankiest restaurant in the theater district.

"A magnum of champagne," Tom ordered.

"Tom, what are you doing?" Kathleen asked.

"I thought we'd celebrate tonight," he answered.

"You never ordered anything to drink before?" she questioned.

"With going to the gala opening I thought we'd make a special night of it," he nervously answered.

"I see no reason to drink to make the night special," she responded.

"Come on, Kathleen what's the harm in having a little bubbly," he joked. Kathleen toasted the evening with her glass of water. Tom drank the entire contents of the bottle alone.

Men in tuxedoes accompanied women in

designer gowns into the lavishly decorated grand theater. The scent of expensive French perfume and men's cologne filled the room. The audience laughed. They tapped their feet to the music. Then as the musicians played *Smoke Gets in Your Eyes* a cloud of white mist came up from the stage floor. It reached out to Kathleen and Tom sitting in the sixth row. Wide eyed, Kathleen watched the stage as at the top of a staircase the gorgeous actress appeared. Gracefully, she descended the steps through the haze.

"This is the most romantic scene I have ever seen," Kathleen said. Her eyes glistening as she leaned over to Tom. His heart raced. His head cloudy.

Tom hailed a hansom cab when they exited the theater. Everything was going as he planned. Kathleen hummed the music scores. The sounds of the horse's hooves clopping on the cobblestones, keeping the beat as the couple gently swayed from side to side as the carriage made its way towards Central Park. The crisp night air was having little effect on clearing Tom's head. He struggled trying to remember the words he had prepared. The driver's sharp left into the park slid Tom across the seat into Kathleen. Clumsily, he tried to rearrange the blanket across her lap and putting it up over her chest. The stench from the old horse blanket mingled with the alcohol on his breath filled her nostrils.

"I'll do it," she informed him, fixing it herself.

"I just want to take care of you. That's all," he slurred his answer. She shook her head. Awkwardly he began professing his love.

"Tom, stop talking of such foolishness," Kathleen ordered.

"Kathleen, I love you. I want you to marry me," he declared.

"You don't know what you're saying," she quickly responded.

"No, Kathleen, I do," Tom said, his head clearing. Reaching into his jacket pocket, he pulled out the blue velvet box. He put the box in Kathleen's hand. She looked at the unopened box.

"Kathleen, will you marry me?" Tom asked.

"No," she answered. No tears...No wavering in her voice. "Tom, I want you to take me home."

"Kathleen," Tom began, but she would not let him continue.

"Here," she handed him the unopened box. "Take me home now," she demanded.

"Kathleen," Tom tried again.

"They'll be no more foolish talking," she curtly answered. With hardly another word between them, they traveled home.

The cold autumn nights quickly turned into the fidget evenings of winter. Arm in arm couples braced themselves together against the snow as they scoured the avenue in search of holiday gifts. Nevertheless, nothing would warm Kathleen's heart. Not the weekly delivered bouquet of flowers she would not accept. Not the telephone message she would not answer, nor the letters she left unread. Tom begged each of her family members to intervene on his behalf. All willingly tried their best, but their words fell on deaf ears.

"I don't care to talk about it," was her constant reply.

"Please, Mr. Donahue," Tom again pleaded. "I

don't know why she won't talk to me."

"I don't know why either," Uncle Jimmy acknowledged. "I'm stopping by the apartment to bring some gifts for her to wrap for me. Tom, I'll try again to talk some sense into her. But I can't promise anything. Her mind is shut on the subject."

"Thank you. I know she loves me as much as I love her. She'll come around," Tom wishfully added.

"Uncle Jimmy, what color paper do you want on this one?" Kathleen asked.

"I like that red paper," he answered.

"I think that will look pretty. I'll use the gold on that box," Kathleen said, paper and ribbons all laid out on the table.

"Kathleen," Uncle Jimmy said. "We need to talk."

"Sure, what is it? Do you want to know what I want for Christmas?" she answered him.

"Tom Walsh stopped over to see me again today."

"You know I don't care to talk about that subject," she answered.

"Kathleen, he's not a subject," Uncle Jimmy told her. "He's a person. A man who loves you and this has to do with your happiness."

"I'm happy," she answered.

"He doesn't know why you're not talking to him. If you don't want to marry him fine. But you two had fun together. Why can't you talk to him?" Uncle Jimmy asked. Kathleen busied herself cutting the gold paper. "Kathleen, I need to understand! He asked my permission to marry you and I gave it, thinking he would have been a wonderful husband for you. How could I have been so wrong?" Uncle

Jimmy asked taking the ribbon from her hand. "I need to know." Kathleen's body stiffened. She looked into her uncle's eyes.

"He drinks," she said.

"He drinks?" Uncle Jimmy questioned what he was hearing.

"He ordered champagne and he was drunk," Kathleen answered.

"Hadn't he ever drank before when you dated?" Uncle Jimmy asked.

"No, if he had I would have stopped dating him as I have done now," Kathleen coolly answered.

"Kathleen, I have known this young man for a year. He's a good man. I have never seen him drunk," Uncle Jimmy spoke honestly. "He was nervous. It's hard for a man to get up the courage to ask the woman he loves to marry him."

"He drank. If it was because he was nervous, there will always be occasions to be nervous," Kathleen reported.

"Won't you give him another chance?" Uncle Jimmy asked as he promised.

"No. I've seen what drink did to my father," tears filled her eyes as she spoke. "I have to watch what it is doing to Elizabeth. I don't want to willingly love another person and watch drink take them away."

"My poor child," Uncle Jimmy said lovingly.

"If you care for me, you'll let this be the end of the subject," Kathleen said.

"No one chooses who they love," Uncle Jimmy's eyes filled as he spoke. "When and if you are lucky enough to have love find you, run towards it. Take it full on into your life. Otherwise, you spend the rest of your empty life yearning for what might have been."

"Uncle Jimmy, why didn't you marry?" Kathleen asked. He stood motionless.

"Kathleen, that is a fair question given the circumstance of our conversation," he uneasily answered. "You have been honest with me and it is only reasonable that I be the same. Now you must concentrate on your decision for your life." Kathleen was sure there were tears in his eyes.

"Why didn't you marry?" She couldn't keep herself from pressing him further.

"I'll pick you up on Saturday morning," he answered. His voice trembled as he added, "then I'll tell you about...Rose." Uncle Jimmy left without another word.

Who was Rose? Kathleen thought to herself watching him from the window as he walked alone into the darkness without his usual lively step. His silhouette was old and frail tonight. *What could she have done to you?*

~ Chapter Thirty One ~

"*Uncle Jimmy, where are we going?*" Kathleen asked.

"We'll be there in a few minutes," he finally answered. For most of the car ride Uncle Jimmy appeared preoccupied by his bad stomach. Kathleen sat quietly looking out the car window. She knew he was worried about telling her about Rose but she let her uncle believe all the indigestion he was feeling was just because he didn't have his usual bacon and eggs breakfast this morning.

Rose... who? She searched her mind for any memory of having heard that name before. *Sounds familiar... can't quite put my finger on it.* Throughout the week, it was easier to keep any thought of Tom from creeping into her mind as she concentrated on Rose.

"Be patient. I'll tell you all about Rose when we get there," he said.

Why hadn't he mentioned her before? Rose ...does my mother or either of my sisters know about her? "I will," she answered watching the streets filling with Saturday shoppers.

"We're here," he announced parking his car. "Here is the only place to properly tell you the full story of Rose O'Toole." Kathleen buttoned the top button of her coat as she and her uncle made their way to the entrance of the Brooklyn Bridge. He had left his top coat in the car saying he felt the heaviness of it was making it hard for him to breathe.

"It is so pretty here," she commented.

"Yes, it always was," he wistfully agreed. "I came to this great land some fifty three years ago. A young lad of nineteen. All full of vim and vinegar, I was." Standing straight and tall as though he had no need for his cane he told of his youth. "I had a grand time, I did. My good Uncle James, for whom I was named, God bless his soul, had for me a job working right here on this bridge. Oh, how proud I was to be building her." They slowly walked along the Bridge's promenade as he spoke. "The labor was hard but, oh, so sweet. Many were the hours I labored in the sun on these very wires," Uncle Jimmy pointing out the locations with his cane as he spoke. He walked slowly to keep from loosing his breath.

"In this grand country everything was possible. I worked as giant machines rolled the steel across the sky like spools of thread. I climbed high on these strains and tied them off. Sitting up there brought me closer to heaven, than I ever thought possible."

"It sounds wonderful," Kathleen said.

"Oh, it was," Uncle Jimmy continued. "I could see the city across the way. I watched the ships sailing beneath me. While I ate my noon meal, I heard stories from sailors of far away places. It was a grand time in my youth." The two stopped for a few minutes under the great gothic arch before they continued towards Manhattan. He leaned back on the stones and rubbed his arm as he spoke.

"My Uncle James and his wife Emily lived in

the apartment your mother and you girls came to. Well they had a son. Sean was his name. We were close in age but closer still in spirit. We had great times together, we did," Uncle Jimmy laughed and shook his head as he reminisced. "Aunt Emily was godmother to her cousin's daughter. It was in your very parlor that I met the love of my life. All pretty and fancy in her Sunday dress. She smiled at me and I felt her capture my heart," his face revealing she still had it.

"Whilst I worked on the bridge, Rose and I courted. She worked at an apothecary. She liked her job well enough but her real loves were painting and baking. Being the friendly young man that I was then, I had dreams of opening a fine restaurant. Rose would make all of our desserts. Kathleen, you never tasted such sweets as she created." Kathleen laughed as he kissed the air.

"Sean was a security officer on the bridge. He loved his job. And to tell you the truth, it was the first job that he did well," he voiced in a serious tone. "At night, when the day's work was done, no one was permitted back onto the bridge. He allowed me to sneak Rose onto it. She was quite a girl. Wasn't the least bit afraid of our carrying ons. She had such a high opinion of me. It was as if, I only had to say it and she knew it to be true. Well, that was my dream."

"It was a good dream," Kathleen said prodding for more information. The color left her uncle's face and stood silent for a while.

"I was far from reaching it. I had saved a little money. The bridge was near completion," he continued. "I had a good reputation as a worker. So, I was approached by a company to work in new buildings installing elevators. This was a golden opportunity for any young man. They promised me a good wage.

I figured it all out on paper. I would be able to save a little more money each paycheck with this new job. I took some of the money I had saved for my restaurant to buy Rose a ring. Sean went with me saying, 'I wouldn't have the sense to pick out a good one.' I told him, 'I knew how to pick out Rose, didn't I?'"

Kathleen listened as he described the intricacies of the heart-shaped platinum setting surrounding the perfect diamond stone. *I never opened the box. What had Tom picked out for me? How could Rose have said no to him?*

"I planned on telling her the good news about my new job and asking her to marry all at the same time. I wanted to ask her here on our bridge. There was a big formal opening to the public planned for May 24th 1883, with fireworks and all sorts of dignitaries in attendance. I thought that would be too uppity a time. The following week on May 31, I was sure the apothecary would be closed. That would be the date of our engagement.

I took Rose for a light lunch. She was prettier than ever. She wore this pink dress with ribbons and flowers and didn't she have a pink parasol to match." A sense of foreboding came over Kathleen when his voice cracked. Beads of sweet covered his forehead. "Everything about her was always perfect," he managed to say. Kathleen stroked his arm comforting him.

"Sean was working security on the bridge that

day," he continued sounding old and tired. "He was waiting at the approach of the promenade when we got there around three o'clock. He laughed and told us 'we need not pay the penny. It was his treat.' " They stopped only yards away from the Manhattan exit, while Uncle Jimmy continued talking.

"There was a rather wealthy older man and his wife with their young son walking on the bridge before us. I took this opportunity to tell Rose how happy he looked. 'How could he be so happy? Wasn't I the luckiest man on the bridge to be with the most beautiful woman in all of Brooklyn?' Rose laughed and replied that his wife was pretty enough.

'But herself looks the happiest,' she told me.

'And why would that be? For sure I'm a much more handsome man than himself,' I answered. Rose laughed. What a wonderful laugh, music for my soul.

'Ah, but look at her son,' Rose teased me. 'Now there is a child, fair of face. Kissed by the angels, he was,' Rose said. Who to know more about the angels than herself?

'A son,' I said, pretending to be in a somber mood. 'You have me there. I'll have to evaluate my life.' We walked along in silence for awhile. I pretending to be thinking seriously.

'I've evaluated my life and in the checking my balance sheet I see I am lacking,' I announced sadly.

'You're lacking in nothing,' Rose quickly came to my defense. The poor girl thought I was serious about it.

'I'm lacking a wife and family, I am,' I said.

'Well, that's true enough. But, that will come in time,' Rose assured me. 'James Donahue, I will not have you saying you're a man lacking anything. I will not stand for such talk.'

'So, are you than asking for my hand in marriage?' I asked her.

'James, I was saying no such thing,' she told me getting all huffy.

'Well then, I'll have to be doing the asking, I can see that.' I went down on one knee, unaware of the crowd around us. 'Rose, the sweetest flower in all of Brooklyn, in all of New York, and I dare say in all of America. Its the greatest of love and affection I have for you. You'll want for nothing. I'll love and protect you for all of your days if you only consent to be my wife.'

Kathleen, I can remember that moment as if it was yesterday. I reached into my pocket and pulled out the ring. As Rose said, 'yes', I placed the ring on her finger. It was the happiest time in my life. Everyone around us cheered. We stood there for a little while talking more about our plans.

The fancy couple that started our talk was in the distance. Their son was only a few feet away from us. It was around 3:30 p.m. and Rose was beginning to become uncomfortable with the huge number of people on the bridge. We were closest towards New York so we began to make our way towards it. We were over there," Uncle Jimmy's voice a little above a whisper as he pointed to the exact locations.

"The child was across from us. The fancy couple still some distance behind us. It was 4 p.m. and according to the newspaper accounts there were some 20,000 pedestrians on the bridge. The narrow stairs leading on and off the bridge was packed. Someone screamed, 'The bridge is falling!' and the crowd panicked. The horde jammed together all pushing as they tried to get off before it fell. Rose ran across to the other side to grab the child. She placed herself over him. I held steady to the side of the bridge protecting both their bodies under mine.

Pieces of clothing and personal items began flying all around us. It seemed a lifetime before the mob stopped pushing and the panic stopped. I felt the pain as my leg broke under the weight of the riot. But I held steady my post to protect the love of my life. I felt the warmth on my leg from what I thought was my broken leg. When it was safe, I stood. Rose did not. As I gently lifted her body, I saw it was her blood on my leg. Her parasol had pierced her chest.

'You can rest assured her death was instantaneous. She felt no pain,' a doctor later told me in the hospital. The young boy under her was covered with her blood but he was unharmed.

I lifted her into my arms and as I did my broken femur and patella broke through my skin. All I remembered next was waking up in a hospital bed. At first, I had hoped it was only a bad dream. A deep depression came over me. There was no reason for me to live. I had promised to protect her for all her life and here within minutes of this promise I had not. I cursed that bridge."

"I am so sorry. I didn't know," Kathleen consoled him.

"I didn't tell my family. How does one write down such horror?" he questioned. Kathleen listened with tears streaming down her face as he continued. His tears mixed with the sweat beading up around his lips.

"One day that fancy man from the bridge came to visit me in the hospital. I almost didn't recognize him. Even without his saying, I knew he hadn't slept since that horrible day. He thought he had everything. It had never occurred to him before just how quickly one could lose it all. What could he say to me? How great was my loss. He had seen how happy we were. He had also seen Rose, at a great price for her and for me, running into harm's way to save his only son. A price he could never repay. The man humbly stood by my bed weeping. He offered me everything he had. Offering me all he had and adding that would still not be enough to repay me.

He knew the value of my loss and that act helped heal me. We talked for some time. I wanted nothing from him. It was Rose's gift to him.

'I need to give you something,' he said. 'I have come here other days and couldn't find the courage to walk into your room. Once I talked to a young man who is your cousin. He told me of the great dream you and Rose had to open a fine restaurant. I beg you. Please find it in your heart to allow me to make that dream come true,' he pleaded. 'I am sure your beloved Rose would want that for you.' That is how I came to open Donahue's." His breathing began to labor again but he continued.

"To me the panicking on the bridge lasted a lifetime. It lasted our lifetime together. It made the happiest day of my life turn into the saddest. She has been in my thoughts everyday since," he looked lovingly at Kathleen. "I don't want you to have such a life."

"You don't have to worry about me," she answered. "I did care for Tom, but I couldn't really love a man who drinks."

"So long as you know what you are doing,"

Uncle Jimmy said.

"I do," she confidently replied. They turned around to walk back over the bridge.

"I've never talked about that day to anyone," Uncle Jimmy confided in her.

"Didn't you talk with your cousin Sean?" she asked.

"No," he answered and they walked in silence for a while. "Sean had left me a letter in the hospital telling me how sorry he was. He was too hard on himself. Thought it all was his fault. He should have controlled the crowd better. I was happy to shift some of the blame onto him," Uncle Jimmy confessed. Kathleen listened. "It really wasn't his fault or mine. I never told Sean that it wasn't his fault. I really should have done that."

"Don't you think he already knows that?" Kathleen asked.

"I don't know if he does or not. Either way, I should have told him," Uncle Jimmy stood and looked at Kathleen. "I'm glad we talked. I'm going to call him to night and tell him."

Kathleen put her arms around him and kissed his cheek.

"You feel all wet. Are you alright?" Kathleen asked.

"It's just my stomach," Uncle Jimmy said. "Did you hear that!" he asked suddenly turning around.

"What?' Kathleen asked.

"My Rose," he whispered. A smile radiated across his face and then he clenched his chest and his lifeless body fell.

Kathleen held him close to her as she had seen her mother hold her father's body. She screamed for help. But there was no use. Rose, his Rose had come to lovingly take him home.

~ *Chapter Thirty Two* ~

"*Mabel, come back,*" Margaret called. "I've changed my mind." Mabel had stopped running and was standing frozen on the steps.

"I don't have to go home?" the four-year old asked.

"No," Margaret said looking into the frail face of her niece. "We'll go back to my apartment. Your mother can pick you up later."

"Yea, I can go back home with you," Mabel yelled. "Daddy's home now."

"Yes, he is. But I'm not ready to give you back just yet," Margaret squeezed the child in her arms, noisily kissing her trying to drown out the sounds of the arguing coming from her older sister's apartment.

"What should we do when we get home?" Margaret asked.

"Let's make a treat for Uncle Billy. He's going to be surprised when he sees me," Mabel answered.

"Surprised? He is going to be delighted," Margaret announced.

"Yes, he will be. He loves me the best in the whole world, doesn't he, Aunt Margaret?" Mabel asked.

Such a good man, my Billy, Margaret thought. *'Margaret can you watch Mabel for a few hours?*

Eddie and I want to go out for the evening.' Three days ago and not a word from either of them... I expected so much more from my sister. But Billy, I couldn't have hoped for any better a man than him. Never a word of complaint... even after all these years those two leaving Mabel with us for days at a time. Not a penny left for her care... Plenty enough money for them to use on drink. Expect when Elizabeth's ready she'll come pick Mabel up.

"Yes, he loves you to the moon," Margaret answered.

"And back," Mabel added.

"And back," Margaret agreed.

"Is Uncle Jimmy on the moon," the inquisitive niece asked.

"No, he's in heaven," Margaret answered.

"Is the moon in heaven," the child quickly questioned.

"Yes, the moon is in heaven. So are the stars and the sun. So no telling where Uncle Jimmy is at up there," Margaret laughed. "Let's go to the butcher's and see what looks good." *Billy has so much love in him. He's going to be a wonderful father when our baby's born.* "I feel so bad for Mabel," Margaret confided resting her head on Billy's shoulder.

"I do too," he agreed. "She's a hell of a kid."

"You should have heard them fighting. I didn't hear it at first, until I saw Mabel stop," Margaret told him.

"She doesn't deserve a life like that," Billy said stroking her hair.

"I don't know what to do for her," Margaret whispered.

"Margaret, why don't we let her live with us?" Billy asked.

"Here?" she questioned.

"Before you had the miscarriage your mother was talking to me about Mabel. It was her idea. She wanted to know how I felt about it before she approached you with the idea. Then you lost the baby, so I thought we should wait awhile before we mentioned it to you. Now that you're pregnant I had wanted to wait until our baby had arrived but now that you've brought Mabel up, how about it?"

"There would be enough room for her and the baby in the little room," Margaret said. "Are you sure?" she asked.

"Margaret, I've given this a lot of thought. I love the kid. We have to do something," he answered. Stretching up, Margaret kissed him.

"I'll talk with my sister when she comes to pick Mabel up," she answered.

"Go in the other room for awhile. I want to talk with your mother," Margaret told Mabel after Elizabeth sauntered in the following afternoon.

"You can't just waltz in here and act as if everything is fine and pick Mabel up as if she were dry cleaning," Margaret irately said.

"What's got your knickers in a knot?" Elizabeth asked. "Did she act up?"

"She's always good. That's not the problem. Elizabeth, sit down. We need to talk," Margaret advised her. "You can't keep dropping her off and then taking off. That's no way to raise a kid."

"Jesus, just because you're pregnant doesn't make you an expert on raising children," Elizabeth retorted.

"This isn't going the way I planned. Let's have a cup of tea and talk over what's best for Mabel," Margaret suggested.

"What's best for Mabel?" Elizabeth yelled. "I'll say what's best for Mabel and me alone!"

"Elizabeth, the way you and Eddie are living is no way to raise a child. We thought it might be a good idea for you to leave her with us," Margaret said.

"You thought! Who the hell are you?" Elizabeth questioned.

"Me and the rest of your family! That's who the hell we are," Margaret snapped back.

"What gives all of you the god damn right to be talking about me behind my back?" Elizabeth angrily accused.

"I'm talking to you now. It would be best for Mabel to stay here with us. You can visit whenever you want," Margaret firmly answered.

"Visit her!... Best for the child!... Damn you, Margaret. No one knows the grief of losing a child. I've lost one. I'll not give up the other!" Elizabeth screamed. "Mabel Sullivan get back in here! Margaret, you're all so worried about her. Tell Mama don't count on us ever coming back to dinner. I don't need any of you. I never did."

Mabel ran into the apartment. "Aunt Margaret... Aunt Margaret!" she cried pulling away as her mother dragged her out the front door.

~ Chapter Thirty Three ~

"Aunt Kathleen," Mabel squealed opening the door.

"Look how big you are," Kathleen delightfully answered bending down to kiss her.

"I'm five now," Mabel proudly announced.

"And so you are. Not too big to give your aunt a big hug now, are you?" she asked.

"Look what the cat dragged in," Elizabeth said harshly.

"Why don't you go and play?" Kathleen hesitantly asked. "I need to talk with your mother."

"She can stay right here," Elizabeth informed the two of them. "I thought it was clear that we don't want anything to do with any of you."

"I need to talk to you in private. I have some bad news," Kathleen timidly said.

"I heard about Margaret's miscarriage some time ago," Elizabeth curtly answered.

"It's not that," Kathleen answered.

"Is it Mama?" Elizabeth's voice softened now as she asked. Kathleen did not answer.

"Mabel, go and play...Is it Mama?" she again asked.

"No it's Margaret?" Kathleen's eyes filled as she spoke.

"Was there an accident? Is she dead?" Elizabeth clutched her chest as she dared ask the question.

"No, it's worse," Kathleen replied.

"Worse?" Elizabeth questioned. "What could be worse than dead?"

"She's dying." Kathleen tearfully answered.

"How could a thirty-five year old woman be dying?" Elizabeth sat down and asked.

"She has cancer," Kathleen answered. "The doctor said she should settle up her affairs. He sent her home from the hospital. He says she only has a few weeks. She wants to see you. That's why I'm here."

"Of course," Elizabeth answered. "I'll go over tonight when Eddie gets home. Will Mama be there?"

"We'll all be there. She can't be left alone. We have planned out a routine for taking turns caring for her," Kathleen answered.

"I want to help," Elizabeth said.

"We knew you would," Kathleen answered while hugging her.

For five weeks, the stench of cancer grew stronger, permeating every inch of the house. The Kelly women dutifully washed away the foul smelling feces that oozed from Margaret's anus. They sponged off the sweat that drenched her body during the periods of delirium. They gave the medications to ease the pain. Diligently they fought in vain. Margaret's skeleton definable. Death... was evident. Dying... was only a formality.

Billy escaped by working. Eddie helped by keeping an eye on Mabel, who now suffered with horrendous nightmares. Lovingly, Elizabeth tried shouldering her share of the care.

Just one drink a day, that's all I need while I'm there, she told herself sneaking the drink. *Just enough to settle my nerves.*

"I know," Bridget said. "I can smell it too. Now is not the time to say anything. Best we don't leave Elizabeth alone to care for her." Kathleen agreed.

"Mom, why don't you and Kathleen go home early tonight? I'll be here to help Elizabeth," Billy suggested.

"It was a rough day, Mama," Kathleen agreed. "Are you sure you are up to it?" Kathleen asked.

"I am," Billy confidently answered.

"Go ahead. We'll be fine," Elizabeth added. "I just gave her medications. She'll be sleeping for awhile."

"I'll be back early in the morning," Kathleen said kissing Margaret goodbye.

Elizabeth flopped down on the couch. Kicking her shoes off, she put her feet up on the coffee table. Billy sat down across from her in the club chair.

"I won't bite. I promise," she said. "Come sit over here and get comfortable," she said patting the couch cushion.

"Your mother looks tired," Billy said sitting down next to her.

"It has been hard for her," Elizabeth acknowledged. "You look tired yourself. How are you holding up?"

"I have good days and bad. Like everyone else," he answered stretching his neck.

"Let me rub that for you," she said getting up

from the couch. "Here does that feel, better?" she asked while kneading his tense muscle.

"That feels great," he answered relaxing a little. "I better go and check on Margaret."

"Stay," Elizabeth responded. "I'll go. I'm up." Billy walked into the kitchen while Elizabeth went to check on his wife.

"Do you want anything?" he called out to her.

"Now that the teetotalers are gone, I could go for a drink. Do you have anything?" she asked walking into the kitchen.

"I have just the stuff," Billy answered taking a bottle from the top shelf of the cabinet. "Get comfortable. I'll bring it in to you."

"To...," he started saying, having given Elizabeth her drink.

"To us," Elizabeth toasted, clinking her glass to his.

"Elizabeth, there is no us," he answered.

"Then, to old times," she replied.

"To old times," he echoed before taking a gulp of his drink.

"Nice and smooth," Elizabeth complimented. "Why don't you bring out the bottle? It's going to be a long night." Elizabeth relaxed her body into the couch's stuffed cushions. They took turns pouring the drinks for themselves.

"Ah, this feels great," she said.

"It does, doesn't it?" Billy agreed. "I don't remember the last time my body felt this good," Billy answered.

"As I remember it, your body always felt good," Elizabeth joked. "We always had a good time together didn't we?"

"We sure did," Billy agreed. "Do you want another?"

"Why not," Elizabeth answered.

"Remember the time we…" Billy began as the alcohol began stirring up the old buried memories and loosening his tongue.

"I can't believe I ever did that," Elizabeth embarrassingly said.

"Well you did," Billy laughed.

"It's good to hear you laugh," Elizabeth said.

"I can't remember the last time I did," he answered.

"Things have been tough for the two of us. Me and Eddie aren't getting along. I should have married you," Elizabeth confided.

"Don't say that,' Billy answered.

"Billy, I have always loved you. Tell me that you stopped loving me?" Elizabeth asked. Billy stayed motionless. "I knew you did."

"I…I don't. I love my wife," Billy answered.

"Then kiss me and prove it to me," Elizabeth said throwing her arms around him. Her mouth seductively touching his. Longingly, he held her in his embrace. Their tongues meeting… their bodies pulsated. They escaped the reality of their lives, as Billy thrust himself inside her warm moist body.

Quietly, Kathleen opened the apartment door the next morning as promised.

"Oh, my God!" she screamed seeing Billy and Elizabeth's naked bodies lying together on the couch. "What the hell…"

"Calm down, stop yelling. Margaret's sleeping," Billy ordered jumping up and beginning to get his pants on.

"It just happened," Elizabeth said buttoning her blouse. Kathleen walked into the bedroom. Margaret was lying on her side facing the dresser. Kathleen leaned down to kiss her.

The pillow under Margaret's head was wet. Her sunken face was cold and mottled. Kathleen searched for some sign of life. No breath... no pulse.... Standing up, Kathleen saw the reflection of Elizabeth and Billy standing by the living room couch in the dresser's mirror.

~ Chapter Thirty Four ~

Provokingly, Kathleen threw Elizabeth's freshly made sandwich in the garbage. Elizabeth wisely chose not to respond. Kathleen continued storming around the apartment cleaning off everything in sight. Not one word would Kathleen say to her. Not one word had she said to her sister since that morning. The wake…the funeral… it was now all over. The family and the friends were all gone. Only the sounds from the rocking chair filled the apartment. Bridget silently cried, tears rolling down her cheeks as she clutched a picture of Margaret close to her chest as she rocked back and forth.

"There's no word for me pain," she told her daughters. "When your father died I became a widow. If I had died, you girls would have become orphans. But to loose a child during one's lifetime…" Bridget began sobbing. "It's so horrible a thought that it dared not be named."

"I know, Mama," Elizabeth tenderly responded.

"Yes, child, I guess you do know," Bridget agreed taking her hand.

"Mama, you haven't eaten all day. Let me make you a cup of tea?" Elizabeth asked.

"That might be nice," Bridget answered.

Elizabeth set Bridget's old copper kettle on the stove to boil. She took down the tea canister. *One teaspoon for Mama, one for me, one for Kathleen, one for Mar... that one will have to be for the pot,* she mournfully thought putting the tea in the infuser. The tea steeped while she set the table for three.

Kathleen closed her bedroom door behind her. Taking off her black dress, she could now morn the loss of Margaret alone.

"Kathleen, come and join us," Bridget called. There was no response.

"Please, Kathleen," Bridget said taping on the bedroom door. Kathleen angrily came out of her room. She deliberately took a cup and saucer out of the cupboard refusing to use the dishes set by Elizabeth.

"Kathleen, don't do this," Bridget pleaded. "It's not her fault that Margaret died the night she stayed with her." Kathleen, trying to keep her composure poured herself a cup of tea.

"There is a special bond that unites sisters," Bridget said handing her the sugar. Kathleen fixed her eyes on the cup in her hand, refusing to respond.

"We're family. Nothing should break us apart," Bridget informed her. "Look at me when I talk to you," she ordered. Kathleen sullenly did so.

"We've had too much pain already. I want you to talk to your sister and make peace," Bridget motherly requested.

"My sister is dead. I have no other," Kathleen heatedly answered.

"Sweet Jesus, please don't say that. Kathleen, talk to her for me," Bridget begged.

Elizabeth fearfully sat motionless listening,

adding nothing in her defense.

"Mama, I'll never talk to her again as long as I have breath in my body," Kathleen defiantly proclaimed.

"Kathleen, have you no pity? I cannot take anymore pain," Bridget responded.

"Pain?" Kathleen questioned. "Mama, there is no word to name having lost a sister either. I thought Margaret would have been in my life forever," Kathleen tearfully sobbed.

I thought Margaret would have been in me life forever, Bridget painfully thought. I *thought me sister Meg would have been also.* Bridget reached over and stroked Kathleen's shoulder.

"But God has blessed you. You have a sister. You have Elizabeth," Bridget comfortingly advised her.

"God has blessed me with Elizabeth!" Kathleen jumped up from the table screaming. "God has nothing to do with Elizabeth. She's from the devil, himself."

"Don't say that," Bridget forbade her. "Margaret wouldn't want her death to separate the two of you. She would want it to bring the two of you closer."

"Mama, you don't know what Margaret would have wanted," Kathleen retaliated.

"I am...was her mother. I know what she would have wanted for us. Sit down, Kathleen," Bridget commanded, motioning to the chair. "You're going to stay here until you make peace with Elizabeth."

"Mama, don't make me do this," Kathleen pleaded.

"I'm sorry," Elizabeth said. "I'm really sorry."

"See, Kathleen, Elizabeth is offering a sincere

apology," Bridget lovingly added.

"Sorry, Elizabeth?" Kathleen sarcastically asked. "Sorry for what?" Elizabeth stiffened in the chair as Kathleen glared at her.

"Sorry you did it or sorry you where caught?" Kathleen irately asked.

"What are you talking about" Bridget asked.

"Tell her, Elizabeth," Kathleen demanded. "Or I will!"

"It just happened," Elizabeth mumbled.

"It just happened? What happened?" Bridget anxiously asked.

"Mama…" Elizabeth said trying to find the words.

"Mama, what?" Kathleen snapped. "Tell her…Mama, I slept with Billy while Margaret was dying in the next room?"

"Oh, me God! Me God…how?' Bridget screamed feverishly pacing back and forth in the kitchen.

"Mama, I'm sorry," Kathleen said. "I didn't want to tell you this way. I shouldn't have."

"Mama, it just happened," Elizabeth offered her only explanation.

"Just happened! What kind of fool do you think I am? Shacking up with your sister's husband doesn't just happen," Bridget irately reproached her. "Sweet Jesus, I left me dying daughter that night in your hands to care for her and the two of you funning it up fornicating. The two of you should be damned for eternity to hell."

"Mama," Elizabeth pleaded.

"Mama? Don't you dare to ever call me that again," wrathfully, Bridget commanded.

"You are dead to me. Get out of me house."

"If I walk out of this door, you'll never see Mabel again," Elizabeth threatened.

"If that's what it takes to revenge me daughter than so be it," Bridget coldly replied. "May you rot in Hell, you whore!"

Elizabeth looked towards her sister. Kathleen contemptuously glared back.

"Then I'll be seeing you two righteous bitches there," Elizabeth shouted, slamming the door behind her.

~ *Chapter Thirty Five* ~

Eight months... thirty-two weeks... or two hundred forty days, no matter which way Elizabeth added up the time the events always came out the same. Each day, alcohol helped as she buried all thoughts of Margaret, Bridget and Kathleen. It eased the pain when Billy left for places unknown, unaware of what he left behind. It insulated her when Eddie quickly obtained a divorce as Billy's baby grew inside her. And the alcohol helped her convince Joe O'Neil, her new husband, that the seven pound, six ounce baby was his five months premature child.

"Mama, can you bring me home a sister when you go to the hospital?" Mabel asked.

"Mama can't pick one out. We have to take what they give me," Elizabeth answered.

"I only want a sister. Don't bring it home otherwise," Mabel replied.

"You little brat," Elizabeth scolded her. "You already had a sister. We'll take what God give us. Joe might like a son."

"Where is my sister?" Mabel asked.

"She's in heaven," Elizabeth answered.

"With Aunt Margaret and Uncle Jimmy?" Mabel asked.

"Yes," Elizabeth answered.

"Why is my sister in heaven?" Mabel began questioning. "Is she coming back? Can I see her?"

"She's in heaven because you killed her, that's why," Elizabeth snapped back momentarily ending her daughter's questions.

"How?" Mabel asked courageously.

"Because you were in such a god damn hurry to be born, that's why," Elizabeth callously answered. Mabel stood fixed in the spot she was standing, unable to comprehend what her mother was saying.

"She was your twin sister," Elizabeth recited the cold facts to her. "When you were born, she got in your way and you pushed her to come out. The cord wrapped around your sister's neck and she was strangled to her death." Mabel starting crying, sorry for what she did. Not understanding but she knew she had done wrong.

"Did my sister look like me?" she finally was able to ask.

"Yes, she did," hurtfully, Elizabeth answered.

"Good. Then Aunt Margaret will find her and take care of her up in heaven," Mabel replied.

"Aunt Margaret, Aunt Margaret, that's all you can say. She couldn't even take care of herself. Don't expect her to be taking care of anyone else," Elizabeth argued with her crying daughter.

On December 5th 1936, Clark O'Neil was born.

"He's so little. What can he do?" Mabel asked looking at her brother in her arms for the first time.

"Don't do much for now. Just eats, cries and craps. But soon he'll be up and running," Joe proudly answered her.

Clark's beginning days were easier than Mabel's were. The O'Neils, unlike the Sullivans, only drank on weekends, as Joe needed to be clearheaded for his work at the shipyards. But the weekends were quite a different story.

"Will ya see to it that you don't kill this one," Elizabeth instructed the six-year old before the couple left for the New Year's Eve party.

"No, Mama. I won't let anything happen to him," Mabel answered.

"Change him and feed him. That's all you have to do," Elizabeth drilled into her. "Plenty of diapers over there and the bottles are in the icebox."

"Yes, Mama," Mabel answered.

"Don't be leaving no smelly diapers around. Be sure to clean them out," Joe added.

"I'll clean them out real good," Mabel replied.

Mabel sat on the living room floor under the sparse Christmas tree. Laughing to Charlie McCarthy's wisecracking jokes on the radio as she built a castle with the blocks Santa brought her. Her baby brother sleeping peacefully as her mother predicted.

"Don't cry, Clark. I'm here," she said picking him up in her arms. "What do you want?" He stopped crying as she walked around holding him in her arms.

"Oh, you are really wet," she teased him. "Almost done. Stop wiggling," he ignored her command as she pinned the fresh diaper. "Do you want a bottle?" Mabel asked struggling to hold him in one arm while taking the bottle out of the icebox.

"Don't cry," she said putting him on the floor. "I'll pick you up again as soon as I get the bottle ready." Mabel filled the small pot with water and heated it up as she had seen her mother do.

"How's that?" she asked him as he sucked. "Must be pretty good," she remarked as he drank the bottle dry. Fed and clean, Mabel tried putting him back to bed but each time she laid him down in the bassinet he began whimpering. Frustrated she had only one last idea. Taking the blanket off her bed, she stretched it out under the Christmas tree.

"Let's pretend we're at the park having a picnic," she said lying on the blanket next to her brother looking up into the branches. "One time I went on one with Aunt Margaret and Uncle Billy and…" she told him. Clark fell asleep listening to her story. His crying woke her up early the next morning.

"Wet again and hungry?" she asked. "Oh, no. You've wet my blanket through and through. I'd better get this cleaned up before mother sees it." *Where is mother and Joe*, she thought. She looked in their empty bedroom. Mabel changed Clark's diaper and gave him a bottle. *What time did mother say they were coming home?* She couldn't remember.

"Did she tell us?" she asked tickling Clark's belly. Mabel put her blanket in the washtub to soak and cleaned up the wet spot on the floor. After finishing rearranging the items under the Christmas tree, she made her breakfast. Clark happily watched her movements as she danced around the house for him.

"I think it's time for your bath," she remarked. Clark smiled. "Do you like baths? I do." Mabel took a damp washcloth and rubbed his blond hair. He wiggled and squirmed. "Stay still and this will be done in a minute. She continued wiping the damp cloth over his body as the water dripped over him.

"See now you're done and you're all cleaned up for the day. Mama will be happy to see that," proudly she remarked. Clark began crying again.

"You can't want another bottle yet," she worried. "There's only one left." Against her better judgment, she gave it to him. "Please stay asleep until Mama gets home," she whispered into his ear as he fell back asleep in his bassinette.

Mabel searched the pantry. She searched the hall closet where Mama hid her bottle. She couldn't find any formula. *I can give him some of the milk from the icebox if he wakes up.* Mabel's plan alleviated some of her anxiety of what to do until her mother came home. *Where did she say they were going?* She couldn't remember. *I'm a big girl. She'll be home soon.*

Mabel heard footsteps making their way to her front door. Eagerly, she ran and opened it.

"Happy New Year, Mabel," her cousin Eileen announced. Eileen O'Neil, was the best thing that her stepfather Joe brought to their family. They were about the same age and shared the same temperament. "Have you seen my mother?" Mabel anxiously asked.

"No," Eileen answered.

"What about Joe?" Mabel worriedly questioned.

"Mabel, let me in," Eileen said walking passed her. "What's the matter?"

"They went out last night and they haven't come home yet," Mabel nervously answered.

"Mabel, they've done that before. They'll be home later," Eileen pointed out.

"I don't have enough bottles for Clark." Mabel informed her.

"Where is he?" Eileen asked.

"He's sleeping. Don't go in and wake him," Mabel told her.

"I won't," she promised.

"I guess, I can give him some milk if he wakes up," Mabel confided her plan.

"Can't do that," Eileen said. "I think milk from a bottle can kill a baby. That's why they get formula. We'll go buy some. Got any money?"

"No. Do you?" Mabel asked.

"Not a penny," Eileen answered. "I'm sure there must be some around here somewhere." The girls searched every inch of the apartment but couldn't find a nickel.

"He's going to walk up soon. What should we do?" Mabel questioned.

"I don't think we should wait for him to get hungry. It takes time to get the formula ready," Eileen self assuredly informed her.

"I don't know what to do?" Mabel's body shook as she spoke.

"We need to get some money," Eileen answered.

"But where?" Mabel asked.

"We can get it from my mother," Eileen quickly replied.

"My mother would kill me. You have to promise me. Swear to me you won't tell anyone about this," Mabel begged.

"I won't," Eileen pinky swore. "Then let's look for your parents. They're probably in Smithy's."

"I can't take Clark out," Mabel answered.

"It's not too cold out. We could bundle him up. I'm sure he'll be fine," Eileen coaxingly said.

"He hasn't been baptized yet," Mabel replied.

"It's only two blocks. What else can we do?" Eileen asked.

Seeing no other choice, Mabel dressed her brother. She held him tightly in her arms as they walked along Fifth Avenue towards the bar.

"Remember the time that drunk gave us a quarter for singing," Eileen asked.

"Yeah," Mabel answered pulling the blanket up over her brother's head.

"Well, if your parents aren't in Smithy's we'll sing and ask other people for money. Then we'll go next door to the drug store and buy the formula," Eileen delightedly offered her solution.

Should only take us one song, Clark won't be out to long, Mabel though, sighing with relief. The girls approached the tavern. A *CLOSED ON NEW YEAR'S DAY* sign hung on the door.

"I don't know what to do now," Eileen lamented.

"Well, we're already out. I guess we should go next door and ask the druggist how much the formula cost?" Mabel nobly said.

"Aren't you Eddie Sullivan's kid?" the clerk asked.

"Yes, sir I am," Mabel answered.

"Where's he been? Haven't seen him around in awhile," he inquired.

"I don't know," she answered.

"Well kid, what do you want?" he asked.

"How much does formula cost?" Mabel asked.

"Which brand?" the clerk questioned.

"I forgot the name," Mabel replied.

"The cheapest," Eileen added.

"Your mother sent you out to buy formula and didn't tell you the name?" a young woman waiting for a prescription asked.

"My mother's home sick. She's sleeping. I didn't want to wake her," Mabel lied.

"That will be one dollar," the clerk said placing the can on the counter.

"We don't have any money with us," Mabel answered.

"You don't have any money. How in the world did you plan on paying for it?" he agitatedly asked.

"Could we sing you a song and do a little dance?" Mabel uneasily asked.

"You sure are Eddie Sullivan's kid. I'll give you that," the clerk said when he stopped laughing.

"Give her the formula," the druggist called from the back room.

"Thank you sir," Mabel said.

"You owe us a song. Don't make it some sad one either," the clerk taunted.

"I know just the one," Eileen said and whispered in Mabel's ear.

"We're in the money, we're in the money," the girls sang.

"We've got a lot of what it takes to get along!" Mabel held on tightly to her brother as she and Eileen danced around. "We're in the money, the sky is sunny…"

"Alright," the druggist said walking in from the back room. "Are you girls planning on making the formula yourselves?"

"Yes sir, we are," Mabel answered.

"Good Lord," the lady waiting for her prescription commented.

"Can you read the instructions on the label?" the druggist continued.

"No, but if you tell us what to do, we'll be able to do it," Mabel answered.

"Child, how sick is your mother?" the young woman couldn't keep herself from asking.

"She's real sick. Too sick to do it herself," Mabel answered.

"Do you have any bottles at home already made?" she questioned.

"No, that's why we came here," Mabel answered.

"John, give me another can, will you? Girls," she continued. "come home with me. I have some bottles already made for my baby. I'll give you a couple to tide you over until I can make some more for you. Just be sure to bring back my bottles when you come back."

"Thank you. Thank you very much," both girls joined in.

"Don't charge Mrs. De Salvo for either can," the druggist informed the clerk.

"If your mother isn't better, come back and I'll make some more for you. Tell her to feel better," Mrs. De Salvo said to the girls as they left her apartment with the first three bottles.

"Did she say where they were?" Eileen asked two days later when Mabel knocked on her door.

"Just said the time got away from them. That's all," Mabel answered.

"Did she ask you where all the bottles came from in the icebox?" Eileen questioned.

"No, she acted as if they should have been there," Mabel answered. "Joe asked me if I needed anything? I told him I needed $5. He took it out of his wallet and handed it to me."

"You should have asked for $10," Eileen informed her.

"Come with me," Mabel said. "I want to buy some flowers for Mrs. De Salvo. I'm going to tell her my mother is better and says thanks."

"Are we going to pay for the formula?" Eileen asked.

"We're going there first," Mabel promptly replied.

"Did your mother say she was sorry and promise it wouldn't happen again?" Eileen asked.

"What do you think?" Mabel answered.

~ Chapter Thirty Six ~

For six years, Mabel protected Clark. He was the only one she grew close to since her cousin Eileen had moved away.

"Sh, sleep under here," she whispered ushering him under her bed the nights Elizabeth and Joe argued. Vowing to herself, she would always be able to provide for her brother she squirreled away every bit of lose change she found lying around the apartment. Only their time spent at school separated them.

"What did you learn today?" Mabel asked the same question each evening as the family sat for dinner.

"You'll never guess who stopped by today." Elizabeth said.

"Who?" Joe asked.

"Eddie," she answered passing the plate of mashed potatoes. "He wants to see Mabel."

"Who?" Mabel asked.

"Don't get smart," Elizabeth snapped. "Your father."

"What'd you tell him?" Joe asked spooning the potatoes onto his plate.

"Told him it's up to Mabel," she answered.

"I don't want to see him," Mabel said chewing

her food.

"Don't talk with your mouth full," Elizabeth reprimanded. "Says he's a changed man and wants to talk to you."

"I don't care if he's changed," Mabel answered.

"Can't hurt to listen to him," Joe advised in between bites of his chicken. "He's your father. Just hear what he has to say."

"Daddy, you're not her father?" Clark asked putting his glass down.

"She has a different father than you. That's why her last name is Sullivan," Elizabeth casually answered.

"Clark, in my heart I am her father. Mabel knows that," Joe affectionately looked at Mabel as he spoke. "Can't hurt for you to talk to the man."

"He's changed. I can hardly remember him to know who he was to begin with," Mabel remarked. "Don't see why I need to have him in my life. It's fine, just the way it is."

"Do what you want," Elizabeth admonished. "He said he was coming back tomorrow morning around ten."

He'll get the message when I'm not here, Mabel said to herself leaving the house early the next morning. *I have no intention of seeing him.*

"Mabel," a male raspy voiced called out her name. Startled, she quickly turned around to see him standing in the vestibule. "I was afraid you might not want to see me," he said crushing out his cigarette under his shoe. "I've been waiting here since six in case you tried to skip out," he said stepping towards her. "I'm your father."

"I know who you are," she answered curtly. "I remember you from your pictures."

"So, I look the same then?" he joked.

"Actually," she said looking him over. "I have to say you look better... not so skinny."

"And look at you, all grown up," Eddie answered.

"I'm twelve now," she informed him.

"You want to get something to eat?' he uncomfortably asked.

"I guess it can't hurt," she answered.

"Twelve years, three months and ten days," he said walking towards the diner. Mabel questioningly looked at him. "That's how old you are. Should I figure it out to the minute for you?"

"No, that's enough," she replied.

"I've been thinking about you a lot for a long time," he hesitantly said. "I've been afraid to come and face you. There's so much I have to make up to you."

"You don't have to make anything up to me. I'm fine," she answered taking a seat at a table.

"I'll have two eggs sunny side up, bacon and toast," Eddie told the waitress.

"And you, young lady?" she asked.

"I'll have the same," Mabel responded.

"Do you remember how we used to dip out toast in the yoke together?" Eddie smiled as he asked.

"I don't remember it," Mabel answered, watching the smile leave her father's face as she spoke. "I still dip my toast in it," she added.

"Do you remember any of the good times we had?" he nervously asked moving the pieces of his silverware. Mabel sat trying to think of an answer.

"How could you?" he timidly remarked. "My drinking always got in the way back then."

"Are you still drinking?" Mabel questioned.

"No. I stopped," he answered.

"So you're on the wagon for awhile?" Mabel observed.

"Not for a while," he said sincerely. "The rest of my life. Can't take one drink. I know that now... How about your mother?"

"I'm not here to talk about her," Mabel answered. "What made you stop?"

"I guess you want the truth?" he asked, looking around at the patrons in the diner.

"Nothing less," she answered.

"I'm not proud of this," he said shaking his head.

"Go ahead," Mabel encouraged him.

"After the bombing of Pearl Harbor," he spoke softly so no one else would hear. "I tried to sign up like everyone else. I went three times to the recruiting station. But each time I went I had to have a couple of drinks beforehand to steady my nerves." He looked for her acceptance before he continued. "The last time I went, the recruiter said to me, 'America needs her men to defend her off our shores and in the home front. And you, sir, are a disgrace both as an American and as a man. Don't waste my time by coming back here.'"

Anxiously, Eddie reached into his pocket for his cigarettes. "No one had ever said I was a disgrace as a man. I haven't touched a sip since," he said lighting the cigarette hanging in his mouth.

"You working?" Mabel asked.

"Todd Shipyards," he exhaled in a stream of

smoke. "That's where I met Frances. She worked in the office back then. Married now for two years. She keeps me on the straight and narrow."

"That's good," Mabel commented.

"She's a good woman," Eddie continued after drinking some coffee. "Her first husband died in the war. Left her with a baby. Want to see her picture?" he asked taking his wallet out.

"Here's Frances," he said handing her a picture of the three of them. "And that's Evelyn. She's three now. I'm the only Daddy she's known...That's why," he tenderly added, "I know how much I've missed." Eddie reached for her hand. Mabel's body stiffened from the stinging of his words.

"What do want from me?' Mabel challenged.

"I don't want anything from you," he vulnerably said. "I just want to be in your life. Let me try to make it up?"

"I guess there'd be no harm in that," she answered.

"You've made me the happiest man in the world," Eddie said, tears moistening his eyes as they stood saying goodbye outside her apartment building. "How about coming to my house next Sunday for dinner? We've moved into an apartment on Thirteen Street, so I could be closer to you."

"I think I can make it," smilingly she answered.

"Great. Frances is looking forward to meeting you," Eddie informed her.

"What time do you want me and Clark to be there?" she asked.

"I thought the first time it would be just us. You understand...just family," he awkwardly answered.

"I understand," Mabel snapped back. "But

understand I don't go anywhere without my brother. It's a family thing."

"I'm sorry, that was wrong of me," Eddie apologized. "I'm having a little trouble with all of this. Bring him. I'm sure it will fine with Frances." Eddie leaned over and kissed her on her forehead. "Three o'clock next Sunday. Good bye for now, sweetheart."

"Bye, Daddy," she answered.

For months, Mabel and Clark went to Sunday dinner at the Sullivan's. Clark's likeable impish charms endeared him to Frances immediately. She doted over him. Lovingly, she sent him home each week with treats. Mabel's compulsory loyalty to her mother prevented any closeness with the woman. Wanting to be obliged to no one, Mabel insisted each week on cleaning up the kitchen by herself. On special occasions, holidays and Mabel's graduation, Eddie took the family out to restaurants to celebrate.

At the end of every visit, he walked them home. Mabel laugh as his jokes teasing her about finishing her first year of high school but mostly he saw the sadness in her eyes.

"There's Mama," Clark said. Looking across Fifth Avenue, Mabel and Eddie saw Elizabeth staggering.

"I'll get her," Mabel answered, dodging the traffic.

"Hi, baby," Elizabeth slurred.

"Mama, let's go home," Mabel said.

"Not just yet," Elizabeth garbled. "I got to find Joe. Can't find him anywhere."

"God damn it, Elizabeth, you're drunk," Eddie reproachfully remarked.

"Daddy, stay out of this," Mabel commanded.

"Yes, Daddy," Elizabeth sarcastically agreed. "Stay out of it. Me and my kids can take care of ourselves."

"Mama," Mabel said turning her attention back on her mother. "I'm sure Joe's home by now."

"Let me help you with her," Eddie offered.

"No. Just go. We can do it," Mabel said putting her arm around her mother's waist.

"Mr. S, we can do it. Mabel can get her into bed." Clark said getting on the other side of his mother. "We'll see you next week."

"I think you'll see me sooner than that," Eddie retorted.

School year finished, only thing left to do is find a part-time job to earn a little money, Mabel thought walking up the steps. Reaching her door, she could hear her aggravated father's voice without opening it.

"I've seen a lawyer," Eddie was saying.

"I don't care who you saw," Elizabeth angrily answered.

"You're an unfit mother," he yelled.

"And now you're a better father," she screamed.

"I've got rights," Eddie said waving papers in her face. "Mabel," his voice softened when he saw her entered the room. "I want you to come and live with me and Frances."

"I don't want to," Mabel defiantly answered.

"You have no choice. Your mother is unfit," he reasoned.

"I won't go," she argued, holding her ground.

"You'll go, if I have to hog tie you and carry you through the streets, you'll go. I don't want you living like this," he disputed back.

"You don't want me living like this. You told me you wanted nothing from me just to make up the past. Don't do this to me," Mabel pleaded.

"I am your father," Eddie stated maintaining his composure. "I have responsibilities."

"Now you have responsibilities," Mabel laughed. "I'm not going with you. I'll run away first."

"Fine, if that's the way you want it," he calmly said. "But if you don't come with me my lawyer advised I should call the police and report your mother's drunkenness. What do you think will happen to Clark?"

I'll take him with me, Mabel thought but didn't answer.

"Just go with him," Elizabeth yelled.

"Mabel, I didn't want this to go this way," Eddie tried to talk comfortingly. "Clark can come over as much as he likes. Nothing has to really change in your life."

"I'll help you pack up some of your things," Elizabeth offered. "You can get the rest another time." Mabel refused her help. As well as refusing to allow her father to carry the suitcase down the staircase.

"It won't be so bad, you'll see," Eddie promised.

"Where are you going?" Clark asked seeing them walking out of the building.

Sunday morning a shrilling noise filled every inch in Mabel's room. Terrified she ran into the kitchen.

"What is that?" she worriedly asked.

"What is what?" Frances calmly replied.

"Don't you hear it?" she questioned yelling over it.

"Stop yelling. I don't hear anything," Eddie said. "Are you ready for church?" Abruptly, the piercing sound stopped, leaving behind an uneasy feeling in the pit of Mabel's stomach.

"I have to see my brother," she announced.

"Not now. We're going to church as a family," Eddie dictated.

For three days and long nights, the piercing sound secretly bounced off Mabel's eardrums. In the dark of night, she could see the creature sitting in the corner howling the high-pitched cry that only she could hear. The horrendous cry only stopped when she was with her brother. Fearfully, she told no one.

"We're going to celebrate the Fourth at Frances's brother's," Eddie announced during breakfast. "They'll be fireworks."

"I'm going to spend the day with my brother," Mabel answered.

"Will you stop yelling," Eddie scolded. "You're coming with us."

"I'm not going with you," she answered defiantly over the mournful sounds coming from the creature. *Why can't they see him sitting over there? Why can't they hear him?"*

"Fine. Don't come with us. But you'll not be stepping one step outside this house, until you stop this craziness" he threatened.

"Who do you think you are? You can't keep me here," Mabel dared him.

"No? Just watch me," Eddie confidently said.

"This should give you plenty of time to think," he said locking her in the closet before they left the apartment.

Mabel sat on the floor. The small amount of light coming in under the door outlined the horrible creature sitting in there with her. Unceasingly he howled. There was no escaping him. She laid her head on the floor trying to suck in some fresh air as the temperature heated. Exhausted she tried to fall asleep. *My brother, I hope Clark is alright.* The unbearable creature kept waking her with his cry.

Outside there was hardly a breeze to be found anywhere in Brooklyn. Elisabeth and Joe joined their friends and the other tenants filling the rooftops. For tonight, the city was promised a spectacular fireworks show celebrating the first July Fourth celebration since the end of the war

"What do we have here?" Joe asked surprising Clark as the boy was taking a drink of beer from one of his friends.

"Boys will be boys," Elizabeth laughed.

"Don't we know it," one of Joe's friends laughed.

"He'll be ten in a couple of months," Joe remarked. "I don't see any reason he can't have a beer of his own."

"Whatever you think," Elizabeth answered.

"I'm sure this isn't the first time you had some. Is it, son?' Joe asked.

"No sir," Clark giggled.

"Well, then finish the glass but don't have any more tonight," Joe told him. "Just the first time he got caught, that's all," he said to their friends when Clark was out of earshot.

Nine o'clock and no more light was filtering in under the door. Only painful cries, some hers, some from the howling creature, filled the closet.

Nine o'clock, Clark finished his beer and joined his friends standing on the edge of the skylight.

"Look! They're starting over there," someone yelled. Clumsily Clark quickly turned. His shoe stuck under the metal edge. Unable to catch his balance, Clark fell forward, crashing through the glass skylight, smashing onto the apartment floor below.

The creature gave out one last furious scream. Mabel shook. The creature left and when he did, she felt an unexplainable emptiness inside her. Exhausted, she fell asleep until the closet door opened.

~ Chapter Thirty Seven ~

"*Mama,*" *Clark's voice eerily rushed* past her ears. Elizabeth quickly turned around... The dropped glass from her hand shattered as Clark lunged forward into the skylight.

"Clark!" she screamed running towards him. "Let me go! Let me go!"

"Don't look," Joe protectively ordered, grabbing her into his arms.

"I have to see my baby," she said pulling away. "My baby...," she cried looking down at Mrs. Johnson kneeling next to his body. "I'm coming. Mama's coming..." Elizabeth rushed towards the roof's only exit. Mrs. Johnson looked up at Joe shaking her head crying. Joe ran and caught up to Elizabeth as she was entering the elderly couple's apartment.

"You don't want to see him like this," Mr. Johnson mercifully told them.

"Where's my baby?... Where's my baby?" Elizabeth asked hurriedly passing by him. "Oh Joe, he's so cold," she said stroking Clark's cheek.

"Elizabeth, he's dead," Joe said, tears running down his cheeks.

"He's not dead!" Elizabeth refused to hear him. "God damn it, someone get him a blanket."

"Here's a blanket," the elderly woman said bringing in one from the closet.

"Where's the doctor?" Elizabeth looked up at the crowd watching them through the broken skylight. "Someone please get us a doctor," she begged.

"Elizabeth, it's not going to help," Joe again tried to console her. "Clark's dead."

"He's not dead…He's not dead. Look, he's still breathing," she said, lying to herself.

"Elizabeth, get up. There's nothing anyone can do. Clark's dead," Joe pulled her to her feet.

"Leave me alone," she ordered. "Why should you care? He isn't your son. He's mine and Billy's." Joe let go of the hold he had on her. Elizabeth knelt again at Clark's side. Joe stood motionless. His tears stopped. The broken glass crunched under his shoes as he walked away.

"Are you hurt?" the police officer asked seeing her covered in Clark's blood.

Am I hurt? How do I answer that? Elizabeth lamented, holding Clark in her arms.

"No, she's not. She's the child's mother," one of the tenants who began filling the apartment said.

"We have to take him," the attendant said. "Is there anyone who can stay with you?" Grief stricken, Elizabeth stood silent.

"I'll bring her to her apartment," one of the tenants offered.

"Here's a number you can call tomorrow to make the funeral arrangements," the attendant said writing down a telephone number on a piece of paper and handing it to her.

Elizabeth painfully watched them place Clark's body on a stretcher. She followed behind as they carried him down the five flights of stairs. She stood silently watching as they put him in the coroner's wagon and then drove off.

"You should go up to your apartment," a tenant advised.

Why? Elizabeth thought. *Clark's dead...Joe's not coming back... Mabel's not there... Billy...Margaret...Daddy...Mama...Kathleen... there's no one....* Dropping the piece of paper, she walked down the street.

~ Chapter Thirty Eight ~

Frantically running home, desperately, Mabel tried to block out her father's words. *It's not true. It's not true.* She had answered him. *You're lying to me.*

"Mabel," he called after her.

"I hate you. I'll never see you again," she had yelled back. *How could he have said something so horrible about Clark?*

"Mabel," she heard the voices of neighbors calling her as past them. But they weren't the voice she was searching for. "Clark, Clark," she shouted racing up the flight of steps taking them two at a time.

"Clark," hopefully she cried out opening the unlocked door. "Mama...Joe..."

"Mabel," the janitor's wife uneasily said standing in the doorway.

"No! No!" Mabel screamed putting her hands to her mouth.

"I'm sorry," the woman responded. Rushing past her, Mabel flew up the other three flights of steps to the roof. The woman tried to catch up to her. Frozen in the doorway, Mabel watched the janitor cleaning up the remaining pieces of glass on the rooftop.

"There's no need of you torturing yourself up

here," the woman breathlessly said, putting her arm on the poor child's shoulder.

"Where is my mother?" Mabel bravely asked.

"No one's seen her or Joe," the janitor turned around and called over to her, "since they took the body away." The cold stare from his wife rapidly put him back to work. "Want me to make you a cup of tea or something," she said leading Mabel back down the steps.

"No...we'll be fine. Our mother will be home soon," Mabel automatically answered standing in her doorway.

"I'll leave you then," the janitor's wife said not wanting Mabel to see the tears beginning to swell up in her eyes.

We won't be fine. Clark, how could you have done this? Mabel questioned aloud walking into his room. *Where are you? Where's everyone?* Tearfully she sat on his bed. Everything he owned was thrown somewhere in the room. *How could I have left you? You needed me,* she fell back on the bed sobbing. *You're here!* Excitedly, she yelled opening her eyes. He was not there, only his lingering sent permeating her nose. *I'm sorry... I'm so sorry,* she wept burying her face in his pillow. For her there was no comfort, only a growing emptiness inside... worn and beaten, she fell asleep.

*Ring...Ring...*the telephone awoke her from a nightmare. Clearing her head, Mabel answered it. A woman was coldly rattling off a list of questions.

"My parent's aren't here.... I don't know...Potter Field?... Three days?... Let me write down your name and number," Mabel's voice broke. The nightmare was real. "My mother will call you back later." Taking her mother's telephone book from the kitchen drawer, Mabel called each person's whose name she recognized.

"Sorry to hear about your brother....Haven't seen your mother or Joe..." was all they each replied.

"He's here," the bartender at Smithy's said. "But he won't come to the telephone."

"Mike, keep him there till I get there," Mabel asked.

"Sure kid. Sorry about your brother," he added but she hung up before he finished. *Joe will know where Mama is...He'll know what to do.*

"Don't know and don't care," Joe slurred his answer.

"Some lady called...We have to make arrangements or he'll go to Pot's field," Mabel maturely advised him.

"Potter's Field," Joe smugly answered.

"She made it sound like a bad place," Mabel said.

"I don't care where they put him," Joe said slamming his hand down onto the bar. "Get me another drink."

"Mike, give him coffee," Mabel ordered. "Joe, you need to sober up."

"Listen Mabel, Clark's not my kid. Never was, your mother says. So I don't care what happens to him," Joe garbled. "Don't be getting me no coffee!" he yelled looking over to Mike. "So best you leave me alone. If you know what's good for you," he threatened.

"Mabel," Mike called her over to the end of the bar. "Go to Gordon's on Fourth Avenue." Mabel looked at him puzzled. "Tell him I sent you. He'll tell you what to do."

"Thanks Mike," she said.

"Don't worry," Mike confidently said. "They won't take him to Potter's Field. Tell Gordon, I'm taking up a collection to help with the expenses."

"Mr. Gordon, I don't want my brother to go to Potter's Field," Mabel nervously said, having no idea of where or what it was. But the woman on the telephone threatened it, if her mother didn't call and Mike was taking up a collection to prevent it.

"That's not going to happen," Mr. Gordon assured her. Mabel relaxed just a little as she sat back in the oversized leather chair sitting across from him at his desk. "Leave it all up to me. One of his parents has to sign this release form and I'll get everything started. Given many a child a good send off with the contributions from Smithy's."

"Mr. Gordon," Mabel embarrassingly interrupted. "I can't find my mother. And Joe wants nothing to do with it. Says he's not Clark's father." The words stuck in her dry mouth.

"Don't worry," Mr. Gordon comforted her. "We can get around that. Just would have been quicker since you're too young." Mabel picked a piece of hard candy from the dish he offered her. "We only need one blood relative to sign to have the body released.... Any blood relative... I'll write it down for you that they won't be expected to have any financial responsibility. Is there someone you can ask?"

"Yes, I have a grandmother and an aunt. We haven't talked to them for awhile," Mabel said, the butterscotch candy melting in her mouth but it wasn't any easier answering the questions.

"Would you rather I call on your behalf?" Mr. Gordon asked.

"No, I'll do it myself. But I'll take the paper letting them know they don't have to pay anything," Mabel said.

"Are they churchgoing women?" Mr. Gordon asked.

"Yes." Mabel acknowledged. "I think they are."

"Good," Mr. Gordon added. "That should make it easier to get one of their signatures. I'll put it down that this will ensure Clark will have a good Christian burial with a priest and all."

"Do you think I should wait another day to see if my mother shows up?" Mabel apprehensively asked.

"What's the longest she been gone before?" he replied.

"Three days," she painfully answered.

"Mabel," Mr. Gordon said. "I think it best we get the form signed today. Don't want there to be any chance that Clark's body gets sent to Hart's Island."

~ Chapter Thirty Nine ~

"*The banshee cry,*" Bridget Kelly sorrowfully said into the telephone receiver. "She got the gift from Peter's side of the family."

"I thought she was being belligerent," Eddie remorsefully admitted. "I didn't believe her. I should have remembered those awful nightmares she had when Margaret was dying."

I could have explained it all to her, Bridget thought but didn't answer. *Peter's cousin had the gift...could always tell when someone close to her was going to die.*

"I'm sorry, Mrs. Kelly, to have to be telling you all this," he continued, uncomfortable with the silence. "I'm worried about her. Can't find Elizabeth. There wasn't anyone else I could think of to help her. She won't talk to me."

"Eddie, thank you for calling," Bridget understandingly answered. "I'll do what I can do."

Tearfully, Bridget hung up the receiver and began searching the house for the scrap of paper on which Kathleen had written her work telephone number. ' *In case of an emergency,*' she said. *Never thought I'd need it.*

Impatiently, she rummaged through each scrap of paper in the top drawer of the secretary, *How could I have let this happen?* she questioned herself. There was no acceptable answer. *Seventy-one years old, you'd think I would have learned a thing or two.* She tried stopping the pain in her chest by sitting in her rocking chair. *'Women are you daft? Why didn't you...,'* Peter haunted her. *I was right. I should have turned me back on Elizabeth.* Bridget's heart ached. *But Mabel...poor child. She's only a little older than I was when I lost Meg... What can I say to her? Where is that bloody number? Peter, for God sakes help me.* She prayed getting up to look further for it. *Oh God,* she cried. *Peter forgive me, I'll be burying a grandson I never saw....*

Ransacking yet another drawer, she found a long discarded picture of the four of them taken before they disembarked the *Franconia.* She stroked Margaret's young beautiful face. *How I miss you? Just to hear you laugh one more time... How much you looked like Meg... Elizabeth, how did I fail you?* She questioned seeing the silly grin on Elizabeth face. *To only be back then...to have the chance to do it all over again... Everything was fine.* She believed it, looking at their happy faces. *God, how cold and callous me heart has become, not remembering all the pain I was in over the death of Peter. Me loneliness... Why was I so stubborn? I had a grandson I never knew...It wasn't worth this. I have a granddaughter I don't know. What do I tell her?*

Bridget jumped as the doorbell rang. "Who is it?" she called out through the open front window.

"Nana, It's Mabel. Mabel Sullivan," a cracking voice called back.

"What do I tell her? That time doesn't ease the pain of grief. It only allows God to put more pain in

our lives, just enough to mercifully make us numb.
Bridget took a deep breath. She wiped away her tears
and patted down her white hair as she unlocked the
front door.

"Nana," Mabel said standing nervously at the
door. Bridget recognized those eyes, remembered
that agonizing look. The same one she had going
door to door looking for some information about
Meg. *Have you seen me sister?' she painfully
remembered. 'Do you know anything about where
she is?'*

"Mabel, do come in," Bridget said.

"Nana, this isn't going to cost you any money,"
Mabel began speaking quickly as she was walking in
the hallway and suddenly she stopped. The house's
scent brought with it a flood of forgotten memories.
Everything was as she had last seen it but she hadn't
thought about this place in such a long time. Of
course, there were times in her dreams she would see
herself sitting on this parlor floor, putting together a
puzzle with her Aunt Margaret and some enticing
aroma was coming from the kitchen. But that was
only a pleasant dream. Now standing here she could
smell the polished furniture and could taste her
nana's apple pie. Mabel tried to hold back the tears
swelling up inside her.

"Mabel, it's a terrible sadness. Your father
called me. I know what happened to your brother,"
Bridget informed her.

"I need you to sign this paper for me," Mabel
blurted out.

"Sign this?" Bridget asked taking the papers out
of her shaking hand.

"Come in the kitchen and I'll make us a cup of

tea," Bridget said leading the way. "Are you hungry?"

"No," Mabel answered. Even with being in this familiar kitchen, the knot in her stomach wouldn't loosen. "I'm not hungry."

"Nonsense," Bridget told her. "You need to eat, especially at a time like this. I'll make you a little something and after you'll have a piece of apple pie. I made one this morning."

"Nana, I think I have to get that paper back to Mr. Gordon right away so Clark doesn't get sent to Potter's Field," Mabel answered.

"Potter's Field," Bridget stopped filling the kettle. She dried her hands and sat at the table to read the letter and the form. Mabel silently watched.

"Mr. Gordon's telephone number is right here on this letter. I'll call him," Bridget said. "You're too pale. You need a little food in you before we go back down to talk to him." Mabel obligingly followed her into the parlor. Bridget dialed the number.

"Good day, Mr. Gordon. This is Bridget Kelly," she politely said. "Me granddaughter Mabel was in to see you this morning."

"Yes, Mrs. Kelly she was," he answered. "I sent her with a form that we need signed."

"Mr. Gordon, I think you may remember me. You had known me brother Jimmy. Jimmy Donahue."

"Yes, Mrs. Kelly," he answered. "I apologize. I didn't recognized your name. I'm sorry about your grandson. It was so tragic."

"Yes, it was tragic. Such a waste of a young life," Bridget answered. "I am signing the form right now. Mabel thinks we need to rush it right down to you. I would like her to eat something first. She looks pale to me."

"Mrs. Kelly," Mr. Gordon advised her. "I don't need it from you today. I can take care of everything by telephone and get the form tomorrow."

"Thank you Mr. Gordon, but don't we need to come in to make all the arrangements?" she asked.

"I have already started them," he answered. "The patrons of Smithy's have offered to cover the expenses."

"Mr. Gordon, that may be all well and good but we'll be taking care of our own. Thank you," she proudly informed him.

"Mrs. Kelly, no ill intent was meant. I'm sure Elizabeth and Joe have donated before to help out other patrons," Mr. Gordon soothingly responded. "Mike called me and told me the money has already started rolling in. What should I tell him?"

"Tell him thank you for me," Bridget said softening her voice. "We'll gladly accept a flower piece from them but save the extra money to use towards someone who'd be needing it."

"Certainly, I'll do as you ask," he diplomatically answered.

"What arrangements have you already made?" Bridget asked

"Mrs. Kelly, this is a delicate matter that I don't usually talk about over the telephone," he sensitively told her.

"Mr. Gordon, I think it best if we continue on with it now," she answered.

"We have three types of white coffins," he tactfully answered. "Considering the fact that it will be remaining closed and given a small budget to work with, I thought it best to use the least expensive. I also planned to use the small room for the viewing.

"The coffin will be closed?" Bridget questioned.

"I called the morgue after Mabel left to inform them that we would be picking up Clark's body to prepare it," Mr. Gordon took a deep breath before he continued. "Clark took a nasty fall. They said they saw no way the coffin could be left opened."

Clark, Bridget heard her grandson's name. "Clark," so painful was it for her to say aloud that she had to stop for a moment before continuing.

"Clark, deserves the best lining you can get. I want the best coffin you have," Bridget ordered knowing it was and would forever be the only gift she bought him. "And it will be held in me home," she said giving him the address and her telephone number. "If that is all, Mr. Gordon?" she asked wanting to get off the telephone before her voice weakened.

"Mrs. Kelly, I have only one more question," he said. "How long do you want the wake to be?"

"As long as it can be," Bridget's quivering voice answered as she hoped Elizabeth would come back in time to say goodbye.

Tomorrow Smithy's would deliver a keg of beer. Neighbors would bring dishes of hot and cold foods. The ladies from the altar society would bring cakes and cookies.

Tomorrow night streams of family, friends and neighbors would come by and give their condolences, never uttering aloud to the family a word concerning Elizabeth or Joe.

Only, "He was such a good boy," would be echoing. Kathleen would kneel next to one of the parish priest as he led the rosary for her nephew's soul. Mabel would grieve alone staring at the unopened coffin and Bridget would mourn everyone she ever loved and lost.

But tonight, as they made room for Clark's coffin in the parlor between the two windows, the three of them talked in the empty house.

"We would like it very much if you stayed here with us," Bridget invited.

"I have to go back home and wait in case my mother comes home," Mabel answered.

"You can leave her a note," Bridget answered. "She'll know where to find you." Mabel ignored the response as she continued moving around a chair in the parlor.

"We'll go home with you tonight. If your mother's there, fine. Then you can stay there," Kathleen suggested. "And if she's not, you can pick up a few things and come back and stay with us."

"Mabel, you're the only family we have left," Bridget added. "And we're all you have. We don't want you to be alone."

"Do you think she'll get mad at what we've arranged?" Mabel asked as they made their way to see if Elizabeth was home.

"Don't see why she should. If she's home, we'll tell her what's been done and we can change anything she wants us to," Bridget said.

"Mama," Kathleen said while Mabel was in her bedroom packing up some of her clothes. "Elizabeth is really something, running out on her kid at a time like this."

"Don't say another word about this. The only one that it will hurt is Mabel and she's been hurt enough," Bridget said looking at the picture in the living room. *So here you are, Clark,* she thought. *I would have been able to pick you out in a crowd. I can see a little of Billy and Peter. Yes, you had Peter's sparkling eyes. There's some of the devil in you. Wasn't there?* Bridget stroked his image. *I'll never hear your voice. I'll never hear your laugh. Clark, I'm so sorry...I never wiped away a tear or cleaned a cut. I never kissed you. I never touched your life....*

"Nana," Mabel said startling her. "I'm ready."

"Did you leave a note for your mother?" Bridget asked putting Clark's picture in her pocket.

~ *Chapter Forty* ~

"*M*abel, *you're the best nurse* I've ever worked with," Charlotte said, sitting across from her at the nurse's station. "You're so good at taking care of others, why can't you take care of yourself?"

"I do!" Mabel retorted. Annoyed she stopped writing her patient's assessment note in the chart. *Why is everyone so concerned about my social life?* The scene being an all too familiar one for her.

"Come on," Charlotte sympathetically said. "You stay at home with your grandmother and aunt every weekend. You never go out."

"But I have," Mabel replied.

"When was your last date?" Charlotte impatiently answered. "Three months ago and did you go back out with him?... No!"

"They need a nurse in 211,"a housekeeper told them as she moped up the hall past them.

"I'll go," Mabel said, eager to end this uncomfortable conversation.

"I know you're going," Charlotte called down the hall after her. "We're picking you up Saturday at six."

"I meant I'll see what they need in 211," Mabel called back. *Charlotte knew what I meant... Maybe it wouldn't be a bad idea to go.* Her crisp uniform crinkling as she walked. Hair pulled neatly back, tightly in place under her cap. Shoes freshly polished, stethoscope around her neck, no makeup, no jewelry, no perfume. Mabel Sullivan R.N. was the picture of the perfect nurse... intelligent, efficient, and caring. With no further thoughts of herself, she tended to needs of her patients.

Her shift done, the ride home in the crowded subway car was always her loneliest time of day. On the days, she was lucky enough to get a seat; she could immerse herself into her reading. However, it was usually the case she had to stand hanging on to a strap above some stranger's head. Those were the days when she could not keep scores of random thoughts from flying in and out of her mind.

Why wouldn't I want to stay home and watch over them? They're getting old. She repositioned her hand on the strap. *They've been so good to me.* They had been good. Not giving her any trouble as she pleaded with them to pay for yet another month's rent as she hoped her mother would still come home, two months after Clark's death. No comments were passed when Elizabeth didn't return. Oh, she did hear the whispers they said at night but never anything bad about her mother was said to her face. *They paid for nursing school. My life's fine just the way it is"*, Mabel thought getting off at the Eight Avenue station.

"The meatloaf is wonderful," Kathleen announced, obviously savoring its taste.

"Nana, it is wonderful," Mabel echoed.

"I simply followed the recipe that Kathleen cut out and left for me," Bridget humbly told them.

"It is amazing what a can of tomato soup can do to spice things up a little," Kathleen delightedly stated.

"Talking about spicing things up," Mabel interjected. "I'm going out Saturday night?"

"Oh, that's nice," Bridget exclaimed. "Where are you going and with whom?"

"Charlotte from work," Mabel answered. "I'm going with her and her boyfriend."

"Just the three of you?" Kathleen asked smiling and raising her eyebrows.

"No. Her boyfriend is bringing his friend, Buddy" Mabel uncomfortably answered. "It's going to be a blind date. Just for dinner and a movie."

"You'll have a good time," Kathleen assured her. "There are some good movies out now to see. I hear Oklahoma is wonderful."

"Do you know anything about Buddy?" Bridget asked.

"He's a plumber," Mabel hesitantly answered looking at her aunt. "They work in the same shop."

"Nothing wrong with dating a working man," Kathleen remarked.

"I know you have thoughts of me finding a handsome young doctor to marry," Mabel laughingly answered. "Like the ones in your romance novels."

"I also read about working men with dirt under their nails, sweat on their brows and strong sinuous muscles" Kathleen quickly replied. "You might like to read one of my paperbacks instead of a medical journal sometime."

"I have people's lives in my hands. The more I know, the better I can take care of them," Mabel retorted.

"Mabel, I'm proud of you as a nurse," sincerely Kathleen spoke. "I just want you to be happy."

"I am happy," Mabel exasperatedly answered. *Why doesn't anyone understand that?*

"What are you planning to wear?" Bridget asked, changing the mood of the conversation.

"I thought I'd wear my blue dress," Mabel told her.

"It looks lovely on you," Bridget approvingly answered.

"Yes, it is flattering on you," Kathleen added. "How about I treat you to a new hair style? I saw a picture of Grace Kelly today and you would look just like her if you had that cut. Let me show you the picture." Kathleen left the table to get the magazine.

"She cares greatly about you,' Bridget said as Mabel rolled her eyes and huffed after her aunt left the room.

"It's a blind date," Mabel angrily stated. "I don't need a new hair cut."

"It's not for the date she is concerned. She...," Bridget lovingly said. "We want you to be happy. We're getting older."

"I know," Mabel replied.

"We're getting older," Bridget continued "and well… we don't want you to be alone."

"Here, look at this," Kathleen animatedly said walking into the room with the magazine in her hand opened to the page. "You would look so much softer and prettier if you had this cut."

"It's only one date. I might not like him," Mabel confessed.

"You just might like him," Kathleen countered back. Mabel took a deep breath and looked at the picture.

"You never get a second chance to make a first impression," Bridget advised

"You'll be a knockout with this," Kathleen expressed her opinion "If Sir Edmund Hillary could climb Mount Everest, surely you can find enough courage to get a hair cut," she challenged.

"Sure, why not," Mabel consented.

~ Chapter Forty One ~

Aimlessly, Elizabeth staggered along the streets of downtown Manhattan. Sufficiently inebriated to numb her memory; sober enough to survive.

"Can you spare some change?" she slurred with her hand opened to everyone she passed.

"You whore...tramp...vagrant...drunken bum," they called her. "Don't look!" men ordered their wives. "There is nothing more disgusting than a drunken woman."

"Disgusting? You want to see disgusting," she screamed back at them vulgarly grabbing her crotch. *Disgusting...* if that was only what she was. The sting of their pathetic verbal attacks did not touch her. *Revolting... repulsive..., horrendous....* From that horrifying night, the night she drank to forget, she knew the truth about who she was. She was...*EVIL!*

Elizabeth huddled in a doorway. Her arthritic fingers unscrewed the cap off the almost empty whisky bottle. *How long had she been here? Ten days...? Ten months...? God... it's been ten years.* She took a swig. *Not long enough.* This was her doorway. She claimed it the first morning she arrived here.

"You have some misery, child," the demons inside her head dredged up the memory of that first morning she came here.

"I am misery," Elizabeth remembered her agonizing answer she gave the stranger. *"I bring it to all who know me."* Desperately she gulped down the last of the whisky.

"Then you're in the right place. We're all the wretched of the wretched. Ain't a soul caring about anyone one of us," the man had said offering her a drink from his bottle.

I am going mad. I have to get out of here. Elizabeth left the doorway that had for so many years protected her from rain and snow. Here she had drunk into oblivion, mercifully passing out and obtaining temporary freedom. But tonight there was no liberation. There was no more booze left. Tonight the demons in her head ran free terrorizing her with hallucinations from the past. Elizabeth wildly flailed her arms trying to stop the bombardment but it was useless. Trembling she watched the dredged up visions of Clark and Mabel.

The street sign read, Delancey Street but this was hell, Elizabeth's hell. She walked on to the footpath of the Williamsburg Bridge. She had found herself here many times. Each time getting a little more courage to end her pain.

No one cares if I live or die... Mabel..., she could not bring herself to think of the only child she had left. *They'd all be better off without me....* She stood by the railing. *To fly for one-minute through the air and there'd be peace... To fly through the air like Ace...If I hadn't wanted him...If I hadn't wanted Billy....my life.... You're right Mama, I should rot in*

Hell, for all I've done. There was no less pain, even after all these years. Tears ran down her dirty face as the demons showed her visions of Margaret's heartbroken eyes and Mabel's little body seizing in the hospital nursery.

"Mama," she could still hear Clark's voice calling out to her. *I deserve no peace for all the pain I've caused. It makes no difference where I burn...* Elizabeth turned and walked off the bridge. *I'll go mad tonight if I don't get another drink.* She walked down the street longingly searching for a drink... from anyone. Just enough to ease the pain and just enough to stop the demons in her head.

Three times the police and social workers had locked her up in a sanitarium forcing her to get her life back. Each time she woke up shackled to a bed with no memory of how she got there days before.

"Three strikes and you're out," the do gooder said the last time she left. *"Don't go back to drinking. You're finally dry. Stay sober or you're going to end up in an asylum."* How could they know that the demons that haunted her in sobriety were worse than a stay in any asylum? Drink was her only solace. It was the only way to anesthetize her pain.

Elizabeth learned how to walk the fine line between sobriety and drunkenness, living in that mellow state, which kept the police at bay.

"Leave that bitch alone," the old officers told the new recruits.

"There has to be some one around here who'll buy a lady a drink," she called out to a group of men driving by. Their car slowed down.

"Sure honey we will," one of the passengers

called out from the back window. Elizabeth walked towards the car. "We're going to a party. Why don't you join us?" he said opening up the back door for her. "Here sit between us and we can party a little on the way."

Why not?... They look like a bunch of average Joe's...Hope there's a bottle in the car...

Quick hand job or fast fuck... Need just enough to get the sound of Clark voice out of my head. Elizabeth sat down in the back seat. Both men squeezed tightly against her, closer than they needed to. The driver quickly drove the car away.

"Here want some?" the man in the front seat said offering her a bottle.

"Where's the costume party?" Elizabeth asked after gulping down a few swigs, seeing each of the men was wearing the same phony wig and beard.

"Slow down and pass the bottle around," the man next to her said. Right turns or left turns, Elizabeth paid no attention to where they were going as they joked and fooled around as the bottle passed between them. Down a deserted street, the driver parked the car behind a warehouse.

"The party's in there?" Elizabeth asked patting down her uncombed gray hair.

"Right up those stairs," one said. "Going to be some good time tonight," another responded. A familiar uncomfortable feeling began swelling up inside of her as she walked up the steps.

"Give me another swig, will you?" she asked.

Inside the warehouse was bare except for a few wooden chairs placed around a soiled mattress on the floor. Elizabeth turned around at once and tried desperately to get back out the door.

"Where're you going, bitch," the driver shouted dragging her by her hair then throwing her down onto the mattress. Begging, she tried to get up.

"You have to stay for the party," another said punching her in the face. Excruciating pain instantly shot from her face and down her body and mercifully, she passed out. For hours or was it days, she couldn't tell, as each time she began regaining consciousness one of them was on top of her or sadistically at her. Then there was nothing...

Slowly, Elizabeth started awakening. Painfully, she tried opening her swollen eyes. Through the small slits, darkness was all she saw. Jammed tightly into some small strange place, she could not move. Her knees cramped against her chest allowing her only shallow breaths from the fetid air around her.

This is it... only nothingness, she accepted her fate. *There was no bright light... no loving family waiting for me... no God to judge me,* Elizabeth laughed to herself *....I'm dead and this is my eternity... to be in a fetal position... Is this inside my own womb that I made vile?... But why can't I move... One can move in a womb... Oh God, I've been buried alive!* Everything around her began to shake.

"What the hell is this?" a man's muffled voice complained through a loud rustling sound. "Christ, there's a dead body in here," the garbage man called out.

"No," his partner answered. "Look, that neck vein is pulsating."

~ Chapter Forty Two ~

For two weeks, The Daily News kept the question of Jane Doe's identity before the public's eye. Each day, on the corner of their front page, they published a rendering of what the police department thought the semi-comatose woman would have looked like before her near fatal beating. Then as a young woman... as a child.... in her middle years... long hair and short... It made no difference. No one in New York came forth to identify her. Bridget Kelly, herself, peering over the pictures in the newspaper with Kathleen didn't recognize any of them to resemble her own daughter.

How could she? With so many facial bones broken, the police sketch artist had no way of portraying the extremely fine features that once graced Elizabeth's face... the face they knew. Under the picture read: 5 foot 2 inch... 110 lbs... 65-70 years old... Caucasian woman. Couldn't be Elizabeth, she was only forty-eight.

Jane Doe was the name assigned to her in the hospital. "It's as good a name as any," she eventually told the doctors when she awoke enough to answer questions. The police, disgusted by her inability or unwillingness to give them an accurate description of the attackers or much detail, dismissed the whole event as one between a pimp and one of his prostitutes. Elizabeth was content leaving it all alone.

"Good morning, Jane," a man said pleasantly while walking into her hospital room. He was a large man with a ruddy complexion, a large head and huge hands. He would have been frightening but for his soft voice. The wrinkled woman standing next to him looked older than her years. "Your doctor said it would be alright for us to talk to you. How are you feeling?"

"I'm fine," Elizabeth curtly answered. "If you're from the police there isn't anything else I have to say."

"We're not from the police," he assured her. "I'm Richie and this is May." Elizabeth nodded. "We know your real name isn't Jane but we don't care what it is. We're here to offer you help."

"Help… where were you a few weeks ago?" she answered sarcastically.

"Your tests show that you've been drinking for some time," Richie continued. "We can help you to stop." Elizabeth shook her head in disbelief.

"Get the fuck out of here!" she ordered. "I don't want to stop."

"If you don't want to stop, that's fine with us," Richie answered.

"I know," May said intensely looking into Elizabeth's eyes. "You're in a lot of pain." Elizabeth felt May's eyes boring deep into her soul. "Or else you would have stopped drinking a long time ago." May stood at her bedside. "Drinking's a disease. You can't stop it all by yourself. That's what we came here to tell you."

"A disease?" Elizabeth questioned.

"Yes, a disease... same as cancer or diabetes...nothing for anyone to be ashamed of," May answered. "Just makes us do crazy things we'd never do in our right minds."

"It's called alcoholism and we're both alcoholics," Richie answered.

"So you two are drunks and just stopped drinking? And now you want me to stop?" Elizabeth mockingly questioned. "What's in this for you?"

"Yes, I was a drunk. But I didn't stop by myself. God helped me," Richie answered.

"Oh! That's what you want... my soul," Elizabeth snickered. "Trust me, God doesn't want it."

"Jane, if you don't want to stop drinking ...don't," May spoke earnestly. "I was where you are... Do you think you can go any lower?" Elizabeth's eyes filled up with the answer. "There isn't any place left for you to go but up," May's eyes softened. "I didn't know that till Richie came into my life... Had to admit it to myself... Couldn't get any lower... Couldn't stop on my own. No one can. It's not that we're weak. It's a disease and we're powerless over it." Her voice strengthened as she continued. "Only God or whatever you want to call that Higher Power has any control to keep you sober... Had to give it all over to him. I'm getting my life back. Didn't think I wanted it back but it was the drink that messed it up. Now I'm sober for thirteen months. Not going to tell you it's easy. Take it one day at a time. That's all there is to it... One day at a time."

"Jane," Richie said. "You survive that beating for some important reason. It couldn't have been just to get drunk again."

"It...," Elizabeth began sympathetically saying. "Must have been hard for the two of you to come here and tell me that you were drunks too. I realize that. I also realize that God gave up on me along time ago. And I don't have much use for him either."

"He's with you now," Richie answered. Elizabeth shook her head in response.

"Jane, you might not be ready now," May said. "But understand that you're human. You were given a life to live. You have a purpose. We all make mistakes...God forgives you... You have to forgive yourself."

"I'm Elizabeth," her voice cracked. "You should go now."

"Can we come back tomorrow?" May asked. Elizabeth nodded. She would have done anything to get them out of the room before her tears fell.

Forgive myself?... I have a purpose... I had two... three children... I made more than mistakes... I could never forgive myself. Nor should I." Elizabeth rolled onto her side and cried.

"Did they come and talk to you about AA?" a nurse asked looking in from the doorway. "Pretty heavy conversation," she empathized, realizing Elizabeth had been crying. "Let me rub your back with a little lotion. That will help you feel better." Elizabeth replied by rolling onto her stomach and not saying a word.

"AA's given a lot of people their lives back. I've seen it for myself," she said warming the lotion up in her hands. "They have meetings here in the hospital every Thursday night. Thinking about giving it a try?" she asked massaging Elizabeth's back.

Elizabeth gave no reply. "You might as well," the nurse said before she left the room. "You can't keep living a decadent life."

"*'You can't keep living a decadent life.'* The nurse's words vibrated through her mind, loosening old crusted-over memories.

'Darling, you must try this one. It is simply decadent,' she heard Mabel Norman inviting her. *So far away from the girl I was then... so young and alive... Can hardly remember being her... How could she have done all that I did?* Elizabeth searched for an answer. *'God forgives you... you have no power over it... you're not weak... it's a disease,'* May's voice reminded her. *A disease I have no control over? ... I have no control over it. A purpose to my life?*

Elizabeth felt Clark's little hand in her hand when the memory of his first step flashed before. Shaking, she remembered the glass of whisky she was sipping on at the time. Shaking, she remembered Mabel's body convulsing in the nursery. *A reason I lived when they thought they'd killed me. Maybe she's the reason? If it is a disease, maybe if I get cured she'll forgive me. I am powerless over it but I owe it to her to try.*

"God," Elizabeth prayed aloud. "There is no reason for you to help me. We know I've done nothing to deserve it. But I am powerless... I need your help!"

~ *Chapter Forty Three* ~

I can't believe him. Mabel infuriatedly thought. *He wears his feelings like a tabard and expects me to do the same.*

"We've been dating for seven months," Buddy spoke softly leaning in towards her sitting across from him at the restaurant table. "And you tell me nothing about yourself."

"I know how long we've been dating," she snapped back at him.

"I want to know you better," Buddy answered.

"You know plenty enough about me," she argued back.

"I'd like to take this to the next level," he said.

"And what, Mr. Fitzgerald, is the next level?" she asked bitterly, Questioning to herself, why did they have to be having this private conversation in such a public place?

"That we promise to date each other exclusively," he answered.

Uncomfortable with the whole conversation, Mabel drank some of her water slowly. *Why should I have to promise that? I haven't dated anyone else since our first date. Can't he leave well enough alone?*

"I'm happy just the way things are," she said

smugly.

"I'm not," he answered firmly. The seriousness in his voice frightened her. "Mabel, I love you," Buddy said taking her hand. "I want the two of us to start planning out a life together. I want to know you feel the same way." She wanted to answer him. Desperately, she wanted to tell him she loved him but something deep inside her kept the words from being spoken. *Is this love I feel?... How can I know?... Dose he really love me?... Can I be certain?*

"Buddy, please don't rush me," she asked.

"Why Mabel? Why can't you let me into your life?" he whispered in her ear after kissing her goodnight at her door.

She could not answer. Watching him walk to his car, she felt the weight of his questions on her shoulders. *Why?* she asked herself.

"Mabel," a raspy male voiced called out from under the corner lamppost. She hadn't noticed him standing there before but she knew instantly who he was. *What is this date?* she asked herself. *Is there some dark cloud over my head? Am I paying for some karmic injustice?*

"Forgive me, but I have to talk to you," her father said.

"Why not?" she conceded. *What is it that Aunt Kathleen used to say, 'when you think things are bad they always get worse?'* "I can give you a minute."

"How have you been?" Eddie asked.

"Good. I'm doing well," she overtly feigning politeness answered. "And you?"

"I'm good and so is the family," he answered. "I'm sorry about...,"

"Is that what you need to talk to me about?

Because I'm not up to it tonight," she abruptly said turning towards the door.

"No, wait... It's about your mother," Eddie quickly informed her.

"My mother?" Mabel said turning back to face him "I haven't seen her since that night. I don't have any idea how you can get in touch with her."

"But I do," Eddie said repentantly looking at her. "A friend of mine saw her. She's working in a mission on Houston Street."

"And why should I care?" she asked.

"Thought you might like to know where she is, that's all. She hasn't had a drink in four months."

"I guess that's something," Mabel disdainfully said. "She had plenty of time to call me then if she wanted to."

"It is something. You're right about that," Eddie answered. "You can tell your grandmother and your aunt if you want too."

"I'm not sure what I want to do, except to go to bed," she answered.

"Guess, it is late," Eddie agreed. "He seemed like a nice boy."

"Good night," Mabel said, turning back towards the door.

"Maybe, I could come around and see you sometime?" he asked.

"Maybe," she answered opening the door.

Locking the door behind her, Mabel turned off the light that had been left on awaiting her arrival home. Nana and Aunt Kathleen both had long since stopped staying up waiting for her to come home with Buddy.

"Such a nice young man," they both highly

approved of him.

What a night, she thought getting herself ready for bed. *If I'm lucky when I get up in the morning it will have only been a bad dream.* She rested her head on her pillow. *How many times have I fallen asleep wishing my life was just a bad dream? It was better... Why is Buddy pushing me?... I should have known that Eddie was going to show.... It's the same as the last time. Everything was going along fine... he comes in and all the pieces fall apart. I couldn't hold anything together back then... Last time I lost Clark...He loved me... I loved him.*

Tears streaming down her face as she thought of her brother. *It was her fault. 'Take care of this one,' she told me. She didn't. She never watched him. She never protected him. She was the one up there on the roof... And she's the one who... I am going to find her. Tell her how great it is she stopped drinking... Maybe then I can put the pieces of my life back together.*

I'll tell her how wonderful. Yes, wonderful, only thing; Mother, it's over ten years too late!"

~ Chapter Forty Four ~

The Kelly family walked home from early mass Sunday morning. It was obvious winter was over; the promise of spring was in the air. Their walk home would not be complete without first stopping at the bakery for rolls and buns. And of course, Kathleen's routine of eating a sticky bun on the way home.

"To tide me over from fasting all night in preparation of receiving the Eucharist," she'd say licking her fingers.

"Mabel, how was your date last night?" Bridget asked filling the kettle with water.

"Was everything alright?" Kathleen asked putting the rolls and buns out on the kitchen table. "You haven't mentioned it at all this morning."

What do I tell them? Mabel questioned herself while putting out the cups and saucers. *Dear Sweet Jesus, I offered up my Holy Communion for the words Do I tell them we're fighting because he says he loves me? Or do I....*

"Was there an argument?' Bridget pressed. "You don't seem yourself."

"No, Nana," Mabel answered. "Buddy and I are..."

"Spit it out." Bridget demanded. "Are what? I'm not getting any younger."

"I saw," Mabel slowly answered. "Eddie last night."

"I'm not surprised," Kathleen commented. "It was inevitable that you would run into him one day. Was he in the restaurant?"

"No," she replied, knowing he could have been there and she too upset to notice. "He was waiting for me when I came home last night."

"I didn't hear you bring him in," Bridget replied preparing the pot of tea. "Must have slept through it."

"I didn't bring him in," Mabel responded.

"Do you want a roll or a bun?" Kathleen asked.

"A bun, thank you," she answered. "Please, Nana, Aunt Kathleen, I need the two of you to sit for one minute. There is something I have to say."

"What is it?" Bridget asked after the two women sat in their chairs.

"A friend of his saw my mother," Mabel blurted it out. Momentarily, Bridget and Kathleen looked at each other then turned their eyes back at Mabel.

"Don't you have anything to say?" she bewilderedly asked.

"No," Kathleen was the first to answer. "What do you expect us to say?"

"Ask how is she? Where is she? Something," Mabel replied.

"I don't care how she is," Kathleen spoke bitterly. "I don't care where she is."

"Nana, she's your daughter," Mabel said. "Don't you care?" She saw a glaze came over her grandmother's eyes.

"The woman you're talking about is not me daughter. She's not me Elizabeth," Bridget reacted coldly. "I told her I'd never talk to her again and I'm a woman of me word!"

"You can't sit here and tell us that you have any concerns about her well being. Do you?" Kathleen interrogated.

"No, of course I don't," Mabel answered. "But there're a lot of things I'd like to say to her."

"She's not worth the time or breath," Kathleen retorted.

Why am I feeling so uncomfortable? Mabel squirmed in her chair. *I knew they didn't care about her. I don't. Why do I feel I should be defending her? I hate her.*

"Do you have anything else you'd like to talk about?" Bridget asked.

"No," Mabel answered.

"Then we can get back to eating our breakfast," Bridget calmly stated "Mabel, be a dear and bring me a jar of preserves from the pantry."

"I'm going to the library this afternoon, want to do some research," Mabel lied, coming back to the table. *Why am I uncomfortable with admitting to them that I am going to find my mother?*

Mabel used her time wisely while riding the subway to Houston Street. She memorized each question she was going to throw at her mother. Five questions, one for each finger, together they made up a fist. One after another, she'd strike her blows by asking the questions. How could you have not shown up for Clark's funeral?.... How could you have left me to make all the arrangements? ....How could you have slept with your dying sister's husband? ... How could you have told a four-year old she killed her sister? ...How could you have left an infant in the hands of a six-year old to take care of him?

She walked up the subway steps and marched the six blocks to the mission. She clenched her fist so tightly she whitened her knuckles. She didn't care about the answers. She'd have her day. She'd force her mother to face the pain that everyone around her felt. She'd bring her mother to her knees. Mabel would make sure of it.

Past the long line of men and women, she walked to the front door.

"You have to wait on line," the sentry at the door said.

"I'm here looking for someone," she informed him.

"Do they want to be found?" he inquired.

"I'm looking for Elizabeth… Elizabeth O'Neil,' Mabel nervously said ignoring his question.

"Don't know anyone with that name around here," he answered shaking his head.

"I was told she works here," she steadfastly said. Nothing… no one was going to stand in her way.

"Doing what?" he interestedly asked.

"I don't know," she answered.

"What does she look like?" he fired another question.

"I'm not sure. She might look a little like me," Mabel answered.

"Do you have a picture?" he asked after scrutinizing her face. She shook her head.

"Don't have a picture. Don't know what she looks like. Don't know what she does. Is there anything you do know about her," he insultingly asked.

"Yes," she said adamantly. "I do know she stopped drinking four months ago."

"Four months ago… Elizabeth…," he bit his lip as he thought. "Oh, you mean Elizabeth. I think her last name is Kelly or something like that."

"Yes," Mabel approvingly agreed. "That's her maiden name."

"She's back in the kitchen. If not, they'll know where she is," he pointed the way as he answered her. "Go straight back to that there door."

The dinning hall was huge with rows and rows of neatly lined up tables and chairs all waiting for the guests to come in and have a free hot meal. A door across the room sprung open, startling her. She turned to see two children come running into the room.

"Come back in here and finish," a woman firmly called after them. Mabel watched as they stopped playing their game of tag and joined the other children and women sitting down eating a meal. *Hadn't expected that, Women yes, but children?*

Mabel opened the kitchen door. Eight people were scurrying about as they made the last minute preparations for the meal. One woman stirred the contents of a large pot, while a man was putting salt into another even larger pot. A young priest appeared pleased with the sauce he tasted. There was an elderly woman preparing a salad while a young man standing next to her was trying to read a passage in a book.

"The word is employable," the elderly woman sounded the word out for him.

It's her. The face, I can tell it now. But the

voice, it's her. Mabel walked over to the counter. "Can I help you?" the woman asked. Mabel stood silently staring directly into her eyes.

"Mabel, it's you," Elizabeth said putting her hands to her mouth.

"Yes, it's me," she answered.

"You're here. You're really here?" she questioned her own sanity as she spoke.

"Eddie told me where you were," Mabel answered rationally.

"I have pictured what you would look like so much that I'm not sure my mind isn't playing a horrible trick on me," Elizabeth confessed. "You're really here?"

"Elizabeth, why don't the two of you go the back room," the priest said. "If you need me I'll be here in the kitchen."

"Father Paul, she's my Mabel," Elizabeth began crying as she talked to him. "I knew this day would come. I prayed for it but when I was ready."

"The Lord picks the time. He thinks you're ready," the priest tenderly answered her, with his arm around her shoulder. His warm eyes smiled at Mabel as he spoke.

Elizabeth led the way, her slow deliberate steps proving how painful each step forward was for her. "I should have asked you if you wanted a cup of tea," she said pointing for Mabel to sit on the couch.

"I don't want anything from you," Mabel curtly answered sitting down in a high back chair across the room. Mabel's words did not miss their target. Instantly Elizabeth began crying.

"I'm not ready," she sobbed shaking her head. Through her gasping for air, she continued. "I can't begin to ask for your forgiveness… I don't have the words…I'm sorry isn't strong enough."

'I'm sorry,' it was almost inaudible, but Mabel heard it and every other. They were not strong words. Nonetheless, they were muscular enough to lift Mabel out of the chair and have her sitting next to her weeping mother on the couch. Mighty enough to open her clenched fist, putting aside the questions that each finger had prepared to throw. Powerful enough to have Mabel gently patting her mother's back comfortingly.

"Don't cry," Mabel said. *The questions… The answers…They don't matter… She's my mother.* "Maybe we should have that tea. Nana says a cup of good Irish tea will cure everything."

"How is my mother?" Elizabeth asked trying to regain some composure. "And Kathleen?"

"They're both well," Mabel answered handing her a box of tissues. "Mama, sit here for a few minutes. I'll be right back with some tea." Elizabeth's eyes swelled up at hearing Mama but Mabel's gentle smile calmed her.

Everyone stopped what they were doing and untrustingly stared at Mabel as she walked into the kitchen.

"My mother wants a cup of tea," she announced, boldly staring back at all of them.

"So glad you're here, Mabel," a woman said putting the tea and a plate of cookies on a tray. "You're all she talks about." Mabel carried in the tray and poured a cup of tea for her mother.

"I heard you've stopped drinking," Mabel said before taking a bite of a cookie. She leaned back into the overstuffed couch. *Who is this woman? She is not*

*the mother I remember. She's not the woman I
wanted to hate.*

"Yes, I have," Elizabeth answered. "Four and a
half months now."

"That's good," Mabel found herself answering.
*What sense would it make to say it's ten years too
late?*

"But tell me about yourself," Elizabeth eagerly
questioned.

"I'm a nurse," Mabel began.

"A nurse," Elizabeth proudly announced. "How
wonderful, you're a nurse. And you like your job?"

"Yes, I love it," Mabel excitedly answered. "It's
a wonderful feeling to help someone."

"Is there anyone special in your life?" Elizabeth
asked with a funny smile on her face.

"There is one special guy. I've been dating him
for awhile," she answered coyly. "Time will tell."

"Take it slow, don't jump into anything too
fast," Elizabeth advised.

"I won't. Don't worry," Mabel answered. *Not
likely, I'll ever rush into anything.* "They treat you
well here?"

"Yes, I share a room with Ruth. You might have
seen her in the kitchen. She's the tall woman with the
reddish hair," Elizabeth answered.

"Yes, she got the tea for us," Mabel told her.

"Ruth is a great roommate. She just finished a
secretarial course and she'll be starting a new job
next week. Would you like a little more tea?"

"Yes, thank you. Do you work in the kitchen?"
Mabel asked.

"I help out there. I work during the week doing
alterations," Elizabeth answered pouring another cup

of tea for each of them. "Been good for me getting back to sewing. I used to do it when I was a young girl."

"I know," Mabel happily answered. "I've seen pictures of you and Aunt Margaret with some of your *creations*. They were quite good."

"Some of them were good. Weren't they?" Elizabeth reminiscently smiled as she answered. "We had a lot of fun back then. That was until the drink took over." Elizabeth put down her cup and looked squarely at Mabel. "I have a disease. I'm an alcoholic. I'm powerless over it. Only God has the power to keep me from it... That's what I was supposed to say to you when I asked for your forgiveness. I've been planning to do just that. But I've been afraid too. Wanted to have a place of my own... something I could be proud of... something I could show you to prove that I changed."

"I can see that you've changed now," Mabel said taking her mother's shaking hand into hers. "I can tell you won't go back to drinking again."

"I would have come to you," Elizabeth said. "I've missed so much of your life."

"It was probably best that I came here," Mabel answered. "Nana and Aunt Kathleen would have made it more difficult for you at their house. That's where I live."

"Guess they'll never forgive me," Elizabeth lamented.

"It will take a miracle. I'll tell you that much," Mabel said knowing the two of them as well as she did.

"Miracle or not, I'm going to have to try to ask for their forgiveness. It's part of our program,"

Elizabeth answered.

"Can you write them a letter or something?" Mabel asked.

"Why?" Elizabeth questioned.

"Cause, I don't see a way they'll ever open the front door to you. They're pretty angry."

"They have every right to be," Elizabeth acknowledged. "I was angry with myself until I accepted the fact that I have a disease. So, I have to find myself a miracle that would make them open the door for me to tell them I'm sorry."

"We have to," Mabel said.

"We have to?" Elizabeth asked.

"We have to find a miracle," Mabel answered. "Don't think I'd let you stand outside the front door by yourself now do you?" Elizabeth did not say a word but lovingly squeezed Mabel's hand in reply.

"So what would make Nana open the front door to the devil himself?" she asked.

"Meg." Mabel answered without any hesitation. "Nana has always carried a terrible sadness in her heart over her sister. She'd open the door. Hell, she'd break the door down if Meg was on the other side."

"You think we could find her? She'd be pretty old by now," Elizabeth doubtingly asked.

"We could give it a try. If we found out anything at all about her, Nana would open the door to hear it," Mabel assured her.

"What about Kathleen?" Elizabeth asked.

"Aunt Kathleen is a hopeless romantic," Mabel laughed. "She loves a happy ending. If you make Nana happy, she'll come around."

"I've learned to trust in God and he brought you here to me today. Maybe it's in his plan that we find Meg," Elizabeth speculated. "Where would we begin?"

"Let me go home and think about it," Mabel said. "I'll come back next week with some ideas and we'll start planning it out then."

"I'll think about it also," Elizabeth said.

"Mama," Mabel said. "You just keep up the good work till I come back and by the way, I do."

"Do what?" Elizabeth asked.

"I do forgive you," Mabel said kissing her mother goodbye.

~ Chapter Forty Five ~

Savoring the energetic feel of the spring afternoon Mabel enjoyed the walk back to the subway station. The songbirds sang their prettiest tunes. The fresh warm air was invigorating. She marveled at how the sun light seemed to radiate off the smiling faces she passed. Only a few weeks ago, she bundled up in heavy clothing trying to protect herself from the bitter cold. Now she felt lighter... somehow freer. Funny, she had not notice the weather this morning.

Where was Mama all these winters? Couldn't think about it before. Can't think about it now, either. She wouldn't allow herself to dampen her mood with thoughts like that. *Must be how Nana handles it. Just puts things out of her mind... Such a pretty block I never realized that before,* she told herself walking up towards her front door.

"I could smell that chicken roasting when I reached the corner," she yelled when she walked in the front door.

"You're in good spirits," Kathleen said.

"God's in his heaven. All's right with the world," she answered.

"Talking about heaven," Kathleen answered her. "Buddy called three times looking for you."

"Did you tell him I went to library?" Mabel asked.

"Yes," Bridget answered. "He has been calling every hour. We expect his next call in twenty minutes."

"He seems upset about something," Kathleen remarked.

"He's such a nice young man," Bridget said for the millionth time.

"Don't worry about him. It will all be fine after I talk to him," Mabel reassured them. *He is a nice young man. What would be the harm in telling him we'll date exclusively?*

"You've been in a good mood all week," Charlotte teased. "Things must be going well for you and Buddy."

"They are," Mabel answered.

"What are you doing?" Charlotte questioned while trying to read what Mabel had written down.

"Do you know anything about Ireland?" Mabel asked.

"Not a thing, except I could find it on a map," Charlotte answered. "Why? Are you planning a vacation over there?"

"Not a trip. I was trying to figure out how one could find someone who lives over there?" Mabel confided.

"They must have telephone books," Charlotte reasoned. "Maybe they could help you at the library."

"That's a good idea," Mabel answered. "I'll stop there on my way home this evening."

I should have thought of coming here myself, Mabel thought as she walked in. Great places libraries, an appealing place for those who like peace and quiet. Here in the company of characters in books one is truly safe to develop relations that would never prove to be hurtful or disappointing. Mabel knew every inch of the library by heart.

"If I wanted to find someone from a long time ago in Ireland how would I go about it?" she asked the reference librarian.

"Good question. Do you have their last address?" she asked.

"I have one from about sixty-seven years ago," Mabel answered. The librarian rubbed her chin and sat thinking for some time. Mabel anxiously waited.

"I don't think I have any resources here to help you," she apologetically said. "The only thing I can suggest is that you write the Irish Consulate and explain what you need and ask for their guidance."

"Do you have the address?" Mabel asked.

" 'Feel free to come back, if I can be of any further assistance.' She said when she gave me their address." Mabel excitedly showed it to her mother as they spoke sitting in Elizabeth's room.

"I have some useful information for you also," Elizabeth proudly announced. "I told Father Paul about Meg and he might be able to help us."

"How?" Mabel asked.

"He has a friend, a Jesuit priest, who is studying over in Ireland. He told me to write everything down that we know about Meg Donahue. Father said he'd send it to his friend and see if he could help us."

"That's wonderful" Mabel commented. "We have two different places to start. We'll get both letters written today."

"And then we'll trust in God's will," Elizabeth

advised.

"Yes, Mama," Mabel echoed. "We'll give it over to him."

"Good day, Mabel," Father Paul's friendly greeting always made her welcome.

"Good day, to you Father. Any word from your friend?" she asked.

"I'll let you know when I have something to tell you," Father answered. "Your mother is waiting for you up stairs."

Over these last four weeks, Mabel came frequently to visit. She knew every inch of her mother's simple room by heart, from her checkered bedspread to the framed Serenity Prayer on the wall. Each visit they talked.

"I'm over fifty," Elizabeth said. "I should be this wise woman with an abundance of philosophical sayings from all I've learned."

"And I," Mabel answered. "Should be married with two children and a dog."

"In time," Elizabeth assured her. "In time." They talked over Elizabeth's successes, Mabel's funny stories from the hospital and of Buddy. Unknowingly, they began putting the pieces of their lives together.

"May I come in?" Father Paul asked.

"Yes, of course," Elizabeth answered.

"I wanted to wait until Mabel was here," he spoke slowly… deliberately. "I need to talk to you both."

"What is it?" Elizabeth nervously asked.

"Let's all sit," Father suggested. "I haven't been completely honest with you," he spoke looking at

Mabel. "I have been in communication with my friend since he first received your letter." They looked back at him bewildered.

"Did he find Meg?" Mabel hesitantly questioned.

"I'm sorry to tell you that Meg is dead," his eyes look down at the floor as he spoke.

"Father, that's alright," Elizabeth tried to comfort him. "We're happy he found out that much."

"How do you know?" Mabel asked, sensing there was more he was not telling.

"My friend has always been a fan of mystery novels," Father Paul began after first taking a deep breath. "In fact he thanked me in his first letter for giving him the opportunity to do some real detective work. He had some time off and decided he would go to Meg's parish and dig up whatever records he could. He cautioned me about saying anything just yet. He didn't want to offer you false hope." He wiped the sweat of his brow as he spoke. Both women listening intently could not understand why he was so uncomfortable.

"In his next letter,' Father Paul continued. "He reported to me that when he met with the parish priest he was astounded to find out that a month before a letter had come to the rectory inquiring about any information regarding Meg Donahue and her sister Bridget." The priest nervously folded his hands and continued. "My friend asked if he might see the letter. 'Providence made me keep it," the parish priest told him. But," Father Paul said adding a little levity, "My friend said the difficulty the parish priest had finding it proved it was more likely his poor housekeeping skills." The women laughed.

"The inquiry was sent by Emma O'Hara on behalf of a Bridey Mahoney," he said reaching into his pocket. "He called me at four this morning with their telephone number. I suggest. No, I urge you call them. You need to hear it from them." Father's eyes looked at the floor as he spoke. "It's all true, what they're going to tell you. My friend verified it himself. He's on his way to the Vatican."

~ Chapter Forty Six ~

Off the Staten Island Ferry and through the streets of Manhattan, Emma drove her new candy apple Chevrolet Bel Air. Her mother, Pat, sat nervously in the front seat criticizing her as she weaved and bobbed through the city traffic. Her grandmother, Bridey, sat in the back seat holding on tightly to the envelope in her hand.

"One more turn and we're..." Emma announced. "Here!" She pulled into a parking space in front of the mission. Anxiously, Elizabeth was pacing up and down the street waiting for them. Father Paul walked along side her offering his support.

"Do you want me to come with you?"

"No," she unwaveringly answered. "They're here!" She had never seen any of them. Only spoken to them on the telephone but instantly she could see, it was them. Father Paul held the door as Elizabeth struggled to get into the back seat.

"Why don't you sit up front with Emma?" Pat asked, being only two years younger but so much spryer.

"Thank you," Elizabeth answered, taking her up on her offer.

"I don't know if you'll be thanking me, when

you see how she drives," Pat advised, relieved she was now safely in the back seat.

"My husband says I'm a good driver. Don't you worry," Emma confidently added, driving away from the curb.

"All I can say," Pat quickly replied. "Is you might be wanting to hold onto my beads and pray while you're up there."

"Mama!" Emma called back giving her mother a stern look in the rearview mirror.

"I'm praying anyway," Elizabeth nervously answered.

"Don't worry," Bridey comfortingly interjected. "The Lord has brought us this far. I don't expect he'll fail us now."

"Mabel what is wrong with you?" Kathleen asked. "I haven't finished reading that paper? You've been acting funny all morning."

"I'm sorry," Mabel quickly answered. "I was just straightening up." *Funny ... I don't feel funny... My stomach's in such a knot... Wonder how Ma's doing? They must be there by now. They should be here any minute.*

"Are you going to stand and look out that window all day?" Bridget asked.

Should I tell them something?... Give them some warning?... There's no way of knowing for sure what's the right thing to do... Have to trust in God... Nana shouldn't be to angry that I didn't tell her. I think she'll understand. They're here!

"I'll be right back," Mabel said leaving the apartment.

"What's all that hubbub out there?" Bridget

annoyingly asked. She hurried with Kathleen in tow to see what the commotion was all about.

"Meg!" Bridget cried seeing Emma for the first time. Her face went pale. Her legs began giving way. Mabel rushed to grab her. "It's Meg," Bridget said. "Oh God, me senses are failing me."

"No, Mama," Elizabeth quickly spoke up. "She's not Meg. This is Emma, Meg's great granddaughter. And this, Mama, is Bridey, she's Meg's daughter."

"Is it true, Elizabeth?" Bridget asked.

"Yes, Mama. It's true," Elizabeth answered.

"Bridey, come and let these old eyes get a proper look at you," Bridget asked. She stroked her face then held her tightly in her arms.

"How did…" Kathleen tearfully started to ask.

"My mother," Mabel answered.

"Elizabeth, you did this?" Kathleen asked. "How?"

"God did it. He only allowed Mabel and me to help," Elizabeth humbly answered.

"I need to sit," Bridget requested.

"Come in side, out of the hallway," Kathleen said ushering them towards the open door. "I'll make us all some tea."

"Am I welcome, Kathleen?" Elizabeth asked.

"Come in, Elizabeth," Kathleen said. "You can help me make the tea."

Bridey sat at the dinning room table and watched every move Bridget made, as if searching for some added knowledge about her mother. Bridget contently looked at their faces. Meg's face… not just a dream or memory.

"How did you find her?' Bridget asked.

"They were trying to find you," Elizabeth answered. "And we found them."

"Trying to find me?" Bridget questioned.

"Aunt Bridget," Bridey said. "Let me try and explain." Bridget nodded. "I was raised here in New York. My parents both passed on a few years back and there was never any mention that I was adopted."

"Adopted?" Bridget asked. Bridey took a few more sips of tea before she continued.

"Last year my aunt in Ireland died. Her lawyer sent me a letter she wrote to me years ago when she was in the convent. She had given it his office to be sent me upon her death. You should read it. It explains everything."

Bridey handed Bridget the envelope. Mabel had her reading glasses already sitting on the edge of the table waiting.

1889

My dear niece Bridget,

I do not know if I do you a service in this act. But in good conscience before God I know I must tell you these facts. It pains my heart that I still can see those piercing blue eyes of your mother begging me, "Please be sure she is taken care of...." I did that to the best of my ability. "Tell her I love her..." this I did not relay. For to relay this was to tell you all the horrible secrets I dare not tell. To say aloud words that dare not be spoken. I can not face you with this. I can not look into your eyes and answer why I let it happen. I only trust and hope in Jesus' love that He can forgive me for what I can not forgive myself.

From a young girl I knew I was going to serve God. During my convent life, my name was Sister

Mary Mother of the Sacred Heart. I was a good nun. I served in our convent in Dublin. At first, I worked in the hospital and then I was given the duty to tend to the souls of the young girls and women who worked in our laundry.

If a young girl or woman found herself with child out of wedlock we were their only sanctuaries. Most came remorseful for their actions. They made their confessions and were prepared to make their penance for their carnal sins.

This was not the way it was with your mother, Margaret Elizabeth Donahue. She was not ashamed for herself or for you. She did not want to bring disgrace to her family but she had dreams for the both of you.

This was unheard of. Once a girl came to us and she had her child, both mother and the bastard child stayed and worked in our laundry until death. There was no other place in our society for them. Meg would not hear of this. She told me secretly that she would take you and run away to America for a new start. I should not have listened to her. I should have been discouraging her. But the words she said to me all made sense when she said them. I was not much older than she was. I had no knowledge of the world outside these convent walls. How could I instruct her?

You were born. Your mother had much trouble. She lost much blood and developed a fever. These girls, in our charge, did not have access to the hospital or doctors. It was our good sisters that helped your mother bring you into this world of tears. She held you for such a brief time but I was moved by her love for you.

We could not leave you with her for your own safety. After two days of sickness, I knew it was close to the end. Meg knew it also. She begged me to promise to take care that you should not have to pay the horrible price of living your life behind these horrible convent walls. That you should not have to pay the price of your life for what the church saw as your mother's sin.

How could I not promise that I would do this for her? How could I do this for her and be honored bound by my vows of obedience? I knew at that moment that I could not honor both. I told her yes. "Tell her I love her and please baptize her Bridget after my sister. Please...please... do that" I did all she asked.

"In the convent yard we have two cemeteries. The one directly to the right side of the church is the blessed cemetery for all the good sisters. Across from there to the right side of the laundry is a small piece of ground with a wrought iron fence around it where the mothers and bastard children are buried in unmarked graves. We were sworn to secrecy not to tell their families of their deaths to spare them the shame. It was into this place your mother was laid to rest.

My dear sister, Colleen was unable to have children. She and her dear husband Timmy were going to America for a new start. I wrote her a letter and asked her to come right away. She came to see me. I took her into the nursery and let her hold you. Together we went into church. She would have given anything to have a child but how could she adopt a bastard one?

I assured her that your parents were married in

the church well before you were conceived. This I do not know to be true. Your mother never spoke of your father to me or to anyone.

I told my sister that because you were only a few weeks old I could write a new birth certificate for you with her and Timmy as parents. I would then document that the girl child of Meg was dead. I don't know what came over my sister but she said yes without ever discussing it with her husband. I did ask that she keep your first name as Bridget as her mother had truly wished.

I was not done with my sins. I had gone this far. I had one more thing to do. I could not mark your mother's grave. But I could map out its location. During my daily prayers, I paced out the steps from the laundry. I paced out the number of steps from the stained glass window of the church. I paced the number of steps from the wrought iron gate. And in case all those items are worn to the ground over the years, I marked down the number of steps from our beloved Mother Assunta's grave to your mother's. I have enclosed that map. Although crudely drawn it is accurate in every detail. I have also enclosed your mother's admissions card.

Having written this all down my deeds are done. I sinned against my vow of obedience. I am leaving the order.

Mea culpa,
Sister Mary Mother of the Sacred Heart

Bridget folded the letter closed. She took her reading glasses off and began wiping her eyes.

"May I read it?" Kathleen asked. Bridget handed it to her.

"There is another letter you should see," Bridey said handing it to her. "It's from the priest that Elizabeth and Mabel sent to find my mother. You don't have to read the whole thing," she said moving her finger along to the point at which she wanted Bridget to start reading.

"Here it is. See… there were groups of women who for reasons such as bearing children out of wedlock worked in different capacities in convents all throughout Ireland. They were called Magdalenes after Mary Magdalene. And it appears that they and their children stayed and died behind these convent walls."

"Do you have the admission card your aunt spoke of?" Bridget asked.

"Yes, here it is," Bridey answered giving it to her. Bridget read each line.

"There's no mention of marriage," Bridget acknowledged. "Or father."

"Mama, do as the priest prays at mass." Elizabeth's voice cracked as she begged for compassion for her aunt as well as for herself. "Look not upon our sins."

OUR sins… the words pierced Bridget's heart as she contemplated on them.

"Do you remember my mother's signature?" Bridey asked. "Is this it?"

Bridget looked over each letter carefully. She knew she didn't need too as before her sat her sister in each of their faces. "Yes, this is her signature. I am sure."

Bridey took the card and emotionally held it close to her heart.

"That's the only thing of your mother's you

have, isn't it?" Bridget asked.

"Yes," Bridey tearfully replied. "I'm hoping you can tell me stories about her. I want to know who she was."

"I can tell you all about her," Bridget willingly replied. "I have lots of stories but first things first." Bridget left the dinning room table and walked into her bedroom. Taking a box down from the shelf, she opened it and lifted up the top tray. She took the contents found there back to Bridey and placed it in her hand. Bridey clenched it in her hand and held it there tightly for some time until she had enough composure to look at it.

"This is beautiful," she cried looking at it pinned onto a lace-trimmed handkerchief.

"It was your mother's favorite," Bridget said of the colorful heart shaped broach.

Bridey asked the question. "She wasn't going with anyone in particular that I can remember," Bridget answered. And gave the names of the few young men who hung around her sister. Bridget told tales from the old days as Emma wrote it all down in shorthand lest her grandmother would forget one word of them.

"It must have been an awful burden that you carried all your life, not knowing where she was or what happened to her," Bridey said as she was leaving.

"It ripped me heart out," Bridget answered. "You've lifted the awful heaviness off me weary body," she said kissing Bridey goodbye.

"We have Elizabeth to thank," Bridey answered. "I couldn't have found you without her searching too."

"Elizabeth, are you sure you don't want us to drive you back?" Emma asked. "It would not be any trouble."

"Thank you, but they invited me to stay a little longer," she answered. "We have some things that need to be said."

"I don't think we need to talk about them tonight," Kathleen tiredly stated. "It's been an emotional day already. We can talk tomorrow. If that's alright with you?"

"I'll come back then," Elizabeth responded.

"Why not stay over?" Kathleen asked. "Your bed's still here."

"Stay, Elizabeth," Bridget urged. "We'll share a quiet night together."

"Like old times?" Elizabeth said.

"Yes, like before…" Kathleen agreed.

"We'll start a new puzzle," Mabel said going to get one from the back closet.

"I haven't done one of these in years," Elizabeth announced. "You still do them every week?"

"Yes and sometimes even during the week," Kathleen answered working on straightening out the pieces before them on the dinning room table.

"They were fun, weren't they?" Elizabeth answered looking at the vast montage of pieces lying before her.

"You didn't think so before," Kathleen said.

"Too boring before," Elizabeth answered. "But now … Funny but I never noticed it before," Elizabeth said holding a piece in her hand. "But puzzles are like families, each piece is unique and alone it looks like nothing. But interconnected they become stronger… become something bigger… and being part of that big picture …. they belong."

"Mabel, I'm sure that's for you," Bridget said when the telephone rang.

"Would anyone object if I invited him over?" She asked.

"Not at all," they answered all searching the table for the pieces they needed.

"Buddy," Mabel elatedly said. "Can you come over now? I'd like you to meet my mother."

Order Information

📖 email orders: info@georgettesymonds.com

📧 Postal Orders: Paradise Found Publishers
P.O. Box 1064, Largo, Fl. 33779-1064
Sales tax: Please add 6% for books shipped to
Florida addresses.

Special note: Author available to be guest at book
clubs, bookstores, libraries, schools and Irish
organizations. For more information visit:

www.georgettesymonds.com